# Despite Herself

## Jessie Chandler

T0405757

## About the Author

Jessie Chandler is the author of nine novels, including the humorously suspenseful Shay O'Hanlon Caper Series. Her crime fiction has garnered a Lambda Literary finalist nod, three Golden Crown Literary Awards, three USA Book Awards, and an Independent Publisher Book Award. As a kid, Jessie honed an interest in crime and punishment by reading Alfred Hitchcock's *The Three Investigators* under the covers with a flashlight. Once in a while you can still find her beneath her blankets absorbed in a good mystery.

# *Despite Herself*

## Jessie Chandler

BELLA
B O O K S

Bella Books, Inc.
P.O. Box 10543
Tallahassee, FL 32302

First Edition - 2025

Editor: Medora MacDougall
Cover Designer: SJ Hardy

ISBN: 978-1-64247-673-6

### PUBLISHER'S NOTE

## Acknowledgments

First of all, this is a work of fiction. I've created my own version of Duluth PD and its inner workings from my imagination. This story isn't a police procedural. Set your sense of disbelief on the bookshelf and allow yourself to escape for a little while.

Over the last couple years my life has changed in ways I never, ever imagined. I've hit my worst lows and have had some of my biggest highs. I've learned to embrace change and not desperately hang on to what was, because what it was isn't any longer. I did that for far too long. The important thing is that I came out the other side, bloodied and bruised, but I'm slowly putting the pieces back together. Writing this romance was the third hardest things I've ever done, but I'll begrudgingly admit, it's helping me heal.

I've been lucky to have some incredibly amazing folks standing behind me and pushing me forward. First and foremost, I want to call out Linda Hill and the rest of the hard-working Bella team. Over the years, these folks have been incredibly patient, supportive, and believed in me and my work when I no longer did. I'm grateful to have you all in my life. Medora MacD, beloved editor. I'm so happy to work with and learn from you again! Thankfully you understand my intentions and the voices in my head better than I do some days, and I appreciate your willingness to go over this damn manuscript again and again and again. Becky, bless your amazing brain for helping me come up with ways to squeeze a romance out of a mystery, characters out of tomato and broccoli, and for the haven you and Deborah offer when I need it.

My journey into the unknown continues. I couldn't have come this far without the support of so many people. April, you've had my back for more years that I can count on my hands and feet, I'm everlastingly grateful for you. Josie Jensen, for being a great beta and checking in. My Minions, MB Panichi, Judy Kerr, and Lori L. Lake, wow. You've been instrumental in keeping me moving forward in life and down the writing road. Your belief in me sometimes makes me wonder if you aren't all crazy. Judy, thank you for our writing zooms on the daily, MB for always being a great cheerleader and feedback-giver, and Lori, for giving me technical advice and allowing me a safe place to recover, heal, and sort the conundrum that's been my life for the last year and a half. Terri Bischoff, thanks for scrambling at the last minute to provide me excellent editorial advice, as always. You kick ass.

Mary, Luzanne, and Susie, you've been my rocks, my sounding boards, and occasionally the ones who've thwapped me upside the head when I needed it. Paige LaDue Henry and the rest of my Grateful HeART Guild—your hearts, and our art—saved me. The link between art and writing is inextricable, and it's time I lived that truth.

Without each and every one of you, I wouldn't be writing this acknowledgment today. Along this line, suicide is mentioned in this story. If you or anyone you know is struggling with thoughts of suicide, national resources are still within reach. As of May 2025, the 988 Suicide & Crisis Lifeline provides free and confidential emotional support to people in suicidal crisis or emotional distress 24/7 across the US and its territories. The line still provides specialized services for LGBTQ+ youth and will remain doing so up to October 2025. If the budget proposal for defunding the specialized services passes, the services will be cut from 988.

24/7 help is also available through The Trevor Project via volunteers, but they can't handle the same volume of calls and chats 988 can. If you or someone you know would like to become a hotline volunteer, check out thetrevorproject.org.

## Dedication

This book is for everyone who thinks they either don't deserve love or are afraid to love again.

## Author's Note

Writing a novel is always an adventure. It's fun, it's frustrating, it's boring, it's exciting. You love the manuscript you're working on, then you vehemently hate it. You think your writing couldn't suck more, and then you put something magical on the page and can't believe those words came out of you. Everything about writing a book is a contradiction. It's like you have your very own *Children of the Corn* video game in your brain trying to kill off your confidence. But, for some reason, you plug on, maybe working around a job and definitely around life's obligations. You sacrifice. Sacrifice time with your loved ones, sacrifice those TV series and movies you want to watch, sacrifice reading a favorite book, and sometimes even sacrifice your own health. Getting up early, staying up late (that would be me), finding an hour here, fifteen minutes there to work on this thing, this masterpiece, this horrible jumble of shit you've created.

Why? Why go through these incredible ups and devastating downs? It's an addiction, writing. The magic of words creates the mystery of worlds, and you're able to fill these worlds with whoever you want and do it however you like. The magic is molding these words into your own vision, your singular dream. The magic allows the story to take you places you might never have gone or revisit the places and people close to your heart. Writing is so personal, different for every person who picks up a pen or opens a document on their computer.

Writing is speaking a truth, spinning a yarn, exploring the unknown, sometimes all at once. There's freedom to be found in both writing and reading. Without words, this world would not be as rich, as colorful, as deeply intense, and personal as it is right now. And right now, the very words we write, the words you read, are coming under the most serious threat of our lifetimes.

It might take three months, or a year, or more to create the work you hold in your hands. These pages are a writer's blood, sweat, and tears. While it might take you a day, a week, maybe even a month to read a book, the work behind the curtain took a whole lot longer. Books are expensive. It's expensive to make books. In the lesbian and queer community, we are so lucky to have publishers who sacrifice everything for us, the writers *and* the readers. I can't stress enough how we must support the people who give our work life. If you're an indie publisher, you're pulling twice the load because you're doing it all on your own.

No one writes for the money. No one publishes authors and expects to make a fortune. We do it for the love of the word. We write for the joy of the process, for the joy of sharing our words and having readers find meaning in our work. We write because it's our oxygen. It's our love. It's freedom. In this freedom we write our collective and individual selves into places where we are often left out, and we share the truth of our lives to the world even as those in power work to erase us.

Please keep buying books. Support our publishers, our authors, and our indie writers. Print books, eBooks, audiobooks. Whatever the form, the more books you buy, the better chance we all have to keep doing the things we love, be it reading or writing or both. These days are fraught with fear of the unknown, attacks on LGBTQ+ books, and challenges to our very existence. Well, fuck the haters. Between the pages of our books you'll find some kind of peace, some kind of hope. Books are sanity when the world is insane. They are filled with solace, escape, determination, and redemption. They are filled with love from an author's heart. They are our truth. Don't let anyone take that from you.

Remember, buying one more book never hurts.

# CHAPTER ONE

"Drink! Drink! Drink!"

The chant was punctuated by the thunder of four sets of palms drumming on a wobbly high-top table, rattling the glass mugs and making the leftover beer in the pitcher slosh. The noise raised the din in the already rollicking Mashed Spud to eardrum-blowout level.

The last of the Spud's signature cocktail went down as smoothly as the first swallow. I slammed the twelve-inch, fluorescent orange, bong-shaped plastic container on the tabletop. Today was a day for finishing it all.

Finally, *finally* I was done with jumping through all the hoops and over the roadblocks brought about by a lateral transfer to the Duluth, Minnesota, Police Department. I was so done. Done with checking boxes and filling out forms. Done with backgrounding. Done with the accelerated FTO program. I'd been on patrol since May. Nine hours ago, the reassignment came down, and off I went to the major crimes unit. It had been a long six months.

Detroit and Duluth might begin with the same letter but were stark opposites. I was more than ready for the slower pace of a metro area ninety-three percent smaller than Detroit's. The previous year, there'd been almost twelve thousand violent crimes in Detroit compared to nine hundred in the Zenith City of the Unsalted Seas. Pretty stark contrast, and I was very much looking forward to a slower pace.

In celebration, my new unit brought me to an actual queer-friendly bar.

Ryan Nash, my oldest friend and now assigned partner, elbowed me. "Can you still hold your liquor, Harrison?" Louder, he announced, "When Bec and I went to college at the University of Minnesota, she was the queen of shots. She could mix a cocktail with one hand and drink everyone under the table with the other."

Another round of pounding nearly did the table in.

"Jesus, Nash." Some things never changed, and I was okay with that.

Nash and I had grown up on the same block, ironclad besties after we banded together and beat up two bullies who'd been picking on both of us and half the class all through third grade and half of fourth. We went on to graduate from the same high school and attended the U of M together.

As kids, we often hung out in a treehouse in Nash's backyard, hiding from the heat of the summer sun, since his pale complexion, thanks to his Swedish ancestry, burned instead of tanning, unlike my own. On a hot summer day when we were fourteen, he was the first one I came out to. The memory was still incredibly vivid. Even now I could smell fresh cut grass and hear the buzzy chirp of crickets in late August.

He'd dramatically flexed his skinny arms. "So that's why you never wanted a piece of this. Actually, I was wondering when you'd figure it out."

That was that. No questions, no comments, only all-in support. He became my wingman when we went out, wasn't afraid of gay bars. He was the first one I'd called when I became engaged. We'd stayed in touch when I left the state, and he was the one to let me know Duluth had an opening when my world exploded.

Laughter faded, and I gave Nash a friendly shove. "You'll make me look bad in front of the boss." These days my alcohol intake was nowhere near the volume I'd sent through my liver at the U. Hitting the bottle had hit critical mass during the breakup of my marriage, but I'd since toned it down. I lifted my drink. "I try and moderate myself better these days. What is this thing anyway?"

Seated beside me was Sergeant Mateo Alverez, his neatly sculpted black beard at odds with his light-brown, very bald pate. Alvarez was usually serious and sometimes dour, but at the moment, his dark eyes glittered with humor. My semi buzzed, now immediate boss clapped me heavily on the shoulder. "Welcome to the Hornet's Nest, Harrison." He gave my bong a poke. "It's a BB. Every rook detective gets one. You're gonna be hooked for life."

He'd told me that years ago, when Duluth's violent and property crimes units had been merged, the team had been nicknamed the Hornet's Nest because no one got along.

"Thanks, I think." First, it felt awkward as hell to be called a rookie after years in law enforcement. Second, maybe these guys weren't as accommodating as it seemed if they brought every Tom, Dick, and newbie to The Mashed Spud. On the other hand, if all the new detectives were christened here, the squad knew what they were getting into, what with the rainbow and trans flags hanging on either side of the liquor shelves behind the bar.

Yeah.

I liked them even more for it.

Nash threw an arm over my shoulder. "Ah, come on, Sarge, she's not a rook anymore. Her training wheels are off."

"Ha ha." I actually felt safe to relax for the first time in the last year and a half. "Why's this monstrosity named the BB?"

"The Bong Bridge," supplied Detective Jen "Just call me Shingo, and yes I'm Anishinaabe, next question" Shingobe. "You know, the lift bridge connecting Duluth to Superior, Wisconsin, across the harbor. Get it? Bong?" She pointed at the bong-shaped container. "Slides down easy and comes back the same way. Sneaks up on you. Trust me, I know from experience."

"Got it." I relaxed even more, joining a bit in the teasing banter while I continued to assess my new partners.

Shingo was soft-spoken until she wasn't. Then it was time to find some ear plugs or make a hearing appointment. I liked her deliberate, calm demeanor, her sense of care for the citizens of the city. I liked her black-eyed, piercing, don't-fuck-with-me gaze, and the way she spoke in measured, confident tones. Dependable, would be there when you needed help. All the qualities of a great cop.

The Sarge was solid and didn't pull punches. I appreciated that.

"Here ya go, Harrison. You slayed the first one." Detective Sean "A-choo" Chu handed me another BB. His nickname came from the fact he sneezed whenever he looked at the sun and was never without a pair of wraparound sunglasses either on his face or on top of his buzz cut.

I eyed the drink, this one in a bright-green container. "Thought you were going to the bathroom."

"Took care of biz. Even washed my hands before ordering that for you." A chorus of groans rounded the table. "Hey, I like your vibe, Harrison. We're here to celebrate. Plus"—he pointed at the luminescent cups on the tabletop—"I think you need the entire rainbow."

I raised the bong. "I do love me a rainbow. Thanks, Chu."

He saluted me with his beer bottle and resettled between Alvarez and Shingo. In his late twenties, energetic and eager, Chu tried to keep everyone up on the latest lingo. When I first arrived, Nash told me Chu's introduction to the unit had been iffy at best. He'd come roaring onto the scene as an immature know-it-all, butting heads with Shingo, his new partner. It didn't take long before Shingo was done with his holier-than-thou attitude and put the smack down. From that point, Chu had gotten his act together. He was quick to laugh, loved to tell the story of his Highland Scots mom and Shanghai-born dad who fell in love in Istanbul, then settled, in of all places, Duluth.

My own parents had been killed by a drunk driver when I was in college. If I thought too hard about what happened, it still took my breath away. I was the youngest and had two older brothers. Unlike my mom and dad, neither of my siblings had been on board when I'd announced my sexual orientation as a teen, and while they weren't overtly judgmental to my face, plenty of discreet zingers flew. After the double funeral, they'd both moved south with their anti-woke wives. I hadn't seen either one of them in person in years. With a pang, I realized how much I missed my mom and dad and how much I'd missed the easy camaraderie of a tight-knit bunch of cops.

Maybe now I could put some of my shredded world back together. Or make a new world entirely. It had been a year and a half since Danna, my wife of twelve years, had thrown a gigantic wrench in the spokes of our relationship. Well, not so much as thrown a wrench in things but blown all we'd built together sky high. She booted me out and moved in the cute, muscle-bound Amazon delivery driver, a Gal Gadot look-alike who was more Poison Ivy than Wonder Woman. I was left with no spouse, no dogs—they stayed behind—and no house. I'd come out of the marriage with my car, a couple of pieces of furniture, and most of my clothes. My life'd become a country song, and I hated country music.

The day I moved out for good, I hit a local watering hole and hit it hard. With nowhere else to go, I walked two blocks to the PD and passed out at my desk. At least I'd been smart enough to listen to the ghosts of my parents reminding me not to crawl behind the wheel.

The captain had been furious when she found me sound asleep the next morning. After some fast talking and a hundred assurances I'd never repeat my behavior, she agreed not to put anything in my official file. That incident had been a wake-up call in a whole lot of ways. On the plus side, I was now healing, back in my home state, with a new job and the freshest of fresh starts.

Shingo gently tapped the neck of her Bud against the radioactive container in my hand. "I'm glad to have you on board, Harrison. Cheers."

"Cheers."

Allowing the conversation to flow around me, I checked out the bar. The usual tang of malty beer, too much cologne wafting off overeager college students looking to get laid, and nervous sweat, probably from the same kids, assaulted my nose. The clientele was queer and queer-friendly, a mix of locals and students. Everyone seemed focused on celebrating Saturday evening's arrival.

Televisions suspended on the walls were tuned to various sporting events, with a decided focus on women's teams. More high marks for whoever was running the place. Tonight, two of the University of Minnesota's women's teams were duking it out on the TVs. Women's soccer was battling Oregon, ahead one to zip, and the Golden Gophers women's hockey team was trailing Wisconsin three-two in the middle of the third.

I loved hockey and played on my high school team and then with the Gophers in college. I kept up on the NHL's Minnesota Wild, of course, and the Seattle Kraken. And now we had the Professional Women's Hockey League's Minnesota Frost. Dumb name, great team. The Frost had been in the Walter Cup finals—the pinnacle series of the PWHL—for the inaugural '23–'24 season and again this past spring. We'd taken the cup home both times.

The interior of the bar was shadowy, dimly lit by strings of multicolored lights arranged around liquor bottles and Edison bulbs hanging in rows from one end of the ceiling to the other. Their glow cast a golden hue on everyone.

Servers slalomed through the crowd as they delivered orders, dodged cocktail tables, and generally avoided plowing into inebriated dancers on a checkerboard of red-and-white linoleum tile. Metallic-red vinyl booths lined one wall, continuing the floor's color scheme. Almost all the tables were occupied, and partygoers were piled two and three deep at the bar itself.

The more I drank, the more my cares vanished. *That's right, Bec, loosen up that stiff spine a little.* After I finished the second BB, I was comfortably tipsy. It'd been forever and a day since I'd had some good old-fashioned fun.

Fun felt damn good.

My bladder prodded me out of my musings. I needed a pit stop and some non-alcohol-fueled liquid. "Yo," I called. "Gotta hit the restroom and grab some water, anyone else?"

A chorus of nopes and no thanks answered that.

I slid off my chair. Nash steadied me as I listed to one side. "Gonna make it?"

"Finding my sea legs. If I'm not back in a few minutes, don't come lookin', I might be cookin'."

Nash raised a brow. "Someone's feeling good."

"Been a minute."

"It has." He ruffled my short black spikes and refocused on the ongoing conversation.

Surprisingly, both restrooms had all-gender signs instead of the usual HIS and HERS. When I was done, I zigzagged to the busy bar, patiently waiting by the server's pick-up area for a someone to look my way.

Three bartenders were hard at it, whipping up drinks and pulling beer from a dozen taps. The crowd was thirsty tonight. *Duh, Bec, bar patrons are always thirsty.*

"Hey, hotness, what can I get for you?" The low voice slid over me like the smoothest silk. My attention whipped from crowd-watching to a pair of bright, greenish-hazel eyes. A woman peered at me from beneath a curly mop of copper hair shaved close on the sides and collar-length in the back. She leaned forward on well-toned arms. Beside her, a door leading from the bar's kitchen was slowing its swing, giving me a clue as to where she'd apparated from.

Those eyes were luminescent. The bar's lighting somehow made them appear as if they were lit from the inside out. For a long second I forgot why I was standing there. The first thing that popped out of my mouth once I dragged my eyes from hers was "I love your hair." It took me two full blinks to realize how stupid that sounded.

The woman broke into a sexy smile and my insides flip-flopped.

"I like your taste. This"—she ran a hand through her curls—"is classic again. Thank god. Now, what's your poison?"

* * *

In my absence, Chu had decided I needed to own the entire bong rainbow and had ordered four more drinks in the appropriate colors. Everyone pitched in to help down the killer brew. Before too long, Nash poured a quarter of his into my bong. From that point on, my cup was in a continual state of runneth-ing over. The hazy thought that I might be sorry tomorrow dissipated like steam rising from a hot cup of coffee.

Two laughter-filled hours later, our little group called it a night.

Alvarez and Shingo had already bailed.

With a sigh, Nash stood. "Well, this's been a good time. Glad you're here, Bec. Want me to walk you home?"

I considered the offer and aimed my wrist at my face. One thirty. I still felt so good. "Nah. My apartment's only a couple blocks away. I'll be fine. Gonna sit here and finish my water."

"You did good tonight." Chu pulled his jacket on. "You got yourself a collector set now. You're dope, Harrison. Glad to have you in the Hornet's Nest."

I waved a hand. "I'm dope. Cool. Back atcha."

Twenty minutes later, I was ready to hit it. I slid off my stool, but before both feet hit the ground, the world gyrated. My head spun like the Kansas twister that lifted up Aunt Em's house with Dorothy inside. My stomach vaulted into my throat.

Oh, no. No, no, no.

I reversed course, returned to the stool, and breathed deep, white-knuckling the table. I'd been so nicely buzzed. Then Shingo's words floated through my Tilt-A-Whirl brain. "Slides down easy and comes back the same way. Sneaks up on you. Trust me, I know from experience."

Damn it. I should've listened.

Someone out of my narrow line of sight began shouting, the tone tense, angry. Someone yelled back, and then a woman responded. I recognized that low voice. She with the luminescent eyes.

That thought spun away as voices continued to rise. Trouble was brewing and I was in less-than-zero capacity to help. I wanted to turn around to see what was happening but knew if I moved my head even a little, I was going to leave a whole lot more behind than I intended.

"I said out. Now."

"Whas your fucking problem, stupid dyke bitch? I was only complimenting those colored-boy homos on their fagness."

All noise in the bar ceased except for the roaring in my ears and their words.

"Arne, get outta my bar or I'll toss you headfirst out the door. This is it. You've had enough chances. You're not welcome here again. Ever."

"I haven't finished my—"

A screech ripped through a rapidly growing ache in my head, followed by a thud, a grunt, a growl, and the sound of what was probably a chair skittering across the floor. I gripped the table harder, then forced myself to look over my shoulder.

The woman had a thin, short man almost half her size on his toes, her hands curled into his shirt. She shook him, stuck her face in his. "Arne, you little asshole, I can't believe you just hit me. You've had the last BB of your life, you sleazy motherfucker. I see you in here again and you're dead meat. You hear me? Dead meat."

He squeaked.

She herded him to the door and helped him out.

That was all the looking I could tolerate. I straightened my head, breathed deeper, and started quietly chanting, "Do not puke. Do not puke. Do not puke."

"Okay, folks, show's over. We're done for the night." From the commanding tone the woman brandished, she either managed or owned the place.

How was I going to get out of here without... Oh god. I didn't want to think about it. Why did I let myself get so carried away? I tried again to stand and again quickly returned to my original position.

Fuck. Fuck. Fuck. My worst nightmare loomed ever larger. I was a puke-a-phobe, a bawling baby when it came to anything barf-related. Don't ever talk to me about the V-word.

*Stop, Bec.* I needed to think about something, anything other than that.

Knuckles rapped my table. "Closing time."

Great. Now I had that Semisonic earworm boring into my skull on top of the hell I was already in. No idea how long I listened to the sounds of tables and chairs being straightened and rearranged. Nausea and the pain were all-consuming. Someone turned the lights up. My head throbbed even harder. Then came the soggy splat of wet rags as tables were wiped down.

I knew I had to go but didn't dare shift a muscle.

A bang by my elbow made me jump. I swallowed hard.

"Come on, I said it was—hey, are you okay?" The luminescent lady again. Her low voice morphed from stern to concerned.

"Uhh" was all I could produce through gritted teeth.

"Can I call someone to pick you up?"

"Uhh."

"Shit." The woman exhaled heavily.

"Boss, you okay out there?" someone called.

"Yeah. Why don't you guys hit the overheads and go ahead and take off."

"We're not done—"

"It's all right. I'll finish up. But will you lock the front door when you go?"

"You bet." Footsteps. A shwap-thunk. "You're sure you're good?"

"I am. Thanks, Clare. I'll take care of whatever's not done."

After a few seconds, the brightness in front of my squinched eyelids thankfully dimmed.

The world went silent.

"What's your name?" The woman's voice was gentle now, at a much more agreeable volume.

"Uhh." Any more than that and I was going to lose it all over the table. *That must not happen. Must not. Must not.* The words rolled in circles around my brain.

Another sigh.

"If you move, you're going to throw up, aren't you?"

"Mmm." Now I didn't even dare open my mouth.

"Jesus. Guess you should've come up for water sooner. Okay. I'll get a garbage can and sit here with you till you feel better. Then we'll either get you upstairs or home."

I didn't reply.

* * *

Every inch of my body ached. I tried to open my eye, but someone had plucked out my eyeball, rolled it around in the sand, then shoved it back in again.

The hard surface under my face didn't feel like a beach. I forced the eye open.

Blurry fairy lights.

The smell of booze.

*Oh, fuck.* I was still at the bar.

Metallic clanging and banging hurt my head. My eyelid slid shut.

Muted memories flitted in and out.

BBs.

Laughter.

One-upping each other with on-the-job horror stories.

Then nothing.

My stomach ached. My sides ached. My back ached. My head was threatening to blow itself off my neck.

I whimpered.

*Death, please hurry and take me now.*

Death gave me the finger.

Little fucker.

I managed to open both eyes. My cheek was stuck to the table. The taste in my mouth was horrifying. Shame and embarrassment oozed down my spine. I had no memory of the cause of my physical discomfort, but I knew exactly what had happened. What would my partners have to say about this? What if Alvarez heard?

*Stop, Bec. One thing at a time. Present predicament takes priority.* More shards of memory from the previous few hours flashed and fled. The concerned look on my reluctant rescuer's face. Her steadying hand as I staggered back and forth to the bathroom.

Her telling me I was going to live when I was sure I wasn't. Right there if I needed her. Her patience. Her kindness. My head in a garbage can too many times. Over the toilet. Cool bathroom tiles under my palms.

The thought of what was probably on those tiles in a public restroom nearly made me gag again.

*Breathe slow.*

*Breathe deep.*

Should've stayed away from the BBs. Stuck with beer. I didn't like beer enough to get wasted on it. But those BBs, they were so good going down.

I never, ever wanted to see another one.

More metallic bangs. Pots and pans?

*Who cares. Get out.*

*Get out now.*

I ripped my cheek off the table, afraid I'd left half my face behind. With less success, I tried to ignore unrelenting nausea. Unsteadily, I wiggled out of the booth. Stood. Stumbled for the door, flipped open the deadbolt, and fled.

One thing was certain. I'd never show my face in The Mashed Spud again.

# CHAPTER TWO

At twenty after four, Theo Zaccardo scrubbed her hands over her face. She'd finished putting away all the previous night's pots and pans and had gathered the garbage, piling bags of it up in the kitchen next to the alley door. Since she'd let her staff go early so she could deal with Little Ms. Barfs-A-Lot, it was on her to put her ship back in shape for a new sailing day.

Exhaustion swamped every cell of her body. It'd been a long time since she'd pulled an all-nighter. Should've called the paramedics and let them deal with the woman right off the bat. Then she would be upstairs sound asleep. She ached from stooping as she did what she could to make sure the poor thing didn't crack her head open on the toilet seat and hauling her to and from the restroom.

But the woman—Theo still didn't know her name—had begged her not to call anyone, she didn't need an ambulance, to please give her a bit more time.

Maybe she was an alcoholic, afraid of repercussions from job or home. Or instead of a drinking issue, maybe she had some kind of alcohol allergy. In either case, heading out to the bar on a Saturday night was a dumbshit thing to do. But no matter how exasperated she'd been, Theo couldn't deny that tear-stained, terrified face. For some reason, her usually nonexistent-for-drunk-ass-customers heartstrings had been plucked. Something about this woman, beyond her now-pitiful state, drew Theo. Maybe it was the exchange they'd had earlier when she had come to the bar asking for water.

She'd always been a pushover for women in distress, especially beguiling ones, and this one checked all her boxes. Dark hair, mesmerizing eyes, a killer grin, and a healthy set of dimples.

She looked again at her watch. Time to send Barfy on her way or get her settled on the couch upstairs, though getting her there would be a bitch.

Theo tossed the rag she'd been using to wipe down the sinks into the dirty bin and exited the kitchen. She'd staged the woman in a booth closest to the bathrooms. The booth was empty.

"Are you kidding me?" She rolled her head to stretch her neck in preparation for round...what was it now? Six? Seven? Much more of this and the woman would probably need IV rehydration at the ER.

With a deep, please-let-this-be-it breath, Theo headed for the bathroom. In two seconds, she was back out. She checked the other bathroom.

Empty.

With the exception of the office, which was locked, the only other place Barfy could be was in the kitchen, and Theo knew for a fact she wasn't there. Had she left while Theo was finishing the washing up?

To the front door she went. Sure enough, it was unlocked. She stepped outside and checked the street in each direction. Barfy wasn't keeled over, at least within her line of sight.

Whatever.

Relieved of responsibility, Theo relocked the door and trudged up the stairs to bed.

* * *

The repeated, bellowing blare of a train horn jerked Theo awake. She swore, fumbling for her phone to silence the only god-awful alarm she'd found that would jolt her brain to consciousness.

The blind-darkened room returned to a blessed state of silence. She let the phone fall to her chest. *Remind me why I allow myself to get into these situations?* Then she answered herself. *Because you are a sucker for a woman in distress, that's why.* Theo was drawn to women with an edgy attitude who could laugh at themselves when the time was right. The woman had been full of edgy attitude, even while being sicker than hell.

The aroma of freshly brewed coffee registered, and she got up and followed her nose to the kitchen.

Tessa was at the table for two, which could become a table for three or four depending on which leaf you had up at any given time. A dragon fantasy novel was in one hand, a mug in the other. When she saw Theo, she set the book upside down on the tablecloth. "Well, don't you look like a rat dragged through the sewer twice over. Coffee's in the pot. Late night?"

Tessa was her youngest sister and The Mashed Spud's accountant. She had the capacity to drive Theo crazy, but more often was her saving grace. A couple of months ago, she'd literally kicked her lying, cheating, sack of shit husband in the balls, filed for divorce, and moved into Theo's spare bedroom. She brought with her some excellent benefits. She was a morning person, exactly the opposite of her sibling. When Theo awoke these days, the comforting scent of java often was filling the apartment. Tess spent her early hours reading and drinking a special blend she ordered up on the regular from Rabbit Hole, a café down in the Cities. It was the best damn coffee Theo had ever tasted. Prior to her arrival, Theo would walk a block and a half to Starbucks each morning to get her caffeine. This new arrangement saved her money, plus she got the pleasure of seeing Tess every single day instead of a couple of times a week. Win-win.

"Yeah, a late night that turned into an early morning. Another fine patron who imbibed too much. I didn't have the heart to boot her." She didn't feel the need to share the fact she'd practically been bribed not to.

"Only one reason you'd do something like that. What'd she look like?"

Theo barked a laugh as she extracted a soup-bowl-sized mug from the cabinet. "Black hair, blue eyes."

"That's all it took. You have such a type." Tessa thrust her own cup toward Theo. "Fill, please."

* * *

An hour later, caffeinated, fed, showered, and somewhat more coherent, Theo descended the stairs and swung open the door leading into The Mashed Spud's kitchen. She flipped the deadbolt on the door to the alley, gathered the bags of trash, and slammed into the door when it didn't open. What the hell? She stepped back and pushed on the door again. It was locked. Had she forgotten to lock it last night and just now relocked it? Considering the havoc of the night before, it was entirely possible. On her second attempt, the door opened and she carried the bags out to the dumpster in the alley.

The sun had burned off most of the morning's chill, and the sky was silky blue. Theo loved days like these, where she didn't sweat half to death or freeze her ass off. Or slip on ice and do a faceplant, something which happened to almost every Minnesotan at least once a year.

She wedged her fingers under the faded black plastic lid, raised it up, and gave it a hard shove. The lid slowly swung like a one-way pendulum and smacked the dumpster's metal backside with a loud bang.

God, it stunk to high hell.

She held her breath and pitched the plastic bags into the chest-high receptacle, exhaling as she walked behind the dumpster to close its lid. *Must be time for pick up*, she thought. *Getting pretty… Shit!*

She flinched and did a double take. Poking out from between the black bags was a well-worn black tennis shoe attached to a very hairy ankle. *Oh, hell. Not again.*

Twice in the previous month the same kid from the local university had crawled into their dumpster and decided to take a nap in the stank. Most likely after a few too many Bongs. Why anyone would make the decision to crash in moldering trash was beyond her. The nearby cardboard recycling container would've been a much less aromatic option. Granted, good decisions probably hadn't been top of mind when he made his choice.

Last time, Theo had told the kid if she saw him snoozing in her dumpster one more time, she'd call the cops instead of sending him on his hungover way. *Guess he chose the cops.*

She grabbed one of the bags and pulled it out, exposing a bent knee covered by stained, ash-gray sweatpants. She gave the bony joint a shake. "All right, bud. This is it. You need serious help."

He didn't budge.

"Hey, buddy. Time to rise and shine." She pulled out two more bags and froze. The world shifted sickeningly.

Arne, the homophobic, racist idiot she'd booted last night, wasn't staring up at her. He wasn't staring at anything.

Someone had scrawled "dead meat" in red letters on his forehead.

She dropped the sacks of rubbish from numb fingers and fumbled for her phone. Her hands shook so hard she almost dropped it as she pushed the three digits.

"911, what's your emergency?"

"This is Theo, uh, Theo Zaccardo. I own The Mashed Spud on Main. There's a body in my dumpster."

# CHAPTER THREE

The repeated chirping of an incoming call dragged me out of an uneasy sleep. Whoever was calling needed to go away so I could get back to trying to ignore the drum line whaling on my gray matter. The ringing stopped. Then started again.

"Shit." I jolted upright, clamped one hand on my forehead, and grabbed the phone with the other. "Hello?"

"Harrison?" Sergeant Alvarez. "You okay?"

"Hey, Sarge." I swallowed hard. "Yeah. Yeah, I'm fine." My voice came out like a croaking toad.

"Sorry to call you in early. I need you to head to the bar we were at last night."

*Oh, shit.* A shot of adrenalized fear crept up my spine. "What's up?"

"Body in a dumpster. Nash is already on his way."

"Body in a dumpster," I echoed weakly. Okay. It was okay. I could deal with that. Slowly, I swung my legs over the side of the bed. Thankfully, the world stayed where it belonged. "Be there as soon as I can."

Fifteen minutes later, after downing four ibuprofen and two glasses of water, finding clean clothes, and trying and failing to tame bedhead, I found a DPD ball cap and was out the door.

I kicked myself for not accepting the walk home Nash had offered. Irony couldn't even begin to cover it. At least the hangover overshadowed my humiliation.

An officer I'd spoken to a few times was stationed at The Mashed Spud's door, holding a clipboard. "Hey, Falls."

Officer Falls gave me a wide, gapped-tooth, hundred-watt grin. "Detective Harrison. Congrats. Moving up in the world, I hear."

"Yup. Look what I wind up with on Day Two." The kid appeared fifteen, but I'd found out she was in her early twenties.

"Probably should give you a heads-up on that. You've got a new nickname."

*Oh, shit.* "What?" The hammering against my temples doubled.

"Detective Detroit. We haven't had a homicide around here for almost a year. Till today. Murder followed you from Detroit. Get it? Detective Detroit. It's Hal Bergstrom's fault."

I wracked my brain. Who the hell was Hal Bergstrom?

Falls read my look of confusion. "He's the county coroner. Everyone calls him Hal."

"Great. Thanks."

"Hal loves a nickname. You know how that goes."

Law enforcement did love nicknames. Detective Detroit wasn't so bad. Coulda certainly been much worse.

She finished logging my name and badge number. "You're all set."

"Thanks." I pulled the door open to face the intense shame I knew was coming as soon as I saw Nash. Or worse, the woman who'd stayed with me all night.

The bar was inky after the brightness outside. For now, the front of the house was devoid of activity, for which I was grateful. I avoided looking down the hall where the restrooms I'd gotten to know intimately were and swallowed suddenly increased queasiness. It'd sure be easy to cruise down that hall and escape through the emergency exit. Then it dawned on my battered brain that I'd trigger an alarm if I did that. Probably a very loud one. Not a good look for a detective on her second day.

Someone had propped open the door behind the bar and I heard the buzz of voices from the kitchen. I made my way toward the sound.

The fading scent of last night's pizza and the sharp smell of liquor wafting from a battered gray trash can which appeared to be a recycling bin made my stomach twinge. *Breathe deep and slow*, I reminded myself as I entered the kitchen and surveyed the room.

Two stainless steel coolers and four rolling racks were loaded with bar kitchen necessities. A countertop pizza oven, a prep table, and a triple sink lined one wall. Red ceramic tile with darkened grout covered the floor. Nash and someone I hadn't yet met, a man dressed neck-to-toe in Tyvek, were in conversation near the back door.

I took a fortifying breath and approached the duo, extracting a pair of blue nitrile gloves from a case attached to my belt, and pulled a pair of shoe covers out of a nearby box.

"Hey, Harrison." Nash did a half-pivot from the short, bespectacled, round-faced man with a wild fringe of white hair. "How ya feeling today?"

"Don't ask," I said as I teetered on one foot and then the other to pull the covers on.

"Ah, yes, you must be the new detective," said the man beside Nash, rubbing his hands together. "Dr. Hal Bergstrom, St. Louis County Medical Examiner, at your service. Call me Hal, but don't call me Al. And skip the doctor bullshit." He actually did a half-bow and stuck out a pudgy hand.

I shook it. "Good to meet you, Hal. Detective Detroit reporting for duty."

Hal's eyes crinkled like a jolly good elf's when he smiled. "I do like a police officer who can take a bit of fun. I've heard much about you from Detective Nash here."

*Oh boy.*

"Don't worry. It was all good," Hal assured me. Then he nodded toward the alley. "All righty then. Let's get down to business so the techs can get to theirs whenever they arrive."

"I've already notified Skippy to call out the crime scene unit." Nash followed Hal outside, and I followed. "They should be here any time."

"Who's Skippy?" I'd met many of the officers in the department, but Skippy was an unknown quantity.

"He's head of the CSU," Hal said. "Sergeant Matthew Skip. Skippy. But he actually likes Jiffy better." Hal let loose a bellow at his own sense of peanut butter humor.

I wondered if Hal might possibly have inhaled a little too much formaldehyde.

Nash said, "Don't worry about Hal, Detective Detroit. You'll get used to him."

"Got it, thanks."

Outside, squad cars blocked both ends of a block-long alley lined with rolling dumpsters and recycling containers for various businesses, leaving a narrow path for vehicles to navigate.

Hal led us to a dented green garbage dumpster. A four-foot ladder stood beside the container, and garbage bags were scattered on the asphalt around it.

"What do we know?" I asked.

Nash produced a pocket-sized spiral notebook. "911 call came in from the owner of the bar, Theodora Zaccardo, at 9:31 a.m. Responding officer is that way"—he pointed to one end of the alley—"and Zaccardo is over there." He jerked a thumb at the black-and-white on the opposite end. "She was taking garbage out and found a deceased male in this dumpster. She removed the bags she'd tossed in. That's why those are on the ground." He pointed vaguely in the direction of the dumpster with his pen. "Here's the kicker. Our DB has 'dead meat' written on his forehead in what appears to be blood."

"Seriously?"

"Dead." Hal snickered.

Why did that phrase sound so familiar? Dead meat. You're dead meat. Who's dead meat? I gave my head a quick shake, then was sorry.

"Detective Detroit," Hal said, "are you okay?"

"Oh. Yeah. Fine." Good old Hal had a sharp eye beneath his droll exterior. "There's something about that phrase. It's so, I don't know, familiar. Anyway. never mind, let's get down to it." *Please, stomach, don't rebel at what is coming.*

The walk-through was thankfully nonproblematic. Based on his preliminary exam, the doc put time of death somewhere between two a.m. and four, maybe five, but wouldn't know for sure until they got the body out of the dumpster and onto a table.

However, he felt fairly sure that the deep wound on the victim's neck was most likely the cause of death. The amount of blood behind the dumpster led him to believe that was where the murder had taken place.

Nash and I left Bergstrom to do his thing and regrouped in The Mashed Spud's kitchen. We peeled off gloves and the shoe covers and tossed everything.

"Why do you think someone would take the time to write 'dead meat' on the guy's forehead?" I grimaced in frustration as I again tried and failed to put context to the phrase.

"Revenge? A warning?"

"Maybe both."

"Could be. Gang ties?"

"Mob ties?"

"Maybe he pissed off the little old lady next door."

"She'd have to be one strong old lady to toss him into that dumpster."

We laughed. Cop humor got us all through some very hard times.

I followed Nash out of the kitchen, into the darker, main part of the bar, which was still devoid of humanity. I was in absolutely no hurry to find out if the bar's owner was the same woman who'd begrudgingly babysat me last night. The thought of my alcohol-induced loss of control brought an uncomfortable flush to my face. My ears heated up like red-hot burners. God, I detested my body's reaction to anger, embarrassment… Well, pretty much any high emotion.

"Nash. Hold on a sec."

"Yeah?"

"How about I take the responding officer and you talk to Zaccardo?"

An expression I couldn't identify flitted across his face. "I was hoping you might take her." He grimaced, then sighed. "I need to tell you something."

"Uh-oh." He sounded serious, not something he usually was.

"It's the teary shit."

"Teary shit?"

"Yeah."

"Wait a minute. Because Zaccardo is a woman, you think she'll be bawling after finding a dead body?"

In the low light, I saw the whites of his eyes as they grew wide.

"No. No, that's not it at all. Not because she's a woman. Well, she is a woman, but it's not that." He cleared his throat. "It's a crying thing. Man, woman, kid. Whatever. She's pretty upset."

"Seriously? You're a cop. Of course you're going to run into howlers." This man I'd known since we were kids was afraid of a few tears?

"I know. Since Sherry and I had Harper last year, whenever I see someone scrunching their face up, getting teary, or...well, crying, I choke up so bad I can hardly talk."

"Are you kidding me?"

He just looked at me.

"What'd the rest of the crew say?" I could imagine them laughing him right out of town.

"The few times I thought there might be a problem, I managed to fast talk my way out of dealing with it." In a quieter voice, he mumbled, "Haven't told another soul. Not Sherry, not anyone."

"Well, shit, Nash. Yeah, I'll talk to Zaccardo. I've got your back." I gave his shoulder a friendly shove. "Your secret's safe. But, man, you gotta do something. Seriously."

"I know. I do know."

We parted ways to walk around the block in opposite directions. I plodded resolutely along the sidewalk, blood again pounding like a bass drum against my forehead, hoping Zaccardo was someone I'd never seen.

A Duluth PD Ford Explorer was parked the wrong way on the sidewalk, streetside doors open. Behind it, crime scene tape stretched from one side of the alley to the other, the shiny yellow strip rippling in the light breeze. A uni got out to meet me.

"Officer…" I leaned in to read his nameplate. "Officer Lieder, I'm Detective Harrison."

"Hey, Detective. Good to meet you. Zaccardo's in the back seat. She's pretty wrecked."

"I imagine. Thanks." Maybe it was a good thing Nash picked door number two. I braced myself and walked around Lieder to the open rear door. A woman wearing a black beanie pulled down over her ears and a faded black hoodie with The Mashed Spud logo sat sideways on the car seat, heels on the doorjamb, appearing to intently study the cracked sidewalk.

I crouched down in front of her. "Hey, Ms. Zaccardo, I'm Detective—" I stopped midsentence when the woman jerked her head up, clearly startled. Pale beneath olive-tinged skin, she peered at me with glazed eyes, eyes that in this light weren't so much luminescent hazel as piercing green.

Those eyes widened.

Mine did the same.

"Detective? You?"

"I…yeah." *Nightmares do come true.*

I stood, retreated a step. She slid off the seat. We stared at each other a few interminable seconds.

*Speak*, I ordered myself. "I'd like to apologize for last night." *Please, Mother Earth, open up right now and I'll be happy to drop right out of sight.*

A shoulder lifted. "Shit happens. How're you feeling? I'm surprised you're upright." A faint glint of humor glittered in those eyes, then disappeared as fast as it came.

"Honestly, I feel like hell. Unfortunately, murder doesn't wait for you to have a solid eight-hour snooze." I pulled a deep breath and exhaled slowly. "Anyway, Ms. Zaccardo, we should get down to it. I'm Detective Harrison."

"Theo."

"Okay. Theo, I need to ask you some questions."

"Yeah." Her face went whiter if that was even possible. She hugged herself.

I thought her legs might buckle. "You want to sit back down?"

"No."

Thankfully, my headache had evolved into a dull, steady throb, and I could think with some clarity. I pulled a notebook and pen from my jacket. Then an unbidden, vague memory flickered through my mind. The warmth of Theo's hand on my forehead as—I shut down that thought fast.

"Are you okay, Detective?"

I looked into those damn eyes, eyes that assessed me in a far too familiar way. "I'm fine. All right, here we go. What's your full name?"

"Theodora Ramona Zaccardo."

"That's quite a handle."

"Why do you think I go by Theo?"

Birthday and address went smoother. Theo was forty-three, living in an apartment above the bar.

"You own The Mashed Spud?"

"Yup. In the family for three generations."

"You live alone?" I had no idea if Theo was straight, lesbian, nonbinary, pan, plain old queer, ace, or whatever, but her appearance indicated she might fall into one of those categories. Even with this oversized hangover, my "Ah-ha" antenna perked up.

"No."

Well, that was that. As if Theo would be interested in someone who'd probably thrown up all over her during an alcoholic blackout. *Jesus Christ, Bec, find your parking brake and set the fucker. You swore off women when Danna clawed out your heart, chewed up your soul, and spit it back at you.*

Back to business. "Who lives with you?"

"My sister, Tessa. She's the bar's accountant. She recently moved in with me."

Something between my shoulder blades released.

*Stop. What's wrong with you? Get your ass back to it.*

"When did—"

"Hey, Harrison," Nash interrupted as his rapid footsteps approached.

I looked up.

He held a large evidence bag in a gloved hand. Inside was a two-foot-long, curved blade affixed to a white plastic handle with brownish stains. "Ms. Zaccardo," he said, "does this look familiar?"

Theo leaned closer. "Looks like one of my pizza rockers. A pizza cutter. Where did you get it?"

"That," Nash said, "is indeed the question, isn't it? Did you use it last night?"

"We have multiple cutters. I don't know if I used that one last night or not."

Nash eyed her dubiously. "Would you be aware if one was missing?"

Theo frowned. "I don't keep track of the number of pizza cutters we've got. Seven or eight, maybe."

Holy shit. Thanks to this sudden, literally sharp reality check, my brain snapped into full-on business mode. "Who worked the kitchen last night?"

"I worked back-of-house."

Nash glanced sharply at Theo. "Just you?"

"Just me, though all the staff have access."

I pocketed my notebook and pen. "I think it's time for a ride to the station for a longer conversation."

* * *

Formalities dispensed with, our person of interest sat slumped at a table in one of DPD's bleak interview rooms.

"All right." Sgt. Alvarez crossed his arms as he peered through the glass at Theo Zaccardo, the shoulders and sleeves of his button-down shirt straining against the well-defined muscles of his biceps and shoulders. "So what you're telling me, Harrison, is you were in The Mashed Spud until four this morning puking your guts out."

My face felt like a red-hot afterburner as I peered at Alvarez's profile in the half-light of the observation room. "Yes, sir."

I'd broken down and explained to Nash and Alvarez the bits and pieces I remembered about what had occurred after the party broke up. Regardless of the embarrassment, nondisclosure would surely bite me hard enough to hurt. Coming clean right off the bat was the best decision, albeit a mortifying one.

"Rigor mortis and body temp puts preliminary time of death somewhere between two and five-ish in the morning," Nash said.

"I hear you, Nash." Alvarez studied my face. "But it seems our new detective has some gaps in her memory, so that doesn't necessarily help. There's potentially a half hour, maybe forty-five-minute gap that Zaccardo hasn't accounted for. Harrison, you sure you don't remember anything else?"

"Almost nothing until I woke up, like I said, at four something and headed home. Except—"

"Yeah, yeah." He grimaced. "I got that part. Okay, you two. Go in and see what she has to say for herself."

Five minutes later, we were seated in the interview room across from Theo, who was intently focused on the Styrofoam cup of coffee I'd brought her. Under the table, one of her knees was bouncing up and down like a jackhammer. We went through all the Miranda warnings one more time, and again Theo refused an attorney.

Both Nash and I had a yellow legal pad, and a thin manila case file was tucked under Nash's.

Theo's unruly red curls were even more untamed now that she was hatless. Her face was still pale, eyes unfocused. I fielded a pang of guilt, wondering if Theo's eyes appeared so hollowed because I kept her up most of the night or if something much, much more serious was troubling her. I hoped for the former but couldn't rule out the latter.

"Ms. Zaccardo," I said, "where were you between one thirty and six this morning?"

"Back to that, are we?" She didn't look up from the coffee cup. I didn't answer.

She sighed, avoiding my eyes. "I was at the Spud. Hit the hay about four thirty, got up at nine, showered, got dressed, ate breakfast. Around ten, maybe a little after, I went downstairs to take the garbage out. Found Arne in the dumpster. Called you guys."

Nash smoothed the top page of his legal pad. "Can anyone confirm your whereabouts this morning, say, let's say between four and six this morning?"

"My sister, Tessa. Like I said, she lives with me."

Nash leaned forward. "Did Tessa know about your altercation with Arne?"

"No. Not till I got up." She still hadn't looked at me. "I did not wake her up to say, 'Hey, honey, I'm home safe and sound, and I had to throw a little weasel out of the bar last night.' Jesus."

"Hey." Nash raised his hands. "We're only asking questions, trying to figure out what happened."

"Sorry."

"It's okay." Nash softened his tone. "Why were you up until so late?"

*Here we go.* My face began yet another slow sizzle.

Theo didn't so much as twitch. "I had a sick customer. Happens sometimes."

For me, being ratted out no longer mattered, although Zaccardo didn't know that. The fact she didn't rat the puker out was a little disconcerting and hugely kind. Jumbled, confusing emotions rocketed through me. The last thing I needed was to get caught up trying to untangle my battered soul. I slammed the lid on the entire emotional conundrum and said, "Please walk us through your morning from the time you got up till you left the apartment."

I jotted notes, asked a clarifying question here and there, but let Nash steer the conversation.

After we twice more made Theo repeat her morning and finding the body, Nash said, "I think we're pretty clear on the lead-up to finding the deceased. Let's move on."

"Yes. Let's." Theo's tone sharpened with the level of increasing exasperation. "I saw the shoe, pulled off a bag, exposed a knee, gave it a shake. No response. Then I removed two or three more bags of garbage." Theo paused to clamp her eyes shut, as if doing so would keep the recollected image off the movie screen of her mind.

I could've told her it wouldn't work.

"I recognized Arne. His neck..." She threw up her hands. "He'd been nearly decapitated, probably with my own goddamn pizza cutter. Jesus. Are you happy now?"

"Ms. Zaccardo, Theo," I said, "we want to make sure to establish as complete a story as we can. We aren't assigning blame." *Yet*, whispered the cop in me. *No way*, argued the not-cop part. But the gap between four thirty and when she got up hung like a weighted shroud.

*Concentrate, Harrison. Do your job.*

A rap on the door interrupted the proceedings. Shingo entered, whispered something in Nash's ear, and retreated, pulling the door closed behind her.

Nash's jaw muscle bulged. He'd always been a clencher when trouble arose. "What else did you notice?"

Theo's voice dropped and her shoulders slumped. "Someone had written 'dead meat' on his forehead."

"Does that phrase have any particular meaning for you?" Nash asked.

It meant something to me. I just couldn't remember why. I watched Zaccardo's lips tighten as she looked anywhere but at either one of us.

"When I threw Arne out of the bar last night..." She took a deep breath.

I straightened. I would've been there for that. "You tossed him? Why?"

"He's a homophobic asshat. He hates me because I'm gay, and a woman, and I own a business. He usually keeps his opinions to himself, always pays his tab. Once in a while, though, he gets— got—out of hand, drinks too much, goes on a homophobic diatribe or a racist rant. Occasionally at the same time. This time he chose to hassle two flaming college boys. I intervened. He punched me." She pointed at her cheek.

Nash and I leaned in. Sure enough, the flesh along her cheekbone was swollen, and a bruise was forming. Another thing

I'd missed last night. And again this morning. "I know it's a little late, but do you need medical attention?"

"No. I'm fine."

"We'll need pictures of that." Nash scrawled the reminder on his pad. "Do you know Arne's last name?"

"I'm sure it's in the credit card receipts, but no, not off the top of my head."

"All right," I said. "What happened after he punched you?"

"I told him he was eighty-sixed and tossed him."

"You didn't hit him back?"

A horrified expression flickered across Theo's face. "Of course not. I did grab him by the front of his shirt, maybe shook him up a little. I dragged him to the front door and kicked him out. It might not have been the gentlest bounce of all time, but it's what happened."

"Do you recall what you said to Arne when you threw him out?" Nash asked, a little too casually.

"I told him I'd had enough, and this was his last chance."

"Is that exactly what you said?"

Theo pursed her lips and closed her eyes. "I told him…" She stopped, a look of terrified resignation appearing on her face. "I told him if he ever stepped foot in my bar again, he was dead meat."

* * *

"Gut impressions?" asked Sgt. Alvarez as we peered at Theo through the two-way mirror. Her head was in her hands.

"She admits she told Arne he'd be dead meat when she booted him," Nash said. "Claims she didn't kill him. Said if she had, she wouldn't be stupid enough to write 'dead meat' on him."

"Good point." Alvarez's eyes were bloodshot. Murder was a picnic for no one. "What else?"

Nash yawned. "If her sister can alibi her I'm inclined to believe her. Zaccardo's an established businesswoman with decades running a successful bar. She's survived the rednecks up here this long without taking someone out, dealt with more than her share of slurs in the past. But Arne did punch her, and we all know once things turn physical anything can happen."

"Harrison?"

I felt Alvarez's dark eyes on me. I had to be logical, well-reasoned. I didn't know the woman aside from our interactions the night before—most of which I couldn't remember—but on a strangely deep, cellular level, I knew Theo hadn't killed Arne.

Regardless, I needed here to be careful not to come off as a knee-jerk, defensive lesbian supporting another probably queer person, either.

"Do I think she has the capability to physically hurt someone if she had to, absolutely. But she's got a lot at stake. The Mashed Spud, her stable position in the community. She doesn't appear to be a loose cannon. It would take some serious muscle to heave Arne into the dumpster. Maybe she could have managed that, but if she killed him behind the dumpster why go through the effort of dumping him in it only to call us this morning to report finding the body? As for the cutter, it's possible someone stole it, maybe to frame her? Or just swiped it to use it. My gut says she's no killer. It feels like whatever happened is way more than a belligerent, drunk asshole and a pissed-off barkeep."

Seconds ticked long and loud in my ears. Then Alvarez shifted from the two-way glass to face us, half his face sallow, the other in deep shadow. "Zaccardo will remain a person of interest. Remind her not to leave the state while this investigation is ongoing, then cut her loose. Harrison, tomorrow ask Zaccardo if the back door to the kitchen was secured last night and talk to the sister about that alibi. Nash, continue working the Arne angle. Once we have his last name, we should be able to find out where he lives."

# CHAPTER FOUR

Theo released her seat belt. "Thanks for the ride."

"Whaddya take me for?" Tessa retorted. "You think I'd leave you with the fuzz, let you stew all locked up in the slammer?"

"Funny." Theo pushed open the door of the Corvette and attempted to lever herself out of the low-slung car without landing on her butt in the parking lot. "You need to do something with this accident waiting to happen before the white shit starts dropping. Navigating Duluth in the winter is bad enough but add a rocket engine and rear-wheel drive and you'll be spinning your tires till spring, if you live through it. You should've taken the Sedona when you bailed."

"Fuck the kiddy hauler. The kids have flown the coop and so have I." Tessa managed to wedge herself out of the car and stagger upright, finally catching her balance on three-inch spike heels. "I spent too many years dragging 'em around in that thing. Besides"—she patted the acid-yellow roof—"this fucking thing is Vinnie's baby. He's not getting it back. Unless it's in pieces." She giggled maniacally.

"All righty then." Theo had hated Vinnie almost as soon as she'd met him years ago, a few hours after he and Tess had driven out of Short Gap—an Iron Range town of three thousand and the place that most of the Zaccardo family called home—and had gotten hitched at the justice of the peace in Duluth.

A fresh-faced eighteen-year-old Tess had waggled her left hand at their mother, showing off a thin, silver ring embedded with a diamond the size of a grain of sand, which was probably nothing more than cubic zirconia. Hell hath no fury like their mother, and it'd taken a month for their father to be even close to civil with Vinnie.

As the truth came out, Vinnie had indeed given off fool's gold vibes. A baby girl came four months later, another girl eighteen months after that, and then a boy, who was, of course, the apple of Vinnie's eye. Which unfortunately was ever-roving, it turned out. He not only had an eye for his wife's boobs, but for the breasts of any woman in his immediate vicinity. Vinnie stepped out more often than he was home, hardly helping to raise his own offspring.

The jerk had pummeled Tessa's self-esteem and tried everything he could think of to alienate her and the kids from the family. But the Zaccardos were nothing if not a tight-knit bunch. They refused to play that game. One of the family members living in the vicinity showed up at Tess's house in Short Gap every single day for the entire first year of their marriage. Vinnie finally got the idea he wasn't going to shake them, and the visits cooled to once a week. Sometimes it paid to have a large family and a stubborn one at that.

Tessa had kept her head down for her children. Theo knew how hard she had tried to make it work and at the same time how difficult it'd been for her to walk away from all she'd known, happily or not, for the last twenty-three years. Since Tess had escaped the jerk, Theo was seeing bits and pieces emerging of the amazing, loving, ass-kicking pre-Vinnie ass-kicker Tess used to be, F-bombs and all.

"Hurry up, big sis," Tessa called and turned around to wait for her. "What the hell happened to your face? I didn't notice before, but you have half a shiner. Did the cops do that?"

Theo managed a laugh. "No, the cops didn't do anything. Arne belted me, and then I threw his ass on the street."

Tess eyed her, as if assessing Theo's honesty. "If they did knock you around, I know a lawyer."

"Of course you do." She bumped Tess's shoulder with hers. "Come on."

Tessa pushed her hands deeper into the pocket of her neon pink-and-purple hoodie as they walked. "You're right, as usual. About the car. I know I'm going to need something better suited for these fucking hilly streets."

"We'll figure it out." Theo pulled open The Mashed Spud's door and let Tess enter. At eight in the evening on a Sunday, the Spud was quiet. "You go on up. I'm going to check in with the gang."

"Okay. Can't wait to hear about the real beating and torture you've endured at the hands of the oppressors."

Minutes later, incredibly relieved to be home and not in jail, Theo dragged herself upstairs. Unwelcome fragments of the distant, awful memories she'd been attempting to hold at bay since she found Arne in the dumpster flickered through her mind. She felt sick, exhausted yet amped, achy, and jumpy as hell. She closed and locked the front door and kicked her shoes off, leaving them in a jumble in the entryway.

"This princess is awaiting her highness's presence in the kitch. Did they take your mug shot and print you?"

"No, and yes, for purposes of elimination, they said. This highness needs to pee. Hang on to your tiara."

Deed done, hands washed, Theo pulled out a chair, then realized something was cooking on the stove. The heady sizzle of ground meat and the aroma of burger and onions woke her up. "What are you making?"

"Anti-Burger on Smashed. I figured you might want some comfort food after your fucked-up day."

"I love you so much."

When Theo and her six scrappy siblings were tots, their parents didn't always have a lot of money. Who needed burger buns, anyway?

A burger became legendary when it was transformed into the Anti-Burger. What kid didn't love anti-whatever-the-usual-boring-thing was? Brown up some ground beef with onions, heap the mess on top of a castle of mashed potatoes. Then the deconstructed burger was crowned with a Kraft cheese single and tossed in the microwave until the cheese melted. Voilà, there was the most delicious creation in the world, ketchup optional. Friends who got to have supper at the Zaccardos' and were served the Anti-Burger were the envy of school for weeks. Now that Theo thought about it, it didn't take much to elevate the ordinary into something mythical when dealing with elementary school kids.

"Here you go." Tess set a plate in front of her.

"I don't know what I did to deserve you." She grabbed the offered fork and dug in.

"You led the way for me, that's what you did. Now, spill your guts."

Between bites, Theo recounted everything.

"So let me get this straight." Tess tucked her straight-as-Theo's-was-curly strawberry-blond hair behind an ear. "Barfy from last night is Detective Harrison?"

"I heard her partner call her Bec," Theo said absently as she scooped up another bite.

"Bec, huh? Is she single?"

"Seriously, after that entire story, that's what you choose to focus on? If she's single?"

"Well, romance might be off the plate for me, but it doesn't have to be for you."

"Romance? Are you kidding me? Did you hear what I said, Tess? The cops think I murdered Arne. She's a cop. Only you would think about a hookup at a time like this."

"I didn't mean a hookup. This is the first time you've talked about a woman who's caught your eye in years."

"Who said she caught my eye? I babysat her while she threw up for hours on end and then she hauled me in."

Tessa held her hands out, palms up. "Okay, okay. Can't I dream of someone else's happy relationship if I can't have my own? Especially yours. You never give yourself credit for what an amazing person you are. You need to let your freak flag fly, girl, and find someone to love on. End your questionable habit of one-night stands. This chick, you light up when you talk about her, even if she did throw up on your sorry self."

"I light up? Oh, no. No, I don't. I do not light up, and she didn't throw up *on* me."

"You do too light up."

"I can't believe we're having this conversation." The glare Theo sent Tess was hot enough to scald.

"Fine. I'm done matchmaking. Happy now?"

"Yes. By the way, you're my alibi for between four thirty and nine this morning."

"Of course I'm your alibi." Tessa narrowed her eyes. "I heard you come in at exactly 4:27—I know because I glanced at the clock—when your shoe slammed against the wall."

"Oh, come on. It didn't quite slam, it was more of a bang." Theo slouched as Tessa gave her a raised eyebrow. "Okay. I did kick my shoes off with more force than usual. I'd lost Barfy and I was frustrated, I guess. I'm sorry-not sorry I woke you, considering. I think they're figuring you were asleep, and I'd have no one to alibi me between half past four and the moment you saw me in the morning."

"I gotcha covered."

The compassion in Tessa's eyes almost made her choke up. "I love you, sis."

"You better."

Theo bit back a yawn. "I'm sure someone's going to show up to ask you about my whereabouts. So we're straight, you heard me come in at—what'd you say? 4:27?"

"On the dot."

"Okay. My alarm was set for nine. It went off, I got up, you saw me then. I ate breakfast, had some of that miraculous coffee of yours, showered, and then headed downstairs to take the garbage out a little after ten."

"You can add to it I can also confirm you were here after the shoe thing and before you got up because you were snoring so loud I could hear you through your bedroom door."

"I do not snore."

"You do too."

"Do not."

"I'll record you one of these days. Maybe you have sleep apnea. I read that's some bad shit."

The snoring joke had been ongoing since they were kids. Although maybe she did saw logs. Whatever. It wasn't like she was sleeping with anyone, and if she did do the sniffle-sniffle-snort-snort, as their mom used to say, it would be even more proof she hadn't attempted to decapitate Arne.

"Snore truce," Theo said.

"Fine." Tessa drew a hand dramatically to her chin and gazed at the ceiling. "It sure seems like someone is trying to frame you. Who was in the bar last night and heard you tell Arne the Ass he'd be dead meat?"

Theo closed her eyes and tried to conjure up the picture. "Detective Harrison. The two kids Arne hassled. Arne himself, and a couple in the back booth. Three guys at the bar, another playing pool, and one hanging out by the juke. Maybe one more person at the bar, but I think she was a regular. Once Arne socked me in the face, I lost it. The rest is a blur."

"At least a few people had to have heard you yell at Arne. I'm sure your exchange wasn't exactly quiet."

"Nope." Theo could still hear herself shouting. "They got quite an earful."

"Rule out Harrison. You said she didn't seem to remember anything about the incident, right?"

"Right. She was way too messed up. I think we could count out the two boys too. I doubt they could hurt a horsefly even if it bit them. The people in the booth were so busy sucking face I'm sure they paid no mind. Took me three tries to get their attention to tell them I was closing up."

"So that leaves the jukebox guy and the three at the bar?"

"And the dude playing pool. Maybe there were one or two additional customers, but like I said, the last bit of closing is nothing but a jumble."

"Maybe if we can figure out who the jukebox, pool, and bar guys were, we can also figure out if any of them have a beef with you. Maybe you had words with one of them in the past and they're holding on to a grudge."

"And they killed a man to get back at me? Right. I've kicked out plenty of drunks, but seriously, would that be worth setting me up for murder? It doesn't make sense."

"Men don't make sense most of the time. I have plenty of experience in that arena. Anyhoo, it can't hurt to talk to your bartenders and see if they know who the guys were. Maybe someone did or said something to catch their attention."

"Okay." Theo yawned again and rubbed her eyes. "I gotta get some sleep." She pushed away from the table and stood. "Thanks for the Anti-Burger. Seriously, thanks for being you. Love you."

Tessa pulled Theo into a hug, then spun her around and shoved her out of the kitchen. "I love you too. Off you go to snoozeville."

Later, Theo lay in bed, covers pulled tight beneath her chin, trying to keep her head above the awful memories that had resurfaced the moment she realized Arne was dead in the dumpster. She'd been able to tuck the horror of that long-ago night into the furthest reaches of her mind for years and bury it so deep it had felt like a fading nightmare.

Not any longer.

# CHAPTER FIVE

"What a day." With a huff, I sat on a well-worn maroon—or burgundy if you worked at Slumberland—leather couch, my first purchase for my first apartment after college. The sofa was one of the few pieces of furniture I'd managed to hang on to after the split. The trusty standby was way more comfortable than the three top-of-the-line couches Danna and I had gone through while binging on *Lost Girl*, *Third Watch*, and *Only Murders in the Building*. It faced the wall a TV would be hanging on. If I still had one.

The glaring absence of a television reminded me hockey season was gearing up and I needed to get something to watch games on, sooner rather than later.

"What a long-ass day." Nash arranged himself in a plaid recliner from Goodwill, facing the room-for-only-one kitchen. Elbows on knees, he tiredly rubbed his chin and gazed around. "Jeez, I like what you've done with the place."

The walls were bare. The only furniture on the living room's hardwood floor was the couch, the recliner he sat in, and a coffee table I'd found on clearance at a no-name furniture store. No bookshelves, no entertainment center, no end tables.

In the postage-stamp dining room next to the miniscule kitchen, a stack of not-yet-unpacked boxes served as an uneven table. Beside it was a rickety church-basement-style folding chair. The only thing that drew any real attention was the 1904 red-brick wall running the length of the apartment and the original wood trim on all the windows.

"Personally, I think the boxes add a certain something. Besides, it's only been six months."

"Have you gotten a bed yet?"

"Why bother? Me and the air mattress get along fine. Did you know they have built-in air pumps these days?"

"Oh, Bec." He shook his head. "Thanks again for offering to feed me. Sherry and Harper will be home tomorrow night. I adore my wife and baby girl dearly, but I was happy when she took Harper for the weekend to visit her parents in the Cities. Thank god grandma and grandpa think that little eleven-month-old pooping machine is the very best thing ever." Despite his words, his face brightened whenever he talked about Harper. "How you really holding up?"

"I'll live. Never again will another BB cross my lips. You know, Nash, I'm always happy to provide a time-out zone whenever you need one. For Sherry too. Turnabout's fair play."

He laughed. "No more Bongs for Bec. Check. Thanks for the time-out offer, always good to have a safe place to hide out. Hey, by the way, I think you did right telling Alvarez about what happened." He shrugged. "Have to admit I thought Zaccardo was surprisingly kind in the way she handled her sick customer."

"Yeah, she was." I half-remembered begging her not to tell anyone about the disgusting situation I'd gotten myself into.

"I should've stayed. I'm sorry."

"You couldn't have known. I had no idea the whirlies were going to hit me like too many New Orleans Hurricanes. Goddamn, it was like going from zero to sixty in two seconds on the Gravity Defier at the county fair."

"Oh, I remember that ride. Bad, bad memories." Nash stared at the coffee table. "I should never have left like that. I knew you were drunk off your ass."

"Hey. Look at me. Seriously."

He lifted his head. His eyes were so dark they were almost black. For as long as I'd known him, he'd always been a sensitive guy. Overthinking, worrying far too much about every last detail. That quality was what made him a good detective, but it was also one of his biggest challenges.

"Come on, Ryan. You've always had my back. I'll always have yours. You've been there for me every time it mattered since first grade. Remember when we messed around down on the railroad tracks laying pennies on the rails and I broke my leg trying to jump on one of the cars for the hell of it? Who dragged me out of there? You. Or when I called and told you Danna was cheating and had booted my ass out, who drove all night to Detroit to help me get my stuff out of the house? You. Who told me about an opening here at the DPD? You. In the end, I'm a grown woman."

I held up a hand as he opened his mouth. "Don't get me wrong. I appreciate the hell out of you. But I have to take responsibility for my own idiocy. If Theo had kicked me out at close, I might've thrown up the two blocks home, but I probably would've made it in one piece. Maybe one potentially very messy piece, but one piece nonetheless. That said, if I'm ever stupid enough to do something like that again, I'd appreciate the backup. I've seen too many people in vulnerable states whose friends didn't step up, and…you know."

"I do know. I know the statistics and the tragic results. I'll listen to my own best judgment next time, not your impaired one. Bec, you've always been the sister I never had."

A moment of silence stretched as I let his words seep in. "You ought to be gay, getting all mushy with feelings and emotions and shit."

The tension broke and we both laughed.

I leaned over and gave him a pat on the knee. "Seriously, caring is never a bad thing. Ever. So, let's be there for each other on duty and off, like always. No sweating the small stuff." I gave him a poke for good measure.

"Ow. Okay. Deal. Your method of eliciting cooperation could use a little less enthusiasm."

"You wish. Let's hit this."

For the next hour we wrestled with the case, jotting ideas on notepads, tossing theories out. After searching through boxes for ten minutes, I found some tape and stuck copies of reports and photos to the living room's bumpy, eggshell-white wall. I added a picture of Theo's bruised face. In it, those luminous eyes were lifeless.

Nash studied our work as I banged around the kitchen looking for a potholder so I could pull a now-hot frozen pizza out of the oven.

He said, "I really can't connect a line from mild-mannered bar owner to murderer over the same kind of dustup that's occurred numerous times at the bar."

"Agreed." I set the steaming pie on a cutting board and chopped it into slices with a pair of scissors. Then I carefully carried it to the coffee table. "Look at that. I didn't even need one of those fancy pizza rocker things to dissect this thing. Honestly, I'll never be able to look at one of those contraptions the same way again." I retreated three steps to the counter to grab paper plates and a roll of paper towels. "What do you want to drink? I have Bud Light, diet Orange Crush, or water."

"You're such a kid. I'll take a Bud."

I delivered the beer and cracked the top of an orange for myself. A thought hit me, and I smothered a laugh.

"What?"

"Shingo's going to have a ball with my misadventure, isn't she."

"She warned you."

"I remember that part entirely too clearly."

"Yup, you're screwed."

"What happened to sticking up for me?"

"You're the one who told me not to worry about the small stuff."

"Nash, I so love when you throw my own words back at me."

"I know."

I allowed myself to sink into the comfort of his familiarity. He was my safe, solid anchor.

We sat side by side on the couch to eat and study the collage of villainy. After downing a couple of pieces, I said, "Let's begin at the beginning. We've got Zaccardo, our for-the-moment prime suspect, except she has an alibi. Well, an unconfirmed one at this point. I'll see what the good sister has to say in the morning."

Nash consulted his notes. "She's owned The Mashed Spud for the last fifteen years. Prior to that, her parents ran it, so she's been around the place most of her life. Originally from Short Gap, a town about thirty minutes northwest of here."

He finished off his crust and grabbed another slice. "Stand-up citizen, belongs to the local Chamber of Commerce. Sponsors boys and girls hockey teams in the winter and two squirt soccer teams and a mixed adult softball team in summer. We know she's weathered years of anti-LGBTQ rhetoric and threats aimed at her specifically and at the bar itself. We now know Arne is Arne Olaf Ivorsen, and he's been a thorn in her side; she can't pinpoint when it started. The man's a homophobic, 'racist asshat,' to quote Zaccardo, and reportedly spewed his opinions like a volcano. Let me think." He chewed a bite. "You were out getting more coffee for Zaccardo, I think, when she told me she's an out lesbian, so right there's a natural point of contention. Ivorsen hauled off and punched her. Sometimes something like that's all it takes."

"She's a lesbian, huh?" Something leaped in my stomach. I ignored it.

"Oh, no. You're not crushing on Zaccardo, are you?"

"No way. Of course not." The little fucker. He'd always been able to read me like one of those comic books he'd always had stuffed in a pocket. "I'm just standing back and thinking things over."

"All right. If you say so."

*Redirect, Bec, redirect.* "Maybe there was something else brewing between Zaccardo and Ivorsen." I swallowed the last of my pop. "Another beer?"

"No, thanks. I'll take some water, though."

I grabbed his bottle and returned with two pint glasses of ice water.

"Thanks." Nash downed half the glass and swiped his sleeve across his lips. "We need to interview the employees. Check out who else was there last night. Get a feel for what Zaccardo's like when she's not trying to put on a good face."

"Right. And the regulars. They'll give us a decent idea what she's like under pressure, assuming any of them will talk."

"Too damn bad you can't remember anything. Could've shed some real-time light on this parade."

"Don't think I haven't kicked myself a million times already, thank you. Put neighboring businesses on the list."

"Got it. Personal bank accounts and the bar's, of course." Nash hunched over the coffee table as he jotted down the plan. "We've established Zaccardo has a motive even if it is a slim one. But then there's her sister, who'll alibi her."

"Let's think about the murder weapon. A pizza cutter—or rocker—as we've learned. We know the Mashed Spud has numerous cutters similar to the one used to nearly decapitate Ivorsen. Zaccardo was working the kitchen Saturday night. Based on the blood behind the dumpster, his throat was slit there, and then he was tossed in and partially covered with garbage bags. Hopefully they'll find useable prints, DNA, or, best case, both, on the rocker or the bags. Easiest way to rule her in or out. And oh, another thought."

Nash looked up at me, pen poised.

"Where does Zaccardo get her pizza cutters? If it's always from the same place, maybe that'll help us figure out if the murder weapon is one of hers or if someone's trying to set her up."

"If someone is trying to set her up, why?"

"No idea." I threaded my fingers and tucked my hands behind my head. "She claims she was in bed during the time Ivorsen was killed."

Nash flipped a few pages. "Says the sister's an early riser, was in the apartment all night, is usually up well before seven."

I stared at our handiwork. "Back to the pizza rocker one more time. If our friendly neighborhood bar owner didn't take out Ivorsen, and the rocker is proven to be one of hers, how did the killer get a hold of it?"

"Good question, no answer."

"Is the alley door to the kitchen locked when it's not being used?" I stared at the ceiling. "If there's only one person working in the kitchen, they'd need to leave to use the restroom at some point."

"Maybe the killer got in however, grabbed it, and snuck out when the ruckus was going down and good ole Arne was being eighty-sixed."

"If that's the case, how did the killer hear Theo tell Arne he'd be 'dead meat'?"

"When the labs get back and the autopsy is finished, we'll know a lot more." He slapped his thighs and got to his feet. "On that note, it's time for me to beat it. Tomorrow, keep me updated on your chat with the sister, and I'll see what more I can dig up at Ivorsen's place. I'll check in with the neighbors too."

"Whoever's done first shoots the other a text and we'll decide what's next."

"Okay. Thanks again for dinner."

"You're welcome."

He gave me a salute and I shut the door quietly behind him. I was fried. Maybe with some sleep I'd have a clearer perspective.

# CHAPTER SIX

Great Big Sea's "Ordinary Day" blasted through The Mashed Spud's kitchen from a wireless speaker on a shelf above the sink. Theo emptied her fourth bucket of mop water down the utility drain and arched to stretch her lower back. It was only nine thirty and she and Tessa had spent the last two hours restoring order.

After Theo was dragged to the cop shop, the crime scene guys had shifted from outside to inside the bar, dusting for prints, spraying luminol, removing whatever they considered evidence, who knew what else. The next day, after they found no trace of bloodstains inside or evidence of an altercation anywhere, the bar was released to Theo, in a complete mess. Amazing how those CSU guys could create such chaos in so short an amount of time.

Since neither Tessa nor Theo had any idea exactly where chemicals had been sprayed, they had to scrub the entire floor, wipe everything down out front and in the back, rewashing every pot, pan, pizza rack, and utensil. Basically anything else that had the slightest potential of contamination.

She dumped Lysol Pro floor cleaner in the bucket and filled it up again with hot water. The only areas left to mop were behind the bar and the hallway leading to the restrooms, the office, and the emergency exit. She yelled, "How you are doing, Tess?"

Tessa was invisible behind a wobbly wall of stainless steel food prep containers. "Making headway. You got one of the racks wiped off so I can stack some of this mess on them, right?"

"I did. The empty one."

"Thanks, Captain Obvious."

The mop bucket clunked across the tile as Theo guided it to the far end of the hall and proceeded to work backward. As she paused to rinse the mop, someone banged on the front door.

With a weary sigh, she propped the mop handle against the wall and made her way toward the door. Deliveries came in through the alley and nothing was scheduled to arrive until two, a resupply of liquor. Probably some Mormons on a mission. She'd seen a few kids in white button-down shirts, ties, and dark pants riding bikes around town.

Theo froze, one hand on the doorknob and the other about to flip the bolt, when she realized who she was letting in. For a split second she considered turning around and walking away even as her insides did a surprisingly juvenile whoop whoop. Good manners got the better of her and she opened up. "What brings the wolf to the hen house?"

"Funny lady. I was hoping to catch your sister for a few minutes. Can I come in?"

"I'll warn you now. She's not in a very good mood. Your people know how to muck shit up with their powders and their sprays. Can't tell what's been contaminated, so we have to do a complete scrub down."

The clang of metal punctuated Theo's comment.

"I know the CSU guys can leave quite a mess. Sorry about that."

As her hackles settled, her pulse shot up. Detective Harrison looked much better than she had the last time she'd seen her. She looked good. *Maybe too good*, Theo thought, as a fierce wave of attraction hit. If this were a random encounter on any other day, she might have acted on her baser instincts and blatantly hit on the woman.

Harrison's black hair was spiked instead of mashed, and her cheeks were no longer deathly pale. At the moment, her eyes were the color of the ocean. Instead of a rumpled polo and jeans, she wore a twill blazer and, from the appearance of the collar, a black T-shirt, which was tucked into a pair of black pants. *Oh no you don't, Zaccardo. You can't sniff around every red-hot, blue-eyed woman. Especially this particular woman. She's looking to haul you to jail, for chrissake.*

A mesmerizing dimple appeared on Harrison's cheek. "Are you going to let me in?"

"Sorry." She took a step back to let her enter, then relocked the door. "Tessa's washing dishes. You might think about helping if you want any answers to your questions."

An eyebrow arched. "That bad?"

"That bad."

"All righty then." She locked eyes with Theo one more time, her gaze all encompassing. "Oh, I do have a question for you, though."

Theo gazed steadily at her.

"Do you keep the back door in the kitchen locked?"

She stared at Harrison for a long second. Why did she want to know? "Usually."

"Was it unlocked the night of the murder?"

"I did have it unlocked for part of the evening, trying to keep up with recycling and garbage, but I was called away about a million times. I thought when my staff left they'd locked it, but..." She trailed off. "It wasn't locked when I went to take the garbage out in the morning. Between Arne and a certain sick customer, well, I was a little distracted and never checked, I guess. Do you think someone snuck in and stole one of my pizza cutters?"

"I don't know, but it's a possibility. Okay, lead me to your sister, Ms. Zaccardo."

Theo opened her mouth to retort, "Theo," when she realized Harrison was teasing. The woman could be a wisecracker when she wasn't throwing up. "You're an ass."

"I have my moments."

"Come on."

Harrison followed her past the bar and through the swinging door into the kitchen.

"Hey, Tess," Theo called as they rounded one of the moveable shelves. "You got company."

Tessa, wearing elbow-high dishwashing gloves, rinsed a round aluminum pan in the middle sanitizer sink, plunged it into the rinse water, and slammed it on the wire rack. The scowl on her face morphed into a look of suspicious comprehension when she caught sight of who was following Theo. "Don't even tell me. You must be the dippy detecto who arrested Theo."

"Tess, Detective Harrison. Detective Harrison, Tessa. Be warned, her vocabulary goes down the shitter when she's upset."

Tessa leaned against the sink and crossed her arms over her soggy T-shirt. She cocked her head, appraising the detective with a blatant once-over. "Holy fuck. Now I understand."

"Understand what?" Harrison peered suspiciously from Tessa to Theo.

"Never mind," Theo muttered. Louder she said, "The detective has some questions for you."

"Oh, I'm sure she does. Detective Dick here wants to chat after her people contaminated every godforsaken thing in here, after she hauls my sister to the goddamn police station and accuses her—"

"Hey," Harrison interrupted, raising a placating hand. "Wait a second. Please. We haven't arrested or accused Ms. Zaccardo of anything. I only need to verify some information with you."

"I'm sure you do." Tessa resubmerged her hands in the dishwater. "What the fuck. Ms. Zaccardo?" Derision lowered her voice. "Didn't she tell you she goes by Theo?"

"Well, yes, but—"

"Don't but me. If you want to chat, you can put the clean stuff away while I keep washing."

The detective shot Theo a "you weren't kidding" glance.

"I'm gonna go finish mopping." Theo exited through the swinging door, wondering who'd be standing when that conversation was over.

* * *

A half hour later, Theo had finished mopping and was halfway done wiping down the bar when Tessa led Detective Harrison out of the kitchen.

"—come on back and help with dishes anytime and remember what I said." Tessa's voice was unstressed, friendly even.

Wow. Had she won Tessa over?

"I won't forget. Thanks for the time."

They shook hands. Tess said, "She's all yours." Without meeting Theo's questioning gaze, she sashayed back into the dishwashing dungeon. Theo stared at the pass-through door as it slowed its swinging and came to a complete stop. What was that supposed to mean? She's all yours? Theo, she's all yours? Or Detective Harrison, Theo's all yours? She tossed her rag on top of the bar. "You seem to have overcome Tessa's anger."

"Once we got over the rough part—us bringing you in—she confirmed your alibi and I survived her inquisition. She's nothing but a big old softie. She answered all my questions, and even some I didn't ask. It's obvious how much she loves you."

Oh, boy. Once Tess became comfortable, who knew what she might share. "The feeling's mutual. But a softie? Tess? Never heard that one before, but she's the best person beneath all that bluster of hers."

"I can see that." Harrison tucked her hands in the front pockets of her pants. "She's a straight shooter, a 'say it to my face' kinda gal."

"She is now. The straight shooter in her was lost for a long time."

"Why are you frowning?"

"Just wondering how you managed to wrap Tessa around your finger so fast, Detective Harrison."

"Rizz," she said. "It's all about the rizz."

"Rizz? Seriously? How old are you?"

"Thirty-seven. Bet you'd like to find out how rizz-ful I am."

Was she honestly having this conversation with a cop?

Yes.

Yes, she certainly was. "Are you flirting with me?"

"I don't flirt. But we can probably be Theo and Bec now."

Well, wasn't that interesting? Theo gave the attraction she'd been fighting some slack. Maybe she could act on her baser instincts after all. "If you don't flirt, I do. Does that mean I'm no longer a suspect?"

"Officially, you're still a person of interest."

"Unofficially?"

"Unofficially, like I said, your alibi is solid."

# CHAPTER SEVEN

Afternoon sun was low in the sky when I parked my squad behind the St. Louis County law enforcement complex. It'd been an interesting day, navigating the treacherous yet fascinating territory between Theo and her sister. The strength of my attraction to Theo surprised me. Wasn't like I'd known her long, but it felt like we'd been connected in some way for years.

A shiver ran down my spine as I badged myself into the police department. October on the North Shore carried a decided crispness, reminding the population the Deep Freeze was only a breath away.

My shoulders felt so much lighter now that the interview with Tess was done. Theo had been right. Helping with dishes had been the perfect way to break Tessa's frosty reception. The woman was a tough nut, as loyal as they came. Initially, her hackles had shot up faster than a skunk's tail. It had taken some nimble discourse and a lot of dish stacking to smooth things out.

Once I assured Tessa—four times—I wasn't out to pin Arne's murder on her sister, that I was only hunting down the facts and nothing but the facts, the tension eased considerably. I listened to Tessa's account of Saturday night and Sunday morning and Theo's whereabouts therein. When Tess finished, it was clear, thanks to an errantly kicked shoe, that Theo was not the one who attempted to separate Mr. Ivorsen's head from the rest of his body.

Tessa was funny, sarcastic, and very direct. No beating around anything with that one. As our conversation wound down, out of the blue, she told me she'd break my knees if I hurt Theo. I assured her that once this case was over, I'd be out of their hair and wouldn't heap any pain on either one of them.

I'd initially thought Tess meant me hurting Theo by tossing her in the clink. But after a protracted, rather awkward pause, with Tess's gaze locked on mine, I realized she meant something a little closer to the heart.

No way. I came here from Detroit to get away from romantic entanglements and heartbreak. I wasn't going to fall into another black hole of so-called love again. Even if Theo did have the most intriguing eyes I'd ever seen.

*Enough.*

I decisively shoved this messy mindfuck aside and pulled open the squad room door. The scent of stale coffee hit first, wafting from a break room the size of a walnut. It was packed with two vending machines, a compact fridge, an old church-style coffeemaker, and a perpetually nasty microwave.

Three rows of four desks were lined up like sentinels on a stained gray battlefield of a carpet, along with an additional row of desks separated by tan-cloth-covered dividers for partial privacy. An eight-foot table was stacked with reams of extra copy paper, miscellaneous supplies, statute books, various forms, and a number of empty or half-empty coffee cups. Why was it that a segment of society always thought someone else should clean up their messes?

A handy but ignored garbage can stood between the table and a Culligan water dispenser.

Some beat cops occupied the unassigned desks, working on reports. Nash's head was visible through the glass window in Sgt. Alvarez's office.

I stuck my head in the door and Alvarez glanced up. "Hey, Harrison, come on in. Good timing, Nash just got here."

I dropped into a padded chair beside Nash. "What's the latest?"

Alvarez shuffled files, found the one he was looking for, and opened it. "First off, the report on the pizza cutter is back. The cutter itself does belong to The Mashed Spud. It has Zaccardo's prints on it, as you'd expect, though it appears the perp tried to wipe it clean. Luckily for us, he left both a partial and a full print behind in the process. CSU pulled a number of matching prints off the garbage bags that were next to the body. We haven't fingerprinted all of the Mashed Spud staff yet or her sister, but they don't match Theodora Zaccardo."

Theo was unquestionably in the clear. She'd be happy to hear that. I ignored the fact I was happy too. "Any hits in IAFIS?" The FBI's Integrated Automated Fingerprint Identification System could return fingerprint results within a few hours on a good day.

A smile cracked Alvarez's somber face. "James Raymond Collins, street name Jimmy Boy. We've got an APB out on him. Midlevel drug dealer, part-time drug mule. Rap sheet's as long as my leg." He riffled through some of the file's pages. "Started out stealing cars, joyriding down in the Cities, then got in with the Low Boys, a street gang based in North Minneapolis. He moved into the drug scene, was picked up a few times for dealing, tagged for assault, domestic violence, was suspected in at least three drive-bys, but nothing stuck. I spoke to a member of the Minneapolis PD's Gang Task Force. They've heard Jimmy Boy was movin' on up. Graduating from pill pedaling to drug running."

Nash asked, "In our area?"

"Sounds like it. When we're done here, I'll talk to Shingo and Chu, see if they've heard any scuttlebutt." Alvarez nodded at them. "Nash, put feelers out as well. Harrison, I know you're still developing confidential informants."

"I am."

"Tag along with Nash, then, and get a feel for some of the neighborhoods." Alvarez rocked back in his chair and tossed the file on his desk. "All right. Let's get to the juice of the day. Harrison?"

"This morning I talked to Zaccardo and her sister, Tessa." I withdrew my notebook. "Tessa Johnson. She's in the middle of a divorce, lives with Zaccardo. Confirmed Zaccardo's alibi, as we anticipated. In light of the fact Jimmy Boy's fingerprints are on the murder weapon, I think it's safe to say we can cross Zaccardo off the suspect list."

Alvarez nodded. "Agreed. Nash, what do you have?"

"Arne lived in one half of a shithole duplex. Going on the last six or eight months, neighbors have noticed an increase in car and foot traffic at his place, day, evenings, and especially at night. He wasn't particularly friendly prior to the increase in visitors—more than one neighbor roundly confirmed he was an extremely unsavory character—and he became belligerent if anyone complained. The dude on the other side of the duplex is a zoned-out junkie too doped up to stand, much less answer any questions."

Alvarez gazed at Nash over steepled fingers. "Got the outer picture. What about the inside?"

"Our Arne had a regular dope-cutting assembly line in his living room. Two-and-a-half kilos of coke, pot, some meth, fentanyl, two scales, baggies. He was churning out a bit of everything. Probably the middleman for whoever's running distribution in the Twin Cities and street runners up here."

"So, the million-dollar question remains." Alvarez rocked forward on his elbows. "Who killed him and why."

"Maybe he was skimming profits," I said. "Or dipping into his own inventory."

"Or both," Nash said. "Could be something completely off the radar, too."

"Good point. Harrison, tomorrow make your first stop the Spud and ask the staff about Arne and the drug angle. Maybe someone knows more than they're saying."

"Can do." Guess I wouldn't be getting away from Theo or The Mashed Spud anytime soon. I wasn't sure if I was happy about that or not.

"Nash, while Harrison chats with the mashed potato folks, you dig into Jimmy Boy from a Duluth perspective. Get in touch with Wiz over at the drug unit."

"Okay." Nash heaved himself out of the chair. "10-4, Sarge. Come on, Harrison, let's take a drive around Arne's neighborhood."

"Sure." The pull of a warm, soft bed was magnetic in its intensity, but duty called. The fallout from the hangover-to-end-all-hangovers was still dogging me.

The phone rang.

"Scoot." Alvarez waved us out as he picked up.

\* \* \*

The incredibly annoying but very effective buzz-buzz-beep from my phone alarm startled me from a dead sleep. I shut it off, took in the cold, gray, sleet-filled morning through slitted eyes, and pulled the covers over my head. When Nash and I had called it last night after driving around Arne's 'hood for an hour and seeing nothing interesting, there'd been more than a nip in the air, but the moon and stars had been visible against velvety blackness.

I'd forgotten how fast the weather could turn up here. I grabbed my phone and found a local channel. A banner across the bottom of the screen screamed, "BREAKING NEWS."

Seriously, what wasn't breaking news these days? I pulled the blankets back up and settled in to find out what the fuss was about.

A red-nosed reporter in a puffy blue jacket with a local Duluth station logo was doing a live shot in Canal Park. Apparently a sudden, overnight rain-into-ice squall had turned the morning commute chaotic. Unfriendly white caps surged atop the slate-colored waters of Lake Superior as she announced that the locals and State Patrol had already fielded over a hundred crashes, spinouts, and cars in the ditch. I felt for the street cops and troopers who had to deal with all of it.

The frigid sights on the TV and the brisk air in the apartment propelled me to burrow even deeper under cover. Though heat was included in my rent, I now realized how little warmth I was in line to receive over the coming months. Detroit had been cool, occasionally downright cold, but it didn't hold a candle to a Minnesota winter, especially the North Shore, with its plethora of white crap, the biting, sear-the-oxygen-from-your-lungs temps, and the howling winds.

The news folks cut to the weather guy, who forecast six inches of snow by the weekend. Winter was settling in and it wasn't even Halloween yet.

*Come on, Bec,* I chided myself before I thought too much about having made a huge weather-related relocation error. *You were born in this state. The old blood just needs a little time to thicken up again.*

Thick blood notwithstanding, it was high time to dig out some warmer clothes. Reluctantly, I abandoned my cozy cocoon and searched through the boxes I hadn't yet unpacked. Fifteen minutes later, hypothermic and frustrated, I gave up and decided a hot shower was called for. Pipes banged as I cranked the lever up and to the left as far as it would go and waited for the water to warm up. Once it did, I stepped in and pulled the curtain around the tub as a fog of steam encapsulated me. The water warmed me and made goose bumps rise on my flesh at the same time. It was then I remembered where my winter clothes were. Folded neatly in a blue bin tucked under the stairs in the house that was no longer mine.

Now I needed to go shopping. I hated shopping. Unless I was on the hunt for a gadget, a book, or some good food. The S-word did nothing but make me crabby.

Out of the shower, I dressed and called the Spud. Theo agreed to round up her staff for a last-minute, eleven o'clock get-together.

* * *

Through The Mashed Spud's windows, I could see Tessa and Theo engaged in a lively conversation with employees perched on stools in front of the bar.

A hastily scrawled sign had been taped to the front door, informing thirsty customers the Spud would open late today. All conversation ceased when I came inside. The Edison lights blazed, bathing everyone in that golden glow.

"Detective Harrison," Theo called as she skirted the bar to meet me halfway. "How do you want to do this?"

God, those damn, spellbinding eyes almost made me forgot what I was doing there.

I focused my attention elsewhere. Elsewhere became an assessment of Theo below the neck. She was clad in a teal, long-sleeved Spud T-shirt with the sleeves pushed up her forearms, and faded blue jeans. The pull I'd felt the first time I'd laid eyes on her hit me full force. The woman was a siren, one of those beautiful, mythical creatures who captivated the innocent with their irresistible songs and lured them to an untimely death. Maybe if I stopped looking at her, I wouldn't get sidetracked with ridiculous siren thoughts. And eye thoughts. And deliciously curvy thoughts.

"Bec?"

"Yes." Theo was going to think I was a walking imbecile if I didn't get my cop face on. "You have somewhere I can talk to your folks one-on-one?"

"Sure. You can use the office. It's right down the hall, past the restrooms you're so very well acquainted with."

"Thanks." I regarded her warily, trying to read her expression without getting sidetracked again. Theo didn't give up a thing. I couldn't tell if she was irritated, amused, both, neither. This one would do well on that TV show…what was it called? *World Poker* something or other.

An hour and a half later, I'd gleaned not much more information than I already had. To a person, the staff agreed Arne was a jackass but, ironically, tipped well. No one knew or would admit to knowing anything about him using or dealing drugs.

The workers not involved in opening the bar trickled out the front door. Tessa had reclaimed the office, and now Theo and I sat side by side on the bar stools.

Doing the interviews had helped me regain my composure. I figured I could maintain it if I didn't get lost in those damn eyes of hers again. Holy shit, I sounded like a romance book cliché. I finished off my on-the-house bubbly water and pushed the glass to the opposite edge of the counter. "Thanks for rounding everyone up on such short notice." I stood, and a shiver ran down my spine, making me shudder.

"Glad to help. Are you cold?" Theo peered at my thin jacket and the button-down beneath it. "You're not wearing much to ward off thirty degrees."

"Gotta pick up some warmer clothes, I suppose. Realized this morning all my winter stuff is forever in Detroit."

Theo's brows raised, either at my obvious disdain for Detroit or the fact my winter gear was not leaving Michigan.

"Honestly, I'd rather break a leg than shop for clothes." I made the mistake of meeting those eyes, now a magical greenish brown.

"I see. You're not a shop-a-holic, you're a shop-a-phobe."

"I am."

Theo gave me a calculating once-over. "I totally understand the feeling. I know a few places that aren't too traumatizing where you might find something you'd like."

"Jot them down for me, I'll check 'em out."

"You will, huh?" She studied my face. "Here's what I think. You'll politely take my recommendations, stuff the paper in a pocket, and forget all about it. In a week or two, maybe a month, someone'll find your stiff, cold carcass and everyone will ask why she wasn't bundled up, since this is Duluth, after all. Cause of death: stupidity."

"So harsh. But true. What are you, some kinda psychic?" How'd she know that's exactly what I'd do? Well, except for the becoming a human icicle part.

Her face split in a wide, crooked grin, and those amazing eyes did their luminescing thing. I felt myself soften a little more. This woman was dangerous, a mesmerist, a hypnotizer, drawing me in like one of Pavlov's dogs. I didn't salivate at the sound of a bell, but one glance from her and I became someone I didn't know. It was as if Theo had wound an invisible rope around my body and was slowly but steadily pulling me ever closer. Somehow, she made me forget all the promises I'd made to myself about staying away from trouble exactly like this.

So pathetic.

"Nope, I'm not."

Her voice jarred me out of my head.

"What?"

"I'm not a psychic. Though I'd love that gift. You forget I own a bar? Teaches you how to read people mighty quick." A sigh whistled through her teeth. "I'll pick you up tomorrow at noon. I assume you'll have a lunch break?"

"Lunch? Well, yeah." I needed to get out of here like a fish needed water.

Theo leaned close enough I could feel her breath on my face. "My duty as a concerned citizen of this city is to make sure the law in my neighborhood doesn't wind up as a stiff, dead in my dumpster, since it seems to be a popular destination of late for the recently deceased. We're going to find you some suitable lifesaving clothes, and you're not going to say no."

I was rendered mute, wanted to tell her she was a bossy bitch, but she'd probably happily own that. I croaked, "I'll buy lunch."

"Deal." She stuck her hand out. "Shake."

I thought about barking but begrudgingly complied. "Gotta go," I said, and scrammed.

# CHAPTER EIGHT

Theo stuck her head in the office. "Bec's gone. We're up and running." She propped a shoulder against the doorframe and hugged herself.

"Okay." Tess spun the chair to face Theo. "How do you think it—what's wrong? You look like you've seen a ghost." She tilted her head and gave Theo a sideways squint.

"I've lost my mind."

That brought out a full-on scowl. "Why?"

Theo stuck out her bottom lip and blew upward, stirring ringlets that'd flopped down onto her forehead. "I told the good detective I'd pick her up tomorrow at twelve o'clock and help her hunt down some decent gear to withstand our notorious winters."

"Wait, what? You're taking Bec shopping? For clothes? You hate going shopping for anything other than women."

"Sheesh. You make me sound like a letch."

"I only speak da troot, as they say up here in dees parts. Seriously, this is entirely unlike the Theo I know and love. The one who holds every woman she's interested in at arm's length.

The master of mutual one-night stands. You must have it bad for her."

"I, well, no. Maybe. She makes my brain crazy. Maybe some other parts too."

"TMI. Relax."

"I swear, it's like I was watching my body double talk to her. Flirt with her, for chrissake. I'm the moth drawn to the flame of death."

"You're serious." Humor faded from Tessa's face. "I've never seen you so discombobulated over a woman before. Maybe you should do whatever you need to do to get her out of your system." She waggled her brows in a bad imitation of Groucho Marx. "I'll never understand why you always shy away from commitment."

Not surprising really. Theo had never talked to Tess about the why of her relationship philosophy, so all she had to go on were her actions.

"Funny lady you are. I'll get over myself. It's only shopping. It'll be fine." Theo straightened and squared her shoulders. "It's for the public good. She can't fight crime as a copsicle."

But maybe Tessa was right, she mulled, heading for the kitchen to put together the weekly food and booze order. What better way to get Bec out of her system than to scratch what itches?

# CHAPTER NINE

A hand slammed on my desk. "What's up, Harrison?"

I jumped. "Goddamn it, Nash, you're gonna give me a heart attack. I hate when you do that."

"I know. That's why I do it. The only time you're totally checked out is when you write up reports, and your reaction is one hundred percent guaranteed." He settled into his chair, the leather of his jacket creaking as he stretched for the ceiling.

It was true. I did tune everything out, ignoring conversations, people walking past my desk, and usually texts whenever I worked on my reports. The sooner I could get them done the sooner I could move on to something a whole lot more interesting. "There." I hit save and print, then yawned. "Done with the paperwork from my visit to The Mashed Spud. Reports are exhausting. And redundant."

"We'd save some serious time if anyone bothered to ask the boots on the ground what would work to streamline necessary paperwork and dump what isn't needed. The PD's records management system is supposed to be upgraded, but that rumor's been circulating the last five years. Find out anything helpful at the Spud?"

"Nope. Arne apparently didn't do business at the bar. Or the kids are excellent liars, as kids can be. But my gut says he kept his nose clean, at least while he was on the premises."

"Probably too busy drinking to do anything else. I don't get the idea this guy was much of a multitasker."

"Nope." I walked over to the printer to retrieve my hard work and dropped the pages in Alvarez's inbox. "You uncover anything workable?"

"Met Wiz at the Coney for a dog with the works. He's gonna have his unit do some checking around."

"Okay. I suppose now you're going to ooze raw onions from your pores the rest of the day."

Nash's white teeth gleamed as he grinned.

"Hey, Shingo." I raised my voice as I saw her walk through the squad room door, followed by Chu, who made a beeline for the break room. "Can I trade you Chu for Nash for the rest of the day? He's got some killer breath."

She dumped a backpack and parked her butt on top of her desk. "What'd he do? Go to the Coney joint again?"

"You're a regular wisecracker, aren't you?" Nash threw a pencil at her, which she snatched out of the air.

"What'd I miss?" Chu approached, his mouth full of some kind of sticky snack, and he flopped hard enough in his chair he nearly upended himself. With his free hand he grabbed into the edge of his desk. "I swear to god, someone's going to get killed in these broken pieces of crap."

"But," I said, "you're the only one who sits quite so... vigorously."

Shingo pointed at me. "Exactly. And for god's sake, A-choo, what'd I tell you about talking with your mouth full?" She gave me one of those can't-live-with-'em, can't-live-without-'em shrugs. "Harrison's trying to dump Onion Boy off on me in exchange for you."

Chu bit off another hunk of what I could now see was a half-devoured Snickers bar. "I'd be down for that. She's nicer than you, anyway."

Shingo fired Nash's pencil at him. It bounced off his arm and landed on the floor. Chu leaned over and grabbed it. "Such violence. You might need some anger management, Shing."

"I'll anger management you if you're not careful, young'un."

Nash laughed. "The love these two have for one another is a beautiful thing, dontcha think, Harrison?"

"It oozes like pimple pus. So, you two lovebirds have any dirt for us?"

Shingo flipped me off and consulted her notepad. "We canvased three blocks around Ivorsen's house. Not many people opened their doors, but we did get a little something from the delightfully nosy neighbor right across the street."

"You'll like her." Chu propped his boots on his desk, careful not to lean too far back this time. "She makes great chocolate chip cookies and has been watching…What was the quote, Shingo?"

"Here we go. Mrs. Goldie Rasmussen, aged sixty-seven, eighteen years in the same residence. She told us, and I quote, 'I've been keeping an eye on that doughy drunk doofus and all his disreputable visitors since the day he moved in.'"

Chu dropped his feet and threw his Snickers wrapper in the trash. "She has two notebooks filled with information on everything she's seen since Arne moved in ten months ago, until he didn't come home Friday night. She's on the job from the time she gets up in the morning to the time she goes to bed, except when she's in the bathroom or out on the town. Even has a chair set up in front of her window with a TV tray desk. I don't know how the buyers, or Arne himself, for that matter, didn't catch on to her nosy shenanigans."

"That there's the shit." I reached over my desk and high-fived Shingo.

"Get this," she said. "In her two books, she made note of license plate numbers, car makes and models, visitor descriptions. Probably more stuff too. We didn't have time to get a real close look, but she sent the notebooks with us. Let's have some lunch and then dig in."

Finally, something solid to sink our teeth into. Then I remembered my twelve o'clock appointment with one I-won't-take-no-for-an-answer bar owner and the grin fell off my face.

I'd have to survive shopping *and* Theo Zaccardo first.

# CHAPTER TEN

Theo pulled into the mostly empty Duluth Police Department parking lot and idled at the curb near the main door. She wondered if Bec would show up. Every once in a while, Theo's big mouth got her in trouble.

This was one of those times. She was seriously attracted to this woman of many faces. Vulnerable, sick Bec who could still make a joke. Serious as sin cop Bec. The more relaxed, half-guarded Bec, like when she'd emerged from the Spud's kitchen with Tessa, laughing.

What would Bec beneath her be like? Her passion, her restrained power unleashed. It would be staggering. If this had been another time, another place, she'd take her self-imposed one shot. But this wasn't another place and another time. Bec wasn't going to be a one-night hookup. The feelings she stirred in Theo were dangerous, in so many ways.

What had she been thinking? She'd practically forced Bec to agree to go hunting for appropriate Duluth-worthy winter gear with her. Bec was a grown-ass woman; she could take care of herself. She knew getting too close to someone with a badge was playing with fire. But Detective Harrison…something about her drew Theo as if she were extra-large magnet and Bec was made of steel.

A knock on the passenger window made her jump, thankfully interrupting her spiraling thoughts. Bec had one hand on top of the car and the other on the door handle. Her black hair was tousled, as if she'd been running her fingers through it. Today she wore a gray blazer and purple, long-sleeved polo. Theo's mouth went dry.

Okay. Maybe a little flirtation wouldn't be out of the question.

Bec yanked up on the door handle again.

Theo fumbled for the unlock button and hit it.

"Holy shit, Theo. I wasn't expecting you to drive a 'Vette." Bec crawled in and shut the door. "This is one hot car."

"It's Tessa's. A goodbye flip-off to her ex." Theo waited for Bec to strap herself in before shifting into drive.

"Nice choice. Have you opened her up?"

"You gonna ticket me?"

Bec laughed. "Hell, no. I might be a cop, but I love speed as much as any red-blooded lesbian with a lead foot."

"I take it you're more a 'do as I say, but not what I do' kinda gal?"

"What happens when I'm off duty is no one's biz."

"Unless you get caught." Theo made a right onto Mesaba and goosed it, the acceleration pressing them both into their seats.

"Now that's some power right there. Can I drive?"

"You'll have to butter up Tess."

"I'll put it on the list. Where are you taking me?"

"Thought we'd check out Duluth Trading. If you don't find anything there, I have some other options up my sleeve."

"Sounds good." Bec lapsed into silence.

Theo didn't know if she should say something or keep her mouth shut. She opted for the latter.

"You know, you didn't have to do this," Bec said after a bit.

From the look of the stiff way Bec held her body and the lack of eye contact, it didn't take a nuclear scientist to see she was uncomfortable.

"I know I didn't. But like I said, the last thing I want is to see you turn into a North Shore ice cube."

"Most people these days don't want to have anything to do with the cops."

"Hey, I have my issues with the po-po, but I also want them to come when I call for help. I know there's more good cops than bad. Trouble, in my opinion, is all the attention goes to the problem children, far overshadowing the decent ones." Theo hazarded a quick look at her passenger. A half-grin flashed and disappeared as fast as it'd come.

"Thanks. Plenty of our citizenry don't understand that. Makes it hard to do our job."

"I can't imagine how hard." *Change the subject, Theo.* "So, what do you think you want to look for?"

"I don't know. A winter jacket, something decent to wear to work and not freeze my butt off, something allowing easy access to my waist. Probably some warm socks, mittens, gloves. A pair of insulated boots. A hat. You know, the essentials."

"I can totally see you in a knit hat with a big pom-pom on the end bouncing around as you chase down bad guys."

Bec laughed and the ice was broken. Maybe this would turn out to be a pleasant experience after all. She hoped so, since she'd instigated it. They fell into a comfortable banter, debating the pros and cons of proper and appropriate and sometimes wholly inappropriate outer wear.

Minutes later, Theo found an open spot across the road from the store and parked. Bec followed her inside.

"Theo, my lady," a six-foot Black man with multicolored dreads and a pink tie-dye T-shirt called from across the shop. "What brings you back so soon after your last shopping debacle?" He wove his way toward them between displays and garment racks.

"Yeah, yeah. It wasn't too much of a debacle once you stuck your nose in it. I'm bringing you business, so be nice. M&M, meet

Bec Harrison. Bec, Mortimer Massy, better known as M&M. He's the general manager and general know-it-all."

M&M sized Bec up. "Girl, it's lovely to make your acquaintance. You're about, what? Five-seven, five-eight?"

She nodded.

"Large in men's, XL in women's?"

"Yup."

"Take that jacket off and hand it to Theo."

Theo wondered if she'd comply. After a half second, Bec shrugged out of it and handed it over.

"Oh crap, girlfriend, you carry a gun." He raised his hands exaggeratedly high in the air.

"Easy, M&M. It's okay. She can't help it, she's a cop." Theo folded Bec's jacket in half and hung it over her arm. "But she's an okay cop. It's cool. She's family."

He planted his fists on his hips. "Like I didn't notice that when you two sashayed into my store. Of course she's family. Now, let me get down to business."

M&M cast a discerning eye over the rest of Bec. "All right, I got you." He winked. "Two measurements I won't announce out loud." He shifted his gaze to her feet. "Size eight in men's, ten in women's?"

Bec's eyes widened. "Eight and a half. How do you do that?"

"An innate talent, darling. Now"—he clapped his hands—"tell M&M what you're looking for."

In twenty-three minutes flat, Theo, laden with two of five bags full of stuff to make sure Bec would stay warm, led the way back to the Corvette. It'd taken M&M ten minutes to round up everything Bec had asked for and ten more for Bec to decide what she wanted out of the offerings. Which was most of it.

Bec said, her voice awed, "That was by far the best clothes shopping experience I've ever had. Not at all painful. I could marry M&M."

"If you were a dude, that might work. M&M makes shopping easy, especially for those of us who detest the chore."

Theo was relieved their outing had been a success. M&M thought Bec was a cool "chicklet" once he got past the cop thing.

He wowed her like he wowed whoever set foot in his playground, with his psychic visual measuring abilities and his bizarre, inborn sense of what a person might give a thumbs-up to.

"Where we going to put this stuff?" Bec asked, her own hands laden with the rest of her booty.

"Don't worry. We have a trunk and a frunk to work with."

"A what-did-you-say?"

"A frunk. It's a funky front trunk. Check it out." Theo popped the trunk and then the hood of the car.

Bec loaded her three bags in the back, shut the lid, and came around to the front. "I'll be damned. Where'd the engine go?"

"No idea. My knowledge is confined to the fact the car starts and goes like a greased cheetah when I hit the gas." Theo wrangled her two bags into the frunk and assessed her handiwork. "Not a huge amount of space, but it works." She shut the hood and checked her watch. "It's 12:35. You have time for some lunch?"

"I do. I've spent the entire morning writing up reports, a painful task I'm not at all fond of. What sounds good?"

"You like Mexican?"

"Always."

"Little Angie's Cantina it is then. Have you been there yet?"

"Nope, I haven't gotten out much. Been too busy with work."

"Time to broaden your horizons. I'm happy to introduce you to some of the finest fajitas this side of the Mississippi. Or the other side too. North of Texas and New Mexico at least."

"I put my hungry belly in your hands."

Theo gave her the side-eye. "That comment could be construed in several ways."

"Oh, I see how it is. Now you want a piece of this."

"Considering I saw you in your polo, pants, and socks, oh baby, you're damn right I want a piece."

Bec put her hand on the dash and half-pivoted to her. "You are a flirt, aren't you?"

"I do have my moments, dahling."

* * *

Angie's lunch rush was busy, but it wasn't long before they were seated in a wood-panel booth upholstered in Southwest Native American, amid the hum of multiple conversations and Mexican mariachi music.

Intricately carved wooden pillars and beams and big eighteen by eighteen, hand-planed, load-bearing columns held the roof up. Neon liquor signs and an awesomely cool, blue neon Cadillac sign contrasted well with warm tans and reds. Southwest paraphernalia like bridles, hats, saddles, and artwork of the region decorated the walls and hung from the ceiling.

The mouthwatering scent and sizzling sound of fajitas made Theo's stomach growl. Bec sniffed, the edges of her nostrils flaring out on the inhale. "Holy moses, those fajitas smell good."

"I know. They're one of my favorites."

A server with her hair swept up in a ponytail, decked out a flannel shirt and incredibly tight jeans approached the table. "Hello, I'm Winter, and I'll be your taking care of you today. What can I get you two to drink?"

"I'm sure you get this question from everyone," Theo said, "but I'm gonna ask anyway. Were you born in the winter, Winter?"

To her credit, she didn't roll her eyes. "I was born in July. I have a sister who was born in February and her name's Summer. Our parents have a rather unorthodox sense of humor."

"Parents can be, shall we say, interesting," Bec said. "How many siblings do you have?"

"Just the two of us, but if there were two more, I'm sure they would've wound up Autumn and Spring, regardless of gender or month born."

They placed their beverage orders. Bec asked, "Can you take our food order now as well?"

"Oh, yeah. Sure. Hit me."

Before Theo could get a word out, Bec said, "We'd like to share an order of fajitas, chicken, beef, and shrimp. Assuming that's okay, Theo?"

"Uh, yeah. Great."

The server gave them a thumbs-up and sailed away.

"I don't know how these kids can remember an order without writing anything down," Bec said. "At least, most of the screwball ones I run into don't have that kind of talent." She paused. "I hope that was okay. That I ordered for both of us. You said you liked fajitas, so I went with it, but it was pretty presumptuous, and I apologize."

"Didn't expect it, but it's okay."

The unexpectedly warm look Bec gave Theo caused butterflies to play tag.

"I can be as bossy as you, Miss I'll Be There At Noon."

"Well played." After a minute of awkward silence, Theo said, "We seem to have spent a substantial amount of time together in the last few days. I know zip about you except you can't hold your liquor."

"Hey, I can hold my liquor. But I was bombarded with BBs thanks to my partners."

"I suppose they forced your mouth open and poured them into you." The corners of Theo's mouth curved up. "Are you're a closet alcoholic, detective?"

"I think I was well on my way during the breakup, but no, I'm not. My problem was your fault. That drink was deadly. Went down like silk."

"Before I knew who you were, I nicknamed you Barfy."

"That's disgusting. Accurate, but disgusting. For the record, I can't remember the last time I've thrown up before that night, and it's a lot harder to recover from a hangover than it used to be."

Winter delivered iced tea for Theo and water for Bec.

"All that aside"—Theo locked her eyes on Bec's—"you've practically got my entire life history, and all I know is you're a cop."

"It's a long story. The short of it is I grew up down in the Twin Cities, wound up in Detroit thanks to a girl. Left Detroit thanks to same girl. Heard about a job opening with DPD, and here I am."

Theo swished the ice around in her glass and took a sip. "That's certainly a short tale. I take it you left said girl for a reason?"

"She cheated."

"Oof. How long were you two together?"

"Twelve years."

"Breakups are never easy, but no need for bullshit like that."

Bec downed a deep swallow of water. "Love hurts. I've retired myself from relationships. Safer that way."

"It is. I'm relationship-avoidant too."

"Do tell."

"Not much to say. Was with someone a long, long time ago. It didn't end well." Theo shoved the once-again-revived memory into her mental trash can and slammed the lid shut so hard she could feel the reverberation in her gut.

"My turn to be sorry."

Theo gazed out the window at the darkly churning waters of Lake Superior. "Thanks. I don't much like talking about it." Or thinking about it. What was she doing telling even this much to a police officer? A hot cop whom she could envision writhing beneath her, moaning in a fog of ecstasy. What was wrong with her?

"Here you guys go." Winter set the requisite sizzling platter between them, along with a red tortilla warmer. "I threw some extra tortillas in for you guys."

"Thanks, Winter," Bec said.

"Hopefully you like 'em. Give me a wave if you two need anything else." Off she charged to tackle her next task.

Relief flooded Theo. Saved from her traitorous brain by fajitas.

# CHAPTER ELEVEN

Theo rolled to a stop in front of the PD. "Thanks again for lunch. I had a good time."

"Me too. I've laughed more in two hours than I have—" I trailed off, not sure I wanted to admit how much fun I had. Meeting the one and only, high-stylin' M&M, hearing Theo hilariously critique M&M's clothing choices, Little Angie's, good conversation. I wasn't sure what had come over me when I ordered for the both of us, but luckily Theo hadn't seemed upset. I wasn't usually so forward, even with my ex.

The company had proved more than entertaining. It'd been refreshing to be hanging with someone who didn't wear the badge or was badge-adjacent. We had the same political views, and it was nice to be able to talk openly about what was going on politically in the country.

"Bec..." Theo interrupted my brooding, her tone tentative. "I seriously don't do this. Ever."

"What?" I could see by the set of her face whatever she was trying to get out was hard.

Her thumb tapped a staccato rhythm on the steering wheel. "I was thinking, which is sometimes hazardous. But anyway, since neither of us are looking for a relationship, how about we gang up, go out and do some fun stuff, have a good time, flirt a little, no strings, just friends. Movies. The Irvin—if you like ships. Hiking. The Depot—we have an amazing train museum. Live music if you're into that. No pressure. There's a ton of cool things to see and do even during the iceberg months." She paused, focused on something out the window. "It's been a long time since I thought of anything except the bar and Tess." She shifted to face me, her expression earnest. "You've made me laugh more than I have in I don't know how long, even if you did haul my ass to jail."

I opened my mouth and shut it again. I felt my face flush, the old ears burn. My "danger, danger" alarm squealed. But the idea of having someone to do some entertaining stuff with—other than Nash and his family—was suddenly incredibly enticing, especially after Theo talked about ships and the train yard. It was as if she'd raided my mind.

The voice in my frontal lobe told the alarm bells in the back of my head to fuck off. For chrissake, I can have a friend who's a girl and that friend doesn't have to be a girlfriend. Theo brought an entirely different lens to look at the world through. She was bubbly, down-to-earth, and had actual empathy for more than her own self-interests, unlike Danna.

But there were so many potential pitfalls with the just-friends scenario. Those eyes, those beautiful eyes in which I'd been valiantly trying not to lose myself. And that goddamn body, curves and strength in all the right places. Solid. Immovable. Irresistible. Her self-assurance drew me in. The woman emanated infectious energy like an airport beacon. That said, the last person who had sucked me in had cost me almost everything. I had no intention of going through anything like that again.

*Get over yourself, Bec. She's offering friendship with no hooks, no claws.* I could do this.

"All right. You sold me. I'm in." *Please*, I begged the gods, the spirits, and the good earth beneath my feet, *don't let this be a mistake.* "For the record, I did not haul your ass to jail." I gave her a pointedly raised brow. "But it might be fun to try my cuffs out on you."

Theo nearly laid me flat with the heat emanating from her eyes. "Oh, I'm not so sure it would be me those cuffs would be used on."

"You like to play it that way, do you?"

"I like it a lot of ways."

This was fun. I inhaled to come back with a crack about ways and means, then realized I was about to get in way over my head. I shot her a regretful grin. "This has been quite an adventure. Thanks." I locked eyes with her for a long moment. "I had a good time with you, Theo."

"Ditto. Let me know when you have some free time, and I'll cook up something exciting."

"Okay. Yeah. I'll let you know. Gotta go." I opened the door and practically leaped out of the Corvette. I paused and leaned back in. "A little advice you may or may not want. I'm sure you already know this, but maybe you should think about stashing this baby before the snow flies. I'd hate to see anything happen to such a fine piece of automotive magic, especially since I didn't get a chance to drive it yet."

"I've been on Tess's case to do that for the last week. Sometimes she's on top of her game, and sometimes she simply doesn't care. Especially if the issue at hand had anything to do with her ex. But don't worry, I'm pretty sure you'll be able to take it out by May. Or maybe June."

"That's an awfully long time to wait."

"Never know. Minnesota winters, as unpredictable as our sports teams. Or predictable, depending on how you look at it."

I watched her rumble out of the parking lot and headed for the front door. I was about to cross the threshold when it hit me like a pie in the face. All the gear I'd purchased was still tucked away in that amazing, blinding, monster car. That hunk of metal should've had Lemon Lightning painted on its sides.

"Shit," I muttered. Maybe this was the universe's way of making sure I saw Theo sooner instead of later—unless I wanted to face the first crappy weather of the season without the proper paraphernalia. *Hard no.*

I badged my way into the police department's inner sanctum, looked up Theo's number, and sent her a text.

**hey, Theo, it's Bec I left my new duds in Lemon Lightning my new name for Tessas vette can I come grab it in the next day or two**

Less than a minute later, she responded. **How could we both have forgotten?**

**shitty memories good company**

**Can I drop your stuff off at your place tomorrow evening?**

**as long as I get out of work at a reasonable time for sure**

The three dots in my message app bounced up and down as she worked on a response. Then, **Shoot me a text. I'm flexible.**

I forced myself not to respond with a comment asking how flexible she could be.

**can do thanks**

A sense of excitement flooded through me. I was giddy, a feeling I hadn't experienced in years. I liked it. *Enjoy it while you can, Bec, because you know this rush isn't going to last.*

# CHAPTER TWELVE

Thursday night The Mashed Spud was, to put it bluntly, dead. Alex, Brooke, and Clare, better known as the ABCs, were three of The Spud's best, most dependable workers. They had everything well under control.

Theo sat at the bar, working on reconciling the liquor sales logs and trying not to pay attention to *Thursday Night Football* on TV. She bit back a yawn. Only seven thirty, and she was ready to call it a night. So sad. Becoming more and more like Tess every day, except, unlike her, she had no desire to open her eyes before ten a.m. or later.

Her phone vibrated against the top of the bar. She picked it up, expecting a text from Tess saying good night. Nope.

**hey I'm outta here if you're at the spud could I swing by and grab my stuff**

Theo perked right up.

**I need to get out of here before I paperwork myself to sleep. How about I meet you at your place? Maybe some fresh air will revive me.**

The thought of getting close to Bec again was anticipatory, edgy, irresistible. *Just play it cool*, she told herself. *Friends. That's it. That's all you can deal with.*

The dots bounced as Bec typed out her response.

The dots stilled.

Theo stared at the phone, drumming her fingers, impatient, breathing shallowly even as she ordered herself to stop.

The rippling resumed.

**okay I'll be home in about fifteen I only live a couple blocks of from the bar if you want to take a walk**

**Yeah, that's perfect. What's your addy?**

Bec texted the info and the apartment number, and Theo got busy putting her work away.

\* \* \*

The wind made it hard to breathe as she speed-walked along Main. A hard shiver worked its way down her spine, making her muscles contract painfully. For once, though, she'd had the foresight to pull on a pair of gloves before she left, and now her insulated fingers were wrapped tight around the handles of Bec's five Duluth Trading bags.

The streetlights cast warm pale-yellow pools on the sidewalk, making her already wistful for spring. By this time tomorrow, there'd probably be inches of white crap on the ground. She'd heard it could be six to eight, beginning in the wee hours of the coming morning and lasting well into the following day. But then they were in for a warm stretch, and most of the snow would probably be gone.

Forecasting the weather here was always a gamble, and the poor weather people were the frequent butt of jokes. In their defense, across the state and especially on the North Shore, the unpredictability of atmospheric conditions was guaranteed. It's what made the weather a staple of conversation throughout the state. *Ya, sure, you betcha.*

And Bec was just a friend.

*Remember that, Theo*, she ordered herself as she found the right apartment building and gratefully pulled open an ornate, glass-paneled door. With a little sleight of hand and some crumpled bags, she crammed herself and her cargo into the cramped entryway.

Inside the foyer, one-inch-by-one-inch cream and caramel-colored floor tiles had been laid in a repeating, diagonal pattern, with larger tiles continuing three feet up the walls. Above that, the plaster had been painted a brilliant white, making the space feel larger than it was. The foyer had the ubiquitous old building odor. The scent wasn't off-putting but a gentle reminder the edifice had seen its share of lives lived within its brick facade.

The interior door was locked, but through it, she could see the stairway she'd need to climb to Bec's second-story apartment. A metal speaker on one wall had a list of last names with push buttons. She found Harrison, and in seconds she was buzzed in.

The beige carpet was vacuumed, and somebody was baking something that smelled suspiciously like chocolate chip cookies. She took the stairs and found 202 two doors down the hall on the right. As she raised her hand to knock, the door opened, and there was Bec.

"You made it."

"I did." *Oof.* Bec looked good. So good. Too good. So very different out of her detective-wear. She was barefoot, in a pair of basketball shorts and a gray Detroit Police Department T-shirt.

Bec stepped back to let her in, then shut and locked the door, allowing Theo a second to assess the rear view. Her shoulders were solid and wide, and the shorts clung very nicely to a curvy ass.

When Bec turned around, Theo met her eyes, then slowly dropped her gaze, following the contours of her chest, her belly, to the hands propped on either side of her waist. Downward, past the shorts to her taut thighs and on to her knees. *Oh dear lord.* Her knees. They were perfect.

*Theo, hold on one second. Knees?* She was a shoulders and back woman. She loved to run her fingers over dips and planes, along the long muscles on either side of the spine. The feel of those muscles rippling beneath her fingertips— *Stop!* She slammed the door shut on that thought.

"I'd ask if you like what you see, but I wouldn't want to be presumptuous."

Theo's head snapped up. "If you aren't asking, then I won't tell you I very much do. Here you go." She handed Bec her bags.

With a hint of a sultry smile, Bec took them. "Thanks for lugging 'em over." She crossed the room and set everything on top of a pile of boxes in what one could barely imagine as a dining room.

"Are those boxes your table?"

"Yup. That was Nash's response too. It works for now. Want a beer? Water? Bottle of Orange Crush?"

"Sure," Theo said before her mouth got ahead of her mind. "Crush me. My second favorite after grape." She took in the mismatched couch, recliner, and coffee table, along with the dining nook and incredibly compact kitchen. She picked the recliner and directed rear to cushion.

"Ironic." Bec rummaged through the fridge. "Grape's my second fave after orange, and either one's gotta be Crush."

Theo couldn't help herself. It was so perfect. "Crush all the way. Yeah, definitely a crush." *For chrissake, Theo, you're flirting with a very dangerous situation on so many levels.*

*But it's so much fun,* she argued with herself. Besides, she had a gut feeling Bec didn't do flings, and that's all Theo would allow. A one-time thing. More importantly, Bec was a cop. An officer of the law. She put bad actors behind bars for a living.

That did it. In a panic, Theo propped her hands on the arms of the chair, preparing to lever herself up and flee, when Bec came out of the kitchen and held out the bottle of pop.

Too late. She lowered herself back into the seat and accepted the offering. "Thanks." She uncapped the bottle in quiet desperation and took a few long swallows, praying the burn of the bubbles would chase away the burn of her thoughts.

"No problem."

Bec seemed oblivious to Theo's confounded state and sprawled on the couch, propping her feet on the coffee table. Now those gorgeous knees were on full display. *Oh, come on, give me a break here*, she thought. *Control your roll, Zaccardo. Conversate.* She swept the bottle in an arc, encompassing the room. "You've got a minimalist aesthetic going."

Bec blew out a long breath. "Not on purpose. I've been concentrating so hard on getting through the lateral move and probationary period at work I haven't had time to think about what to do with the place, much less the energy to make it happen." She upended her bottle of pop, throat contracting and releasing hypnotically as she swallowed.

It was all Theo could do not to stalk over to the couch and pounce. *You do not pounce on just friends.* "If you want—when you have time—I'd be happy to help you sort stuff out, organize, whatever." Did that just fly out of her mouth? It sure did.

Bec dropped her feet to the floor and leaned forward, the soda bottle dangling between her fingers. "Yeah, I might take you up on that. Sooner or later."

"Just let me know."

The heated tension in the room eased, and the conversation moved from living in the North Country to dealing with all the snow, which led into an animated discussion about which winter sports they enjoyed. Downhill skiing was her answer to that question. Bec was into hockey, and she liked rugby, football, and the WNBA. Before she knew it, an hour had passed.

After Bec's third yawn, Theo stood. "I think it's time for me to go and for you to hit the sheets."

Bec made a face. "I suppose. Thanks again for carting my load over." She rose, held out a hand. "I'll take that bottle."

"No problem." Theo slapped the empty plastic container into her palm. "Thanks for the pop and the chat. It was nice to get away."

Bec trailed her to the door. "Come on over any time you need a break."

"I might take you up on that," Theo said, echoing Bec's earlier words. She put her hand on the doorknob. "Lemme know when you're off again and feel like doing some unboxing."

"My next day off is up in the air, but I'll catch some free time here and there. I'll text. I hate calling, so don't take it personally."

"You and me both. Talking on the phone is highly overrated." Theo pulled the door open and stepped into the hall. "See ya."

With a wave, Bec gently shut the door behind her.

Theo skipped down the stairs and out onto the sidewalk. The more or less unplanned visit had gone better than she'd expected, aside from some uncomfortable moments and the weird knee fetish she'd suddenly developed. Although, if she had to be saddled with a staring affliction, at least knees were better ogling material than boobs. Not that she didn't love boobs, but knees were much less problematic if you got caught staring.

At The Spud, business had picked up. Half the tables were full, and three-quarters of the stools in front of the bar were occupied.

Tessa was perched on one of them, head down as she either played on her cell or had her nose in a book. The perfect sitting duck.

"Whasssss up, sis?" Theo said near Tessa's ear. She leaned out of the way in case Tess snapped her head back, which she did.

"Jesus Christ. You scared the crap out of me."

"Sorry. Couldn't resist." Theo slid onto the stool beside her and saw that a book had won out over the phone.

"Where were you? I came out to ask you something forty-five minutes ago. You haven't responded to any of my texts."

*Oops.* "Sorry. I shut off the ringer earlier." Theo tried to bite down a grin but couldn't stop herself. In a singsong voice, she said, "Wouldn't you like to know where I was?"

Tess assessed Theo. "That's why I asked, dope. Why do you have that sneaky-ass grin on your face?" Then her eyes went wide. "You went to see Bec, didn't you?"

"Somebody had to bring her the stuff she bought at Duluth Trading. Besides, I was curious about her place."

"I'm sure you were curious about her place. All right, sister mine. Cough it up."

# CHAPTER THIRTEEN

Big fat flakes of snow spiraled out of a dark, marble sky as the weather guy on the radio said, "The temps will stay below freezing for the next forty-eight hours. Snow is expected to continue to fall throughout the day, tapering off early tomorrow morning. We're expecting somewhere between six and ten inches, in multiple snowbursts. The evening commute will be slow, so plan ahead. Welcome to early winter in Duluth, my chickadees. Now, I'll throw it back to you, Kelsey. What's new for our Haunted Halloween Haunted Ship tour?"

Nash made a move to turn the radio off.

"Wait a sec. I want to hear about the Haunted Ship thing."

"Okay." He put his hand back on the steering wheel. "You're—"

"Shh."

He shut up.

"—bonfire," said a woman's voice, "outside there'll be food trucks, lots of Halloween lights all over the Irvin. Inside, for those of you looking for a little fear-charged adrenaline, the haunted tour has been redesigned this year to be spookier and more exciting than ever. Strobes will be in use, so anyone who's sensitive to them, beware. The Haunted Ship is open Thursdays to Saturdays, running through October 31st, so you still have a couple of weeks to check it out. Switching gears, on to the jobs report—"

I hit the off button.

Nash glanced at me. "You still love to be scared shitless?"

"Of course. Danna hated that kind of thing, so it's been a while, but yeah."

"Afraid to say I'm with Danna on that one. Don't look at me to go with you."

"Still haven't gotten over the time I left you in that cave?" I hadn't thought about that adventure in years.

"Bec, you left me in there with a snake. You know how I feel about snakes. And my flashlight batteries died."

"I came back." Thinking about this now made me realize I'd been a pretty big asshole.

"Not till the middle of the night."

"Oh, come on. It wasn't even midnight yet."

He glared at me.

"Nash, I'm older and wiser now. Truly, I'm sorry about leaving you behind."

"I could've died. Abandoned with a viper."

"I'm sorry I left you with the snake, and no, you wouldn't have died. The big fella was a hognose, and they aren't venomous."

Nash pulled into the parking lot of a run-down bar in Hermantown. "Don't care if it was venomous or not. I nearly had a heart attack, and if that'd happened, I wouldn't be sitting here with you right now." He cut the engine.

"That's a very good point. It was a royally awful thing to do."

"Thank you. I forgive you. For now." He killed the engine and opened the door. "Come on. My CI should already be here."

Snow came up to the ankles of my new boots, the soles squeaking as I hurried after Nash. Good thing Theo stopped by last night. I pulled my stiff but well-insulated jacket tighter around me. I never would've considered a coat like this until M&M demonstrated the movability built into the shoulders and arms and told me I'd be toasty despite the cold and wind. He'd been right.

The dive bar was the kind of place people were drawn to when they wanted to be left alone with their booze to ruminate over the crappy hand life had dealt them. The lighting was the usual bar-dim, which helped to hide the unkempt, almost spartan interior. Old bar filled my senses, the malty odors and the faded, but undeniable scent of cigarettes. *Gross.*

Two guys slouched at the bar, nursing mugs of beer. The liquor-slinger sat on a stool, playing some kind of handheld game.

Tabletops flaunted stains like battle scars, and from the sticky sheen, I didn't think they'd seen a rag in recent memory. The requisite booths were situated along one of the walls. Nash headed directly for the only occupied one and slid into the seat across from a person who had a hood pulled over their head. I followed him.

"Brady," Nash said, "this is my new partner, Detective Harrison."

Brady's face was shadowed by the hood. With the poor light, I couldn't make much out.

"Nashy, you banging this one? She a hottie." A woman spoke in a voice so gravelly it sounded painful. Her "this" sounded like "dis," the accent of the deep Iron Range.

Nashy? Hoo boy, he wasn't going to live that one down.

"You know I have a wife and a kid. I'm not banging anyone, period."

"A wife and a kid don't usually stop no man."

"You have a point, Brady," Nash said. "All right, you texted me you had something on Jimmy Boy."

"Spoke like a man, always to the point, no goddamn foreplay."

"Time's ticking, so either you do or you don't." Nash's tone was even. I'd always admired his calm presence, even as a kid. Nothing much rattled him.

Except snakes and tears.

She scratched her forehead. The back of her hand was marred by circular scars. "How much ya got for me?"

He said, "Depends how valuable your information is."

She shifted. The hood fell. Her face was world-weary, gaunt, riddled with scars. She could've been thirty or sixty.

"Your Jimmy Boy, he be part a that Bloods gang now. He grooved from sellin' to runnin' dope up here from the Cities. Dumps it, he go back, he do it again."

"We already know that." Nash gazed at her expectantly.

"You no fun at all, Nashy."

"Brady." Nash's don't-fuck-with-me-tone came out to play.

"Fine. Ya don't have ta be a hard ass. The scuffle butt is"— drops of spittle flew as she spoke—"he was sent up here ta deal wit' some dumbass who been cuttin' and distributing for the Bloods. But then dis guy, he started doing the old skim-skim."

*Arne, you naughty boy.*

"Where is Jimmy now?"

"He makin' runs 'twixt here and there again."

"Can you find out when his next run's going to be," I asked, "and where the drop is?"

"Maybe."

Nash pulled out a fifty and snapped it. "If you can find that out for us, I've got another one of these for you." He set the bill on the table.

"Nashy, you know I do whatever I can to help ya." Fast as a whip, she nabbed the bill, pulled it into her sleeve, and slid out of the booth. We followed suit.

"I know you do, Brady. Thank you. I have some baby stuff in the car if you want it."

Brady leaned toward him. "Whatchu got?"

"Formula, baby food, blankets."

"Good stuff. Can always use that at the Community Shelter. You nice when you nice, Nashy."

"I do what I can."

"I know ya do. You one of the good guys, even when you act all hardass. I help you if I can too. I owe you my boy's life." She threw her arms around him and he stiffly patted her back.

"Come on. Let's load you up."

She followed us out to the car, and Nashy handed her three reusable bags full of baby goods.

"You have a lot to carry in this snow, Brady," I said. "You want a ride?"

"Naw, thanks. I got dis, only going tree blocks." Brady tootled off, making her own path to the sidewalk.

"What was that?" I asked once we were safely in the car with the heater blowing.

"What was what?"

"Why does Brady owe you her kid's life?"

He pulled out into the street. "Three winters ago, I found her living down by the train tracks in a corrugated tin and cardboard shelter." He grimaced. "God, that night was cold as shit, below zero. I heard a baby crying, followed the sound, smelled smoke. Found this little shack she'd built. She had one of those camping stoves, had rigged a chimney to vent it outside. Might've worked okay if the weather had been twenty degrees warmer. She had a five-month-old baby boy, was trying her best to keep him warm, but it was a losing proposition. After some fast talking, I got them into my squad. Don't know how it happened, but found a place that very night that took them in, with a possibility it could become a long-term thing if she stayed off the dope. The baby wound up with a serious respiratory infection, so my intervention was good timing. The kid pulled through, and Brady made the decision to shake the drugs. She's had a hard life, but in the end decided to make the effort to do right by her son and save herself in the process. She still lives there, helping the women and kids who show up. The staff says Brady's an odd duck, but she's dependable and good with the clientele."

"That's some story. Nashy, you're a regular hero."

"You are not allowed to call me that."

"Nashy? Or hero?" My words were sarcastic, but my tone was warm. "Scuffle butt says you're a good human."

"Very funny." Then the good human showed me the bird.

# CHAPTER FOURTEEN

With the click of a button, the last of the Spud's food order was placed. Theo yawned and stretched, checked her watch. Lunch time. She rummaged through the fridge and made herself a turkey and cheese sandwich and grabbed a banana off the counter.

She pulled up her email and ate while she weeded and deleted and responded to what needed attention. One of the subject lines was IRVIN, THE HAUNTED SHIP. Best haunted house ever, in her opinion. She loved all pre-Halloween festivities, but loved Halloween itself even more, since the day was also her birthday. Time to break out the holiday decorations. And the hat. Years ago, an artist friend had given her a gift he'd made—a two-foot-tall, black foam hat. It was supposed to be a potato but looked more like the pointy end of a rotten yam. She loved it nonetheless and wore it every year, even it if was too big and kept tipping forward, periodically blinding her.

Her usual rituals had gone out the window since the day she found Arne. All that had seemed irrelevant in light of what had happened. This year, for instance, likely would be the first time she'd missed going to the Haunted Ship in more than a decade. Maybe two.

She found herself clicking open the email anyway.

*Thirteen days left to get yourself scared silly on a haunted ship before Halloween. The Irvin is a Great Lakes iron ore freighter retired in the 1970s, refurbished into a floating museum. The ship is docked at the pier right off Canal Park. A tour leads hapless victims through the haunted ship, complete with character actors and highly detailed scenes.*

The email continued, but Theo hovered the cursor over the delete button. Then something made her reread it. An idea began to form in the back of her head and soon was knocking on her front door. Maybe Bec would be up for a little floating terror. The Haunted Ship might be the perfect activity for just friends. Theo grabbed her phone before she could rationalize why this might be another bad idea.

**An email came through and it made me think of you.**

*No, too sappy.* She backspaced and tried again.

**Hey, Bec. The Irvin's been turned into a haunted ship for Halloween. It's open evenings till the 31st. Wondering if you might want to get freaked with me?**

Was this the right thing to do? Was she playing with fire? Not unless she wanted to play with fire, which, in this case, she did not. No sultry looks, best to do no flirting at all.

For god's sake. She was a grown-ass woman. *Get your usual swagger on, Theo, and knock off this pussyfooting around.* She shoved the rest of the banana in her mouth, hit send, and returned to the business of thinning her inbox. Easier said than done when her eyes kept straying to her phone screen. What if Bec wasn't interested in haunted ships? *Then, Theo,* she lectured herself, *something else will come along.*

Delete, delete, delete.

*The ringer. Turn the ringer on so you don't miss...anything.* She did, then bobbled it when text alerts immediately pinged. "Shit," she muttered as the phone hit the floor.

She picked it up and scrolled the list. Lots of junk. And one from Bec. She opened it.

**how did you read my mind heard about this haunted ship thing on the radio earlier. nash wants nothing to do with it love haunted anything**

"Yes," whistled through Theo's teeth, and a rush of adrenaline flooded her, making her hands tremble as she responded.

**I have powers you can't imagine. Tessa won't go near the ship whether it's haunted or not, and I go every year. Sounds like we're a perfect match.**

She hit send, then reread what she'd written.

Crap. That last line made it look like she was trying out a come-on.

**what kind of powers do you hold that I can't imagine I like to use my imagination**

That text was followed up with, **supposed to be off this coming Thursday evening does that work**

**I'm not sure what kind of—things—you like to imagine. Maybe one day I'll find—**

Nope, way too much. She backspaced. *Stick to the facts as you understand them.*

**Hang on, let me check the schedule.**

*Holy shit, Zaccardo. You're truly, honestly a dimwit.* Theo was so distracted by her dimwittedness, she forgot what she was doing.

*Thursday, you moron. Check Thursday.* She reopened her laptop and pulled up the Spud schedule. Usually, the ABCs worked a day during the week and at least one of the weekend days, sometimes both. A few clicks, and the tightness in her shoulders eased. The ABCs worked four to close on Thursday. Theo figured Tess wouldn't mind being on call in case anything came up, especially if it was because Theo was hanging out with someone.

**We're good to go.**

No response for forever and a day, then, **awesome sounds like there might be food there you want to do that or will you have eaten**

Bec would be coming from work, probably hungry. Theo loved food trucks with the best of them, but knew when people lined up, as they usually did at events like this, it could take a half hour or longer to get served.

**I can wait till you're off. Love me a good food truck, but when there's a crowd up in these here parts, there's never enough trucks to service everyone fast enough. To save our asses from becoming blocks of ice, I propose we grab a fast bite at DCI once you're off, then we can head to the haunt.**

Theo's leg jiggled under the desk as she waited for a response.

**sounds good to me what's DCI**

**Only the second-best Coney Island hotdog joint since my beloved Original Coney Island restaurant, established in 1921, closed. Now all we have left is the Deluxe Coney Island. DCI.**

The response took less time this go round.

**oh yeah got it. nash loves that place he always shows up with mega onion breath. you like onions**

Theo stared at her phone, trying to formulate a cohesive sentence. Was she asking? Why? Was it an offhand comment? Maybe Bec liked onions.

**Yeah, you can leave DCI with some serious halitosis. I'm not a fan of raw onions, so I shouldn't blast you out.**

**hey sweet same page**

Theo stared at the texts. For the life of her she couldn't come up with a thing to say. So completely, utterly unlike her. She settled on: **Yes, we are.**

**how do we go about getting tickets for this extravaganza**

Ah, a question she could work with.

**At the ship. They're open until ten thirty, and the tours take about twenty minutes.**

Who knew those little squiggling dots could be so mesmerizing?

**sounds good if all goes well I should be off by six. want to meet at the restaurant? I'll let you know if I'll be late**

**10-4, detective. Be careful out there.**

She eyed the words and added a thumbs-up.

Bec sent one back.

Theo slumped over the table, feeling like she'd run a marathon. At least, all things told, the conversation ended better than it had begun.

She and Bec were going on a friend-date. *Friend. Remember that six-letter word.*

# CHAPTER FIFTEEN

Thank god today was Haunted Ship day. The week had dragged on so long it might as well have had a ball and chain attached to it. No hits on the APB on Jimmy Boy, either here or in the Cities. He'd gone to ground like the vile little vole he was. Since I was without any ongoing cases other than the murder at the Mashed Spud, I bounced between Nash and Shingo, helping with whatever I could on their mysteries. I was more than happy to assist, but nothing I did kept my mind off Theo and Case of the Body in the Dumpster. And Theo and those breathtaking eyes.

Brady, Nash's CI, hadn't come through with anything yet but did relay she might have something soon. Which meant my evening was free and clear.

I'd been looking forward to this day and the company who came along with it. My brain looped the texting conversation between Theo and me almost a week ago. I'd wound up being more flirtatious than I intended, but, for some reason it was so damn easy with her. I could imagine her cheeks turning beet red and the bright sparkle lighting up those eyes.

The sun was out, slowly sinking into the west as I drove home, glinting off snow piles along the side of the road. The weekend storm had dumped about six inches, but in true Minnesota fashion, by the next day everything had been plowed and, thanks to temps in the fifties, the roads were now clear and dry. Earlier, I'd checked the weather. The high of forty-three would cool off to a balmy thirty, so it would be a bit chilly, but not too cold for tonight's festivities.

I found a parking place not too far from my apartment. A good omen.

Inside, I changed and flopped on the couch. Still an hour and a half before it was time to meet Theo at the Coney place. I was starving. Maybe Theo was available, and we could eat now.

I held my phone over my face as I typed.

**Im home done early if youre free we could grab a bite earlier**

Theo didn't answer right away, so I pulled up the Irvin website and read all about the huge ship's Great Lakes history. Before too long the phone buzzed.

My heart did not speed up. Not a bit.

**Ah. You're one of those hangry people. The way to your heart is through your mouth, then?**

I grinned.

**unless you want a belligerent Bec**

**I imagine a belligerent Bec is a bitchy Bec. We certainly don't want that. I can meet you any time.**

**heading out now**

I considered adding a comment about what could get me out of a bitchy mood, then thought better of it.

\* \* \*

I arrived first and parked right in front of the restaurant, letting the warm, now almost hot air blow on me. The street was quiet, and I soaked in the warmth. The restaurant had a Deluxe Coney Dog sign and a green-and-white awning which shaded the front windows. OPEN in red neon beckoned the hungry.

A boxy blue-and-white Chevy pickup from somewhere in the nineties pulled up behind me, Theo in the driver's seat. Hopefully she'd talked Tess into storing that awesome beast car somewhere safe.

I got out and so did Theo. She looked toasty in an insulated flannel, jeans, and winter boots.

We met in the middle between the two vehicles and headed for the door.

"Glad to see you driving something other than the canary," I said.

Theo laughed. "It was a tough sell, but I looked up the resale value on it and she changed her mind about risking it PDQ."

I stopped with one foot on the curb. "PDQ?"

"Don't you remember those convenience stores? PDQs?"

"Nope. What's it stand for?"

Theo fully faced me. "You're kidding, right?"

"No," I said slowly and peered at her suspiciously.

"You'll get it pretty darn quick."

"What?"

Now she looked at me as if I'd lost my mind. "PDQ. Pretty darn quick."

The lightbulb flashed. "Oh, FFS."

Now she had the great wide eye of incomprehension.

"FFS. For fuck sake."

"Oh, FFS. Touché." She gave me a playful shove.

"Hey, disorderly conduct."

"I'll bet I can wiggle my way out of a ticket."

"Now you're bribing an officer of the law, ma'am?" I looked her in the eye. In the light, hazel had morphed into the piercing green that made my heart catch.

"You gonna punish me, officer?" Her tone was low, seductive.

I didn't dare respond. A heavy beat thudded, not in my heart, but further down south. FFS, all right.

We arrived at the front door and grabbed for the handle at the same time, shoulders colliding.

Theo hip-checked me out of the way and pulled it open.

"Seems you got a little violent streak in ya there, barkeep. Maybe you should take up hockey."

Her only response was an upraised brow. "You can get it next time, hangry girl."

"Promise?"

"Only if we go dutch."

"Deal."

We both laughed, and she pushed me inside. The aroma of hotdogs, onions, and Coney sauce hit, and my mouth watered.

The restaurant was three times as long as it was wide. A laminate yellow counter with a dozen stools waiting to be filled—probably not till next spring—ran half the length of the eatery. Hotdogs warmed on a flat, stainless griddle in front of the window facing the street. They were aligned in a neat column from brown and crispy at one end to recently-slapped-on-the-grill pasty on the other.

Booths with thick, Kelly-green padded seats, and a row of tables, two abreast, filled the restaurant. Vintage or vintage-looking diner chairs were tucked neatly under the tables.

A white board displaying the restaurant's logo across the top offered up the day's specials, handwritten with a marker whose skimpy output indicated an imminent need for replacement. Behind the counter, two Hamilton Beach triple spindle mixers patiently waited to blend ice cream into shakes and malts.

We both picked the #2 special, two Coneys, no onion, cheese please, with fries and a drink. A friendly college kid took our order while another woman tucked the dogs into buns and decked them out. The finished product landed on our tray before we got our change.

Theo grabbed the tray, I scooped up the drinks, and we settled into one of the many available booths. Hopefully, come suppertime, people would swarm in and buy a shit ton of hotdogs.

The first Coney went down like a rocket, one bite right after another, me pausing only to chase it with my soda. I scowled, trying to remember what new word Chu had been trying to teach us to use instead of awesome. "Fire. That's it. These Coneys are fire."

Theo's mouth was stuffed, and she almost choked on a laugh.

After gobbling up my second dog, I wiped my lips and chin with three napkins, checked my shirt to make sure I wasn't wearing any Coney sauce, and tossed the napkins in the cardboard serving tray. I finished before Theo, probably because I'd gotten in the habit of bolting my food before a call came in.

I chewed on a French fry, covertly studying Theo as she finished hers. She ate with obvious relish, totally enjoying herself. Not enough people paid attention to the small pleasures in life, and for me, good chow ranked right up there.

"Bec?"

I jerked my gaze from her smooth throat to her eyes, realized she'd caught me red-handed. Or would that be red-eyed? "Sorry. Daydreaming. You're fun to watch while you eat. Oops, did I say that out loud?"

She blessed me with a playful grin, and her eyes crinkled in good humor. I didn't think I'd ever seen her smile so widely in the short time I'd known her. Her eyes sparkled, full of life. "Yes. Yes, you did say that out loud. What can I say? I love to eat."

"Oh, you do, do you?" This would be way more fun if I was teasing Theo-more-than-a-friend instead of bantering with Theo-just-a-friend. *But that's what Theo is*, I reminded myself. Just a friend. An incredibly hot bundle of happy friend. Exactly the way I wanted it.

Theo flushed but didn't break our gaze. Her voice dropped an octave. "I do."

Thoughts of just-a-friend fled as fast as a bunny trying to outrun a pack of starving dogs. My mouth was suddenly parched.

She stuffed the rest of her Coney into her mouth, grabbed her pop, and finished it.

I couldn't think of anything else to say except, "Ready to roll?"

# CHAPTER SIXTEEN

Twilight was in full bloom by the time Bec found a parking space in the gravel-filled Bayfront Festival Park lot. They'd decided to leave Theo's truck at DCI and ride together. Fortunately, the lot was less than half full on a Thursday, and the walk to the Irvin wasn't far.

"Wow," Bec said as she matched pace with Theo, her breath coming out in white puffs. "The ship is huge. Well, okay, maybe not huge-huge, but it feels huge-huge."

"I got ya. Docked right here, it dwarfs everything it's next to. For some reason, old planes, trains, automobiles, ships—jeez, that sounds like a movie sequel—are my jam. They, I dunno…" Theo paused, searching for a way to describe her feelings. "I'm in awe. The amazing things people were able to accomplish without any of our so-called modern thingamajigs."

She studied Bec's profile, trying to gauge a reaction. Instead of gauging, however, she became distracted, admiring the curve of Bec's jaw, the way her dark eyebrows followed her brow line in a sweeping curve. The short hairs curling gently behind her ear.

"I think I know exactly what you mean."

Bec gave Theo a friendly nudge. Theo stiffened, feeling as if she'd been hit by a bolt of lightning that crackled through her head, down her spine, and burst out of the soles of her feet.

For an instant, she wondered if Bec felt it too. Then rationality came knocking. *Come on, Theo. Electricity, lightning?* They were literary tropes in romance books. Life was not a novel.

But, nagged an inner voice, it did happen. She'd felt it. Right through her jacket. Had Bec? *You and your bright ideas, Zaccardo. Let's do stuff as friends since neither of us is looking for a relationship.* What had she been thinking? *Go ahead, Theo, you can completely ignore an obviously budding attraction to Bec that would inevitably blow back on you. Have you lost your flipping mind?*

*Knock it off,* she ordered her inner, apparently uber-hormonal fifteen-year-old self. *Pull your head out of, well, wherever it's stuck.*

Bec had an intensity about her which drew Theo to her like a golden retriever wanting some love. The good news? She wasn't a dog, and she wasn't looking for love. Was. Not.

"Theo?"

"What?" The stiff breeze coming off the water hit hard, and for once she welcomed its sharp sting of reality.

Bec's head was tilted, expression of confused humor on her face. "I said it's not lip service. My fascination with monstrous modes of transportation."

There went those goddamn dimples again. All Theo's concerns evaporated. "I know it's not lip service." Theo shouldered Bec back, wondering if the zing would repeat. Thankfully it did not. *See, Theo, all in your imagination.*

They rounded a curve and came face-to-face with the William A. Irvin, a mechanical monster rising from the deep. High above, lights on the various decks glowed green and purple, and a huge orange-and-black banner draped over the side welcomed those looking to put a little fear into their lives.

The sidewalk and thirty feet of snow-trampled grass spanned the distance between the street and the ship, stretching along the entirety of its six-hundred-foot length. Character actors prowled through the crowd, in turns scaring and then chatting with their prey. Three food trucks were at the curb, serving up BBQ, Vietnamese, and Big Bubba's Burgers. The lines weren't too long, either because Halloween events began later at night or because the winds gusting up to twenty miles an hour off the lake were enough to scare folks away. Theo was okay with that. Fewer people to deal with was always good.

They crossed the street and hopped up on the curb. Almost every inch of snow was well-packed by hundreds of feet. Kids ran wild, screaming, yelling, and generally creating happy chaos.

Bec grabbed Theo's gloved hand as she surveyed the space, and gave it a hearty squeeze. "It's like a carnival. I love the carnival. But this experience will be better than any carnival because it's floating. Thanks for thinking of this."

Never had Theo seen anyone so excited about touring a creaky old boat, except, perhaps, herself. Bec's enthusiasm flooded her, seeping into every pore. The freedom she felt was astonishing. For this instant in time, fuck responsibilities. To hell with decorum. She was going to have a great time.

She tightened her mittened grip on Bec's hand, pulled her in, and wrapped both arms around her, twirling them in ever faster circles, laughing with joy. *This is it*, Theo decided. *Enough worrying*. Tess always told her not to overthink. How many times had she heard her say, "Live in the moment, sis." She could. Yes, she could, goddammit. Could ignore the almost uncontrollable urge to lean in and brush the smooth, warm skin of Bec's neck with her lips.

Any further thoughts flew straight out of Theo's smoking brain then as Bec wrapped her arms tighter and increased the pace of their staggering spin. Her feet came off the ground and they giggled hysterically.

Bec lost her footing and down they went.

Theo landed directly atop her, laughing so hard she couldn't form a coherent sentence. She rolled off Bec onto her back, hand over her mouth as she attempted to stifle her mirth. Their eyes met, and they both dissolved into another paroxysm of hilarity.

A kid in a winter jacket two sizes too big and a stocking cap advertising the Bentleyville Tour of Lights stood over them, his mittened hands on his hips. "Are you guys okay?"

"Hey, buddy." Bec's voice was tight as she fought to keep a straight face. "We're fine." As she said the word "fine," they both lost it again.

"Adults," the kid muttered and walked away.

Bec made it to her knees, then her feet, and pulled Theo up.

"Thank you." She swiped ineffectually at the tears streaming down her face. "Someone must have dosed us with laughing gas."

"Avast ye, me maties," Bec shouted, raising her arm as if she were wielding a sword. "Find the nefarious nincompoop and hang 'im from the yardarm, then feed 'im to them fishies!"

# CHAPTER SEVENTEEN

The crowd emerging from the Irvin was giddy. Enthusiastic chatter and the sound of some poor kid bawling their head off echoed off the ship's hull. All in all, the experience had been awesome.

We'd made it through the gauntlet, laughed a lot, yelped a little, and I had to admit to screaming once. Theo was slightly more reserved, but not by much. I was pretty sure she had a good time too. Whoever oversaw this event deserved major kudos, as well as all the stage builders who created the haunted spaces on various decks and, of course, the actors themselves.

With our arms companionably linked, we stumbled off the last step of the gangway onto solid ground. Theo dragged me toward one of the food trucks.

"You hungry?" I asked hopefully.

"After all that nuttiness, you know it. Plus, the s'mores hot chocolate at Big Bubba's is the best. They fill the top of the cup with mini marshmallows and take one of those small torches and toast 'em up. Comes with graham crackers for dipping."

"Sounds great." We queued up at Bubba's, and I assessed the menu. "Think I want a burger, too. They smell so good."

"They are. Want to split?"

"Sure. As long as cheese and fries are involved."

"Cheese on the burger or cheese on the fries?"

"Any and all."

Theo laughed. "What about fried onions?"

"Oh, yeah. Mushrooms too if they're sautéed and don't come out of a can."

"They are sautéed, no can."

"Bacon?"

"You are a woman after my own hungry heart."

A flush of warmth began in my stomach and crept upward. "It's been a long time since anyone wanted to share anything with me. My ex-wife pretty much hated everything I liked."

"Well, we're of the same burger and fajita mind, anyway."

I basked in the glow of Theo's words. She was the diametrical opposite of my ex. After the first few years of our marriage, Danna began to care less and less about me and more and more about herself. Theo was, what? Refreshing? Yes. That's exactly what she was.

Fifteen minutes later we were in my car with the heat on high.

"OMG," I croaked after the first bite. "This is beyond good."

Theo licked her thumb. "Right? Glad you like it. Bubba's burgers have always been bomb-a-rific."

"Bomb-a-rific?"

"Yup. The nieces and nephews say the weirdest things. Bubba and I—"

"Wait." I held up what was left of my burger like a stop sign. "Bubba's someone's actual name?"

"No. His name's Kevin Smith. But I've called him Bubba as long as I've known him. Everyone does."

"Ah. The only Bubba I knew was a schoolyard bully. In fifth grade, he was picking on some of the younger kids, and Nash and I yelled at him to stop. He called me a dyke and I punched him in the eye. I didn't know what the word meant, but the way he sneered it…" I trailed off. "Nash pulled me off him. He didn't harass anyone after that."

"You were a defender of the underserved even at that tender age. Did you get in trouble?"

"Nope. He was too embarrassed to admit a girl slugged him. Even now I don't know what it is that fires up my intolerance for injustice."

"Sounds to me like you were born to be a cop. So when did you figure things out?"

"Looking back, I'd always had plenty of crushes on hot actresses. Demi Moore, especially in *G.I. Jane*. Seriously sick. Halle Berry, Sandra Bullock, Melissa Etheridge."

"I'm with you on Halle, Demi, and Sandra. I guess we both have a type. Good thing I'm a redhead."

"So I'm not attracted to you?" I nabbed a fry.

"Exactly."

"I'm an equal opportunity hair color lover. Except for blondes." I wanted to add I found absolutely nothing wrong with redheads, especially curly-haired ones, but figured that might get me into more trouble than I was looking for.

"Equal opportunity, huh?"

I made a face. I was so tempted. *No, Bec, bite that tongue.*

"Your ex was blond, I take it?"

"Yup. On that note, time for a diversion. Enough about me. Tell me more about your Bubba."

"My Bubba. Poor Bubba. A few years ago, we'd struck an agreement for him to take over The Mashed Spud's kitchen. We'd serve a limited menu, pretty much the same thing he's got going with the food truck."

"What happened?"

"Had to come up with about twenty grand to turn the Spud's frozen pizza kitchen into a functional space for a chef. You know, the fancy grill and an oven, the whole exhaust system, that kinda thing. I didn't have enough cash, and Bubba's credit was tanked. We decided to let the idea go. In the long run, I think he's making out better with the truck. He can go where the crowds are."

"I'm sorry it didn't work out."

"What's meant to be is meant to be. Usually there's a reason something turns out the way it does."

I finished my half of the burger and fries and wiped my fingers. "I've felt that way too, sometimes. But it's hard to keep believing that in my line of work. I see so much senseless tragedy it's hard to reconcile. I mean, what's the reason a kid is beaten to death by a drunk father? For what reason is a university freshman raped? Life can be unfair as hell."

"Yes, it can. I get where you're coming from. The bar is kind of a microcosm of the society you deal with at large. You see the best and the worst. The Mashed Spud's kind of like *Cheers*, where everyone knows your name. Which isn't always a good thing."

"No, it's not. Though I never really watched that show. I was too little when it first came out, never got into the reruns."

"You young thing."

"Come on. I'm only six years younger than you."

"My twenty-fifth high school reunion is coming up, not that you could pay me to attend. Wow. When I think about it, I feel ancient."

"What year did you graduate?"

"2001, A Space Odyssey."

"Ancient, my ass. Nothing about you suggests you're ancient. Aside from the haircut. But since *Stranger Things* came out, hockey hair is back in, so that assumption is out the window."

"Look out, folks, this one's a mullet wiseass. I must say, I do wear my age well. Must be my fancy, fifty-step beauty routine."

"Fifty steps to a brand-new you. At eighty-two."

"Sounds like a commercial. Maybe we're on to something. Hey, do you remember having a conversation with me about my hair the night of your unfortunate BB reaction? You came up to the bar for some water, made a comment you liked my hair. Do you remember what I said?"

She cocked her head, those hazel-y green eyes sparkling, sending an electric shock straight down my spine. I sat up straight and tried not to squirm. *Think about the sky.* But the sky was dark. *Then think about stars. Or black holes. Like your memory.* "I have no idea."

"'This'"—she ran a hand through her curls—"'is classic again.'" An amused expression settled on her face.

"Well, you are a classic. Age is an attitude, and I love yours."

"If age is an attitude, I've got plenty of that. Time for some dessert." She pulled the cup of hot chocolate out of the holder and unsealed the lid. Perfectly toasted marshmallows filled the top. She broke off a piece of graham cracker and scooped up some of the goo. A strand stretched all the way to her mouth, then broke off, trailing a white line down her chin.

In another time, another place, I would've leaned over and taken care of that. Instead, I busied myself with my own cup. Steam rose when I took the lid off. "Smells like camping." After the first bite, I was sold. "Oh, yeah. This is so good. You advise well."

"Thank you. Maybe I should charge Bubba for promotion." She finished off the cracker. "Being involved with you—" She held up a hand. "Let me clarify. Being involved with you as a friend, I've been thinking about the job you do, dealing with people at their lowest, meanest, and, not to be too flippant, but sometimes at their deadliest and deadest. I don't know how you do it."

I paused, a dripping graham halfway to my mouth, trying to figure out how serious she was. "My alarm goes off, I get up, and I go to work. Piece of cake."

"Funny. No. I mean, how do you turn your brain off of the stuff you confront every day and go on to enjoy your hot chocolate like the world isn't all fucked up?"

I took the bite, thinking it over as I chewed. "The world is all fucked up. I learned the hard way when I was first on the job that if I obsess over all the crap we deal with on the daily, it's a destroyer. A therapist helped me sort shit out. She taught me how to compartmentalize and keep functioning, and then later, go back in and air the dirty laundry, so to speak. She saved my ass and my job."

"I'm glad you had her. Was she back in Detroit?"

"Yeah. She's retired, but we still exchange emails occasionally. I have a new one here I like."

"Nice. I don't think many cops would admit to having a therapist if what I see on TV is any indication of the truth."

I took a sip of the hot chocolate. "I don't advertise the fact I talk to a shrink, but, if asked, I'll tell it like it is. I figure it's kind of like being gay. You can hide it, or you can live honestly, and that honesty could make a difference in someone else's life. Or my own. Cops are twice as likely to die by suicide as they are be killed in line of duty, and women, it turns out, are less willing than the men to seek out help, counseling. I refuse to be a statistic."

Theo peered at me with wide eyes. "I never realized how big a balancing act you need to do. Remain grounded, don't become a raging psycho. Harden yourself to deal with the worst of the worst and still be able to go home and be a loving human with a heart."

"Some cops can't do it. Some can. There's stuff you get used to. A lot of it you don't. But if you don't find a way to process, it'll chew you up, change you. I've worked hard not to let that happen. Really hard." I gnawed my lip, debating whether or not to give voice to what I was thinking. *Fuck it.*

"I was with Danna over a decade, but in less than two weeks, you understand me better than she ever did."

That comment slowed Theo's chewing, and she regarded me for a long moment. "That's a goddamn shame, Bec. You deserve so much more." She lifted a shoulder. "Guess you arrested me so I could be your sounding board."

"For the love of nothing holy, I did not arrest you. But you are a great sounding board. Somehow you make it easy."

"I'm easy in ways you'll never know."

What could have become a dark, melancholy moment vaporized, and just like that, we were teasing and sharing funny work stories. I told her about a streaker case I had early in my career in Detroit, a repeat offender who hit a different downtown business for three months in a row before we nailed him. And another about the time I had to go undercover as a prostitute and wound up in a motel pool after fighting with one of the johns. I might've been a drowned rat, but I bagged the vermin.

She told me about full moons and crazy drinkers, about a guy who'd decided to go-go dance on one of the tall tables on New Year's Eve and became the hit of the party. He'd donated all his tips to the bar staff, and he hadn't even been drunk. Of course, she also had to poke me with a story about the time a drunken, ungodly sick cop had kept her up all night.

It was easy to let myself go with Theo, to simply enjoy the food, the conversation, the company. Spending time with somebody who was interesting, empathetic, generally happy with their life, someone who had their own opinions and could share them in a nonconfrontational way—*looking at you, Danna*—was soul-affirming.

I glanced at the clock on the dashboard. Almost two hours had flown by. The parking lot had filled up, and the old Irvin was probably rocking the fear factor. "I suppose I should bring you back to your car. Thanks for suggesting this. I've had a great time."

The warm expression on Theo's face suggested she had as well. "Me too. It's been a long minute since I had a chance to forget everything and do nothing but be present. You helped me make it happen, Bec. Thank you."

"Feeling's mutual." I put the car in gear and pulled out of the lot. "If you need to be dumped on your keister in the snow again, I'm your gal."

"You need a friendly ear, I'm yours." She inhaled to speak, held it, then blew the breath out. "Please don't take this the wrong way."

I gave her a wary side-eye. "Okay."

"I love your smile. You're a cop with a big heart, except for when you arrest me, and I love how you love to have fun."

"Ohmigod. I—"

"Yada yada. I've heard it all before." She pressed her lips together as she tried to repress an irrepressible smile. "To my car, James."

"Yes, milady." I dropped her off and drove home, relieved I'd made it through the evening without making too much of a jerk of myself or totally losing my mind and jumping Theo's bones.

*Did that thought just hit my brain?*

*Yes, Bec, it did.*

*Uh-oh.*

# CHAPTER EIGHTEEN

Theo rolled out of bed after hitting the snooze button four times, trying to hold on to rapidly disappearing fragments of her dream. It was a hot one, she remembered that much, starring herself and a woman who eerily resembled Bec, in the backseat of Theo's old blue '80s Caprice Classic. That car's back seat had been an exceptional place for messing around. She'd been sorry to see it go after the engine caught fire on the side of Interstate 35.

*Not good, Theo, to be dreaming about someone you can't touch.*

She spent a little extra time in the shower, thinking maybe a little self-satisfaction would stop her mind from going where it didn't belong. It didn't help.

She dressed and wandered into the kitchen.

Tessa had her chair balanced on two legs, a paperback in hand, coffee cup in the other. "Good morning. It's—" The chair legs hit the floor, and she consulted her phone, which lay face down on the table so notifications wouldn't distract from her reading pleasure. "It's only nine thirty and you're on your feet. Impressive. How'd last night go?"

Tessa knew she was going to meet up with Bec and, of course, was as nosy and curious as always, god love her.

"Fun. They did an amazing job on the Irvin as usual. I introduced her to Bubba's."

Tess set her mug carefully on the table. "Come on. Give me the nitty-gritty and don't leave anything out. Did you kiss her, have a little make-out session?"

"Oh my god, Tess. No. I did not kiss her. She did not kiss me. We did not make out." Aside from goofing around, which had been delightful.

"Ha ha. Cough it up."

She tried to order her thoughts as she filled a coffee cup. "We had a good time. In another world, I'd be interested in something more."

"Are you planning on being a confirmed bachelorette the rest of your life?"

"So what if I do?" Theo snapped with an uncharacteristic sharpness that surprised her as much as it did Tessa.

"Hey, hold up. I didn't mean to offend you."

"No, I'm sorry. I didn't mean to bite your head off."

Tess leaned toward Theo. "What's wrong?"

"Nothing."

"You never snap at me. What's going on, missy?"

Theo had long hated herself for her decision not to be completely honest with Tessa. She was up-front about everything else. Well, mostly everything. Just not the thing which had driven her to live her life as she did. If Tess ever found out— *No, don't think about that.* "Don't 'missy' me, missy."

"Brat. So, what happened?"

Theo tested her coffee. Perfect. "We had a great time. Bec's something. Sweet, ornery, a hellion at times."

"So what's the problem?"

Theo related the acceptable parts of her dream.

"So let me get this straight, knowing you as I do. You are having some"—she did air quotes—"'feelings' for Bec. You two had a great time and you like-like her."

Theo opened her mouth, but one mom look from Tess shut her up.

"You think she might be interested. But you can't hook up because now she's your friend. You don't hook up with friends. Ever. Yeah?"

"Well, yeah. We made a deal to do stuff. As friends." She sneered at the look of sheer disbelief on Tessa's face. "We did. Bec doesn't want a relationship any more than I do."

Tess threw up her hands. "There's the answer. You two can hit it and quit it since neither of you want a relationship. Fuck buddies. Could it be more perfect?"

Theo closed her eyes so Tessa wouldn't see her roll them. "No. No," she said more forcefully. "That's not perfect. My rule—"

"Yeah, yeah. Your fucking rule. No strings. Friends don't get the chance for no strings."

"Exactly. So in that vein, I was thinking…"

"Really." If Tess could have been any drier, they'd be in the middle of the Sahara.

"Really. I think more often than you might think I think." *Okay, Theo, fly by the seat of your unthinking pants.* "Let's invite Bec over for a game night. Easy, fun. Lots of laughs." Safeguarded by the presence of Tessa, she could hang with Bec and wouldn't have to worry about any awkward moments. Genius.

"I see." Tess used her coffee mug to hide a smirk, but the mug wasn't big enough. "I've got your number. You want me to be a chaperone so you two don't fall into some crazy hinky dinky on the couch. Or in your bed. Are you serious?"

"Well, yeah. Besides, Bec's hilarious. You'll love her."

"She's not afraid to pitch in, I know that." Tess regarded Theo. "Fine. When do you want to do this, this—this…" She snapped her fingers as she tried to come up with the right word. "Farcical situation?"

"Farcical? Good word. Not for this situation, but in general. I'll have to remember it for crossword puzzles. Anyway, as soon as possible. Monday. I'll text her." Theo could not keep the smile from her face. "Knew I could count on you. Gotta run." She bolted from the kitchen, heard a thwap and a thud, probably Tessa's book bouncing off the doorjamb and falling to the floor.

"You missed!"

# CHAPTER NINETEEN

A text from Sgt. Alvarez woke me. I squinted at the time. 7:23 a.m.

**3:00 my office Ivorsen update**
**okay**

I scrolled through the rest of my texts. Spam, one from Nash regarding the plan for the day, a bunch of political fundraisers asking for money. And then Theo.

**Hey Bec, thanks for the great time last night. Wondering if you might be interested in coming over Monday evening after work for dinner and maybe play some board games with me and Tess or cards if you hate board games, or have a bullshit session if you hate playing any kind of game. Which would be odd, but possible.**

My heart began thudding. Before I talked myself out of it, I thumbed, **love games monday should be good**

**Great!! Let me know when you're close to leaving work.**
**will do have a good weekend**

I stared at the plaster ceiling, thinking about games and then about the previous night. I was filled with a jumble of joy and uncertainty. The Haunted Ship and the after-party in my car had been full of merriment and introspection. The more I got to know Theo, the more I liked her. She knew who she was, comfortable in her own skin. She didn't give off any run-for-your-life vibes. She was mature but hilarious, serious, kind, cared about the people in her life and the world at large. She wasn't narcissistic or self-involved. Pretty much summed up what I'd wanted and what I didn't get in my failed relationship.

*But you pay to play*, I reminded myself. I was not going to take the chance of paying again. All I needed was to make a file in my mind and fill it with all the ways Theo was enchanting, sexy, beautiful, beguiling, spellbinding, and whatever else she might be that might lead me to destruction-by-love. Then I needed to slam that file drawer shut, lock it, and lose the key. No going back to debrief any of it.

Beyond all that sticky business, I'd forgotten what having some good, old-fashioned fun felt like. Simply going out and doing something silly or entertaining, no bars, no booze, and sharing the experience with someone I liked had made me happier than I'd been in a long time.

Now I wanted more of it. My therapist would be proud.

Without a doubt, Theo and I had a connection, as much as I didn't want to admit it. Did I not want to admit it? Playing mind games with myself was becoming a daily habit. Could blossoming friendship stir up feelings similar to new love? Been a long time since I'd made a friend. The breathless excitement of waiting for a text, anticipating what's next, the intoxicating feeling of being understood on an intimately deep level. Whatever was happening between the two of us was doing a number on my emotions, but I fiercely liked it as much as it fiercely scared the crap out of me.

All this friendship thing lacked was the physical part, which I could work around, right?

*Right.*

I rolled over and punched my pillow. Despite myself, I was attracted to Theo. Yes, I was. To her personality. Her wit. Her kindness. Her bod—

*Okay, hot shot, cool your jets. You can appreciate the beauty of her body without including carnal knowledge.*

"But, Bec," whispered my evil, shoulder-riding gremlin. "Can you stand to appreciate her body from afar? Without caressing those perfect curves, without feeling the softness of her skin under your hands? Without feeling her lips on yours, without tasting her mouth, without the soft swipe of her tongue? Without ever hearing her say, 'I love you' in the throes of passion?"

"Shut the fuck up." I fired my pillow across the room. It hit the wall and landed on top of the boxes I'd made into a half-assed dresser. I stomped into the bathroom and took a long, cold shower.

* * *

I walked into the squad room at two on the dot after spending most of the day with Nash running down names connected with Mrs. Rasmussen's license plate list. Alvarez was in his office, on the phone, door shut.

Shingo looked up as I passed by. "Hey, Harrison, how was the day off?"

I parked myself at my desk, and she spun around to face me. "Good. Did the Irvin haunted tour with a friend. Laughed a whole lot, was introduced to Big Bubba's Burgers." I wondered what she'd say if she knew I'd been with the person who found Arne's body.

"Oh yeah, Bubba's. The best. Did you have the s'mores hot chocolate?"

"I did. The guy's a genius."

The squad room door opened, and Nash came in, followed by Chu.

Shingo half-turned. "Trouble by two."

Chu tossed his messenger bag on his chair. It nearly bounced off, but he saved it by the shoulder strap. "I take offense to that comment."

Nash propped a hip on his desk. "We ran into each other in the hallway, and here we are."

The banter ended when Alvarez's door opened. He boomed, "All right, you yahoos. Get yourselves in here." He spun around and did a close imitation of my stomp to the bathroom this morning as he returned to his own chair.

Once we were assembled, he said, "Sorry to squeeze you all in, but between kissing other people's asses and keeping ours covered, my time is limited these days." He looked even more worn out than he had the last time we'd checked in.

"First," he said, "the chief is breathing fire because the mayor is crawling up his butt to solve Ivorsen's murder. The mayor is being hounded by Visit Duluth, the visitor's bureau. They want no negative press regarding the city or our department when they roll out this season's 'Welcome to Duluth, The North Shore's Safe, Exceptional Winter Wonderland' marketing campaign. Can't scare off the tourists by letting them know there's a murderer-slash-drug slinger running around. Yada yada." He exhaled noisily. "Goddamn, I hate politics. Departmental politics, city politics, tourism politics, national politics. I'm ready to go back to street patrol."

No wonder he was looking so rough.

"Only new thing I have is Hennepin County has finally shared some information, which I'll get to in a minute. Where are we on this thing?"

Nash said, "My CI got a hold of me yesterday. Jimmy's supposed to be on the move up here with more dope very soon. Could be tomorrow or a week from now, but as soon as she hears she'll give me the 411. Still working through the list of drop-bys Arne's neighbor gave us. Generally, lots of low-level drug users. No one admits to seeing, much less knowing, Jimmy Boy Collins."

Shingo said, "Chu and I are recanvassing Ivorsen's neighborhood and triple-checking known drug houses. No news, but we did Narcan three people and send them to St. Luke's."

"Good work. Fucking fentanyl. All right." Alvarez leaned forward, the muscles in his forearms rippling. "Here's what I know, and it jibes with your CI's information, Nash. Now that Jimmy's iced someone, he thinks he has stature. But his bosses are pissed because they wanted Arne to go away quietly, not be found in a bar's dumpster with his killer's prints on the murder weapon. So, like Nash's CI said, he's back to running the goods up and the cash down. Frankly, I'm surprised they haven't yet cut their losses and taken him out."

Chu said, "Maybe he's something to someone and that saved his ass."

"Could be. The APB on him is out but doesn't do much when we don't know what vehicle he'll be using. If Nash's CI can get us a date, time, and place, we'll have a decent shot to bring him in. Bonus if we squeeze him to name names. We could potentially blow this particular drug pipeline up."

Alvarez rubbed his eyes and dropped his hands to the table. "We apprehend a murderer, save Visit Duluth's outreach marketing campaign, take the pressure off the mayor, and allow the chief to get back to whatever it is he does in his fancy office. Christ. We're not just cops, we have to be fucking miracle workers."

# CHAPTER TWENTY

Theo's intention to finish with her share of Monday's work by four was a success. Time to get upstairs and work on game night dinner. She'd found a fajita stir-fry recipe on the Internet and figured it would be a safe choice, since she was sure Bec liked fajitas. As she ascended the steps, Bec texted.

**hey, gonna be a little late but should be no later than seven thirty**

**No problem. Whatever time you get here will be great.**

**thanks cant wait**

Theo's stomach fluttered, the feeling a little edgy and a lot holy shit.

**Me too. Tessa's looking forward to grilling you some more. I apologize in advance.**

**ha not a problem gotta go see you soon**

She opened the apartment door. "Tess?"

"Kitchen."

The aroma wafting from the kitchen made her mouth water. She rounded the corner and stopped dead. The counters were covered with every pot and pan she owned. "What's going on here?"

Tess rounded on her, wearing a blue apron bearing the words YOUR DAMN OPINION ISN'T IN MY RECIPE in bold white letters.

"Nice look. My opinion is I want to eat your recipe. What are you doing?"

"What's it look like? Cooking."

"I told you I had this."

Tessa belly laughed. "You burn water, and you told me you had this yesterday. Did you even notice the chicken needed to marinate for at least two hours?"

"Well, no. I—"

"Case closed. Out of my kitchen."

"I won't argue." Theo headed into the living room to set up the card table, but that was already done too. She yelled, "Did you play house all day or what? Thanks for setting up in here."

Tess appeared in the doorway between the kitchen and the living room, wielding a huge butcher knife. "You evil ogre, be gone with you. What are these accusations spewing out your pie hole about playing house?" She waved the knife at Theo. "If you're not careful, I'll carve your tongue out and stick it up your nose. I'll have you know I also reconciled last week's receipts, did payroll, and paid for last week's liquor delivery. All before you got up this morning, little troll."

Theo laughed too hard to come back with a decent response.

"That's what I thought." Tessa flounced away.

"Thanks, Tess, for making life easy for me."

"Don't you forget how nice I am, or I'll skewer you and broil your innards right in front of your paramour."

Theo stuck her head in the kitchen. "Paramour?" That Dungeons & Dragons-esque romantasy was going to Tess's head. "I've told you four hundred times. Bec isn't my paramour. Or my love interest. Or my main squeeze. Or my significant other. Or my thing on the side. You behave when she gets here."

"Whatevs."

* * *

At ten after seven, Bec texted.

**heading your way Nash is gonna drop me in the alley be there in five**

"Hey, Tess, I'm heading down to let Bec in the back door."

Tessa was splayed on the couch with her head on a pillow, one leg stretched out and the other on the floor. Her nose was buried in a book called *Broken Blade*. Of course it had on its cover a guy brandishing a sword, someone who looked like that long-haired Italian guy on the front of a gazillion trashy romances from the '90s.

Tess waved her off and didn't bother to answer.

Theo tromped downstairs, happy the evening was moving along smoothly. The stools around the bar were full, and her staffers were efficiently serving them and those out on the floor. She pushed through the swinging door and cast a critical eye around the kitchen. The kids were doing a great job of keeping things caught up here too. Holiday raises were in their future.

Theo unlocked the door and went outside to wait. She leaned against the wall in the golden puddle of light cast from the fixture above, thinking about the benefits of having a good friend and reminding herself to watch her mouth. The fresh air felt good, but the evening chill quickly worked its way through her T-shirt, raising goose bumps on her arms.

One good thing about cooler weather was a much-reduced stench from the garbage dumpster, a thought which inevitably led her to memories of finding Arne. She shuddered.

Headlights bounced crazily against brick as a dark-colored SUV pulled into the alley and rolled to a stop. The passenger door swung open and Bec emerged.

"Thanks, Nash. Don't worry. I'll behave." She slammed the door, and Nash waved at Theo as he pulled away.

Bec will behave? Behave while playing games or something else entirely? Interesting. Then she put the brakes on. *Don't do this to yourself, Theo.*

"Hey. You didn't need to wait out here. Aren't you freezing?"

"Only a little. Come in where it's warm." Cold fingers fumbled with the key before she remembered it was already unlocked. Something happened to her brainwaves every time she was near Bec, and this time was no different. She got them inside, threw the deadbolt and spun around.

Dressed in black from neck to feet, Bec was a striking figure. Her hair was flattened, as if she'd been wearing a hat. "You look like you're on a mission."

"It was a mission all right. Yearly qualifications. I didn't want to take the time to go home and change."

She slowly ran her gaze over Bec again. "I'm not sorry you didn't." This woman was scorching.

This *friend* was scorching.

Bec was a scorching friend.

*Theo, knock it off.*

They stared at each other, neither speaking, ragged emotion ricocheting between them.

Bec took a step closer.

Everything around Theo disappeared until the only thing filling her senses was Bec. Barely restrained energy pulsated between them, the waves intense, unrelenting.

The battle inside her raged. Bec was a friend. God, she was beginning to hate that F word.

Then all willpower shattered. She grabbed the stiff cloth of Bec's jacket and jerked. Bec crashed into her, slamming Theo against the door. Then her mouth was on Bec's, and, oh god it felt like coming home. Theo slid her palms up to cup Bec's face. Her lips parted, admitting Bec's tongue. The fire that she had tried to ignore every time she came near this woman threatened to consume her.

The urgency was almost painful.

Theo reversed their positions, molding her body against Bec's, feeling everything, everywhere.

Bec's arms crushed her, hands tangling in her curls, holding her with a kind of barely contained power she'd never before felt.

She was drowning.

Bec was the only one who would save her.

Blinding passion drove the need to feel Bec's skin under her palms. She burrowed beneath the jacket, caught a handful of shirt, and yanked. The instant the hem cleared Bec's waistband, her fingers hungrily slid across her ribs to her back, and she held on. Muscles covered by hot, smooth skin tensed and released as Bec moved against her.

Someone moaned, either herself or Bec, she didn't know which. All she did know, with every thump of her racing heart, was that she had to have more. As Theo's palm skimmed the small of Bec's back, she found herself spun around and pinned once again against the door. Whatever minuscule amount of control she had vanished. With a moan, she groped for Bec's belt.

Blistering lips slid away. Theo almost cried out at the loss, but the urge dissipated when Bec's mouth came to rest against the spot where her neck met her shoulder. The first swipe of her tongue and then a soft suckle buckled Theo's legs. Now the only thing holding her upright was Bec.

The firestorm between them raged.

"Theo," someone shouted. "Hey, Theo! Where are you? Oh. Holy shit. Sorry!"

Bec retreated so fast Theo nearly hit the floor.

"Clare." Theo blinked, trying to find her footing and her brain at the same time.

"Jeez, Theo," Clare said. "You'd think you were a horny college student."

Her face was so hot it felt like it might slide right off her bones. Finally she managed a breathy "What's up?"

"Saw you sneak in here. We ran out of Johnnie Walker Black. Wondered if you'd seen any. Not that you're doing much seeing of anything right now."

"Jesus, Clare." She scrubbed her face with her hands. "What ever happened to kids being seen and not heard?" She waggled her head, trying to shake some sense into it. "I stashed a bottle in the cellar night before last. More will be in this week's shipment."

"Be seen and not heard? This is the 2020s, boss. Not the 1920s. Thanks." With a flirtatious wink, Clare rolled a cart aside, pulled open a trap door, and disappeared down the steps.

Theo looked at Bec.

Bec looked at Theo. Then retreated two steps. "Not sure what just happened, but it was…"

"Yeah, it was."

Bec shifted her shoulders and tried to tuck her shirt back in. "I'm totally not sorry, but I know this isn't what we agreed. I should go."

Blood was returning to Theo's head. "I'm not sorry either. Come on. You're not going anywhere." She grabbed Theo's sleeve and dragged her through the kitchen, up the stairs, and into the apartment.

Tessa was still on the couch. As they banged their way inside, she sat up. "What the holy hell happened to the two of you?"

# CHAPTER TWENTY-ONE

"Coming in hot, but the sizzle has fizzled." Tess set a platter of steaming fajitas and sliced veggies on the table.

"Holy cow," I said. "These smell fantastic."

"Why thank you." She rummaged through a drawer and pulled out a couple of serving spoons and set them on the platter. "I think they're going to be okay."

"Oh, come on, Tessa. Your cooking is always good. I have no idea how you do it." Theo edged around Tessa and opened the fridge. "Bec, what would you like to drink? We have water, lemonade, not homemade, or Orange Crush."

I gave her a nod of appreciation.

"I remember things." The heat in Theo's eyes had been banked but wasn't fully extinguished.

The comment jolted me. "Pop. Yeah, I'll have pop. Thanks." My mind was still so blown, my body so stunned by what had been offered and then ripped away I couldn't fully focus on anything. I couldn't even recall how Theo had explained anything to Tess before she whisked us into the kitchen for dinner.

Tessa said, "Pour me a lemonade and sit. There's not enough room in here for two of us to be bumping butts."

"I thought the big sister, me, was supposed to boss the little sister, you. Not the other way around." Theo secured drinks for all of us and got out of Tessa's way.

Tess set warmed tortillas, sour cream, salsa, refried beans, and cheese on the table. "You boss me around the bar, I boss you around the kitchen." She bobbed her head at Theo. "This one was going to cook for you." The tone of her voice made it abundantly clear what Tess thought of Theo's culinary skills. "She kept saying she was all over it, but she had no idea she needed to marinate the meat beforehand, much less how to put everything together. Left to her own devices, you guys would've been eating frozen dinners."

Theo grinned widely. "All true. But we'd have figured something out. Come on, now. Eat."

Viscerally, I could still feel the heat of that mouth, the searing graze of those fingertips. I successfully stifled a groan and concentrated on the mouthwatering aroma of chicken, peppers, and onions.

Everyone loaded up and dug in.

"Tess, this is amazing." I took another big bite, coming closer to getting a grip on things.

"Thank you. Not bad, if I do say so myself."

"Um hmm," Theo managed as she shoveled food in her mouth, most likely so she wouldn't have to speak.

Although my gray matter was coming back online, my body remained in shock from what had transpired. I tried to block out the fact that blood still pumped furiously through my veins. I shifted to ease the almost forgotten, yet intimately familiar ache.

The application of a shoe to my shin startled me. I looked up from my plate.

Tessa was staring expectantly at me.

Theo widened her eyes and popped a loaded tortilla chip in her mouth.

"I just asked what's going on with the dead guy in the dumpster." Tess jabbed her fork at me. "You okay?"

"Yeah, fine, just a lot on my mind. Arne Ivorsen, yeah, I can't get into a whole lot, but I'll give you a sound bite." I told them we were working leads involving a gang from the Cities, and drugs were involved, since that was public knowledge. "Sorry I can't get into more, but that's the gist."

Tessa nodded slowly. "Lots of cross-jurisdiction complications?"

"There are. It's better than it used to be, though."

"In any case," she said, "thanks for busting Theo out of the clink."

"Oh, god." I gave Theo a dirty look. "You've sicced your sister on me now too?"

She smiled sweetly and took another bite.

I debated on setting the record straight for Tess. Then decided to let it go and embrace the fact this false arrest scenario would be the running joke for as long as I was associated with these two. I finished off my fajita and scooped more chicken onto my plate.

Tess handed me the tortillas.

"Thanks."

"She's a great cook," Theo said, as if coming out of a coma. "That's why I let her stay here."

Ah, she speaks. I tilted my head and raised a brow. She ignored me.

"Bullshit. You let me stay here for my java beans and my coffeepot."

"Good point," Theo said. "I never expected Tess to land here, but I'm very glad she did." Those magnetic eyes met mine, the embers still banked.

I held her gaze. "I guess things happen when you least expect it," I said, then gave her a smug smile.

Theo kicked me under the table again.

After a dessert of chocolate chip caramel brownies, we gathered around the card table in the living room. By now I was aware enough to take in my surroundings. The apartment was all hardwood and old-world charm, painted a warm terra-cotta in the living room and buttery yellow in the kitchen we'd vacated. I wondered what colors the bedrooms and the bathroom would be if the bright theme held up throughout the house.

"Bec, you up for a round of Cards Against Humanity?" Tessa asked. "You're probably exhausted."

"Nope, I'm great. The game's hilarious." I was tired but having more fun than I'd had in, well, since a few days ago at the Haunted Ship with Theo. Hanging with both of them was strangely comforting. So easy to be around. It was a good time watching them alternately tease and then prop each other up. They hooted and hollered, were obnoxious and introspective, all in the span of a single conversation. I was envious, but happy they were so close.

Theo doled out the appropriate number of white "answer" cards Tess and I would use and pulled a black, fill-in-the-blank or finish-the-statement card for herself. She read it and rubbed her hands together. "Okay, here we go. 'At the end of the rainbow, you'll find…blank.'" She laid the card on the table so we could read it.

"This'll be good," Tess said as she sorted through her stack and plucked one, placing it face down on the table.

I considered my options and tossed a card on top of Tessa's. Yesterday, I wouldn't have dreamed of making the choice I did. Today? Things had changed. I couldn't get the feel of Theo's mouth out of my head. Her tongue, her hands, all electric on my skin, and I was having too much fun to care what it all meant.

"By the way," Theo said, "we have special Zaccardo rules. I'll pull one extra white card and mix it up with both of yours. Adds a little more depth to the game when only three are playing. I'll mix them up, and if I choose the card I drew, I get the point." Theo pulled a card, added it to mine and Tessa's, and put her hands behind her back.

"Can't tell you," Tess said, "how many alternate rules we've made up for a million games over the years."

"If we hadn't"—Theo placed the cards face down on the table—"we'd still be playing the same game of Monopoly from 1995."

Tess snorted. "Truth."

"Considering the very little Theo's told me about your family, you guys seem pretty tight. I'll bet a game can get mighty rowdy."

"Oh yeah," Tess said. "We're tight all right, until a game or cards come out. Then it's everyone for themselves."

"Here we go." Theo lined the black card up with the three upside down white ones and read, "'At the end of the rainbow, you'll find…'" She flipped the first card. "'A level of incompetence we haven't seen yet.'"

"Fits the shitshow in the Oval Office," Tess said. "Maybe the fuckhead will start shitting rainbows."

"Good one, Tessa." I held my hand up for a fist bump. "It could mark the start of National Pride Night."

"That's a dream." Theo flipped the next card. "'At the end of the rainbow, you'll find…it's too hot to sit like a lady.'" She lifted her head, caught my eye as she narrowed her own, and gave me a slight nod. She knew exactly whose card it was, and now the game was afoot. I returned her acknowledgment with a wide smile.

She broke our locked gaze. "Last but not least, 'At the end of the rainbow, you'll find…Congratulations. Someone stole the weed.'" Theo leaned closer. "Stole the weed. Oh, my god, how about stole the pot of gold instead?"

The three of us dissolved into giggles. I managed, "Either we're all overtired or Tess spiked those brownies with some weed," which led to another round of hysteria.

"Okay." Theo blew out air and wiped her eyes. "I gotta go with incompetence because that's too goddamn perfect. Although the pot/weed card was great too. Who's is it?"

Tess raised her hand. Theo flicked the card to her and placed the other in a discard pile.

We played for an hour, and then I called a stop. My sides ached from laughing, and tomorrow was going to come way too fast.

I folded up my chair and set it against the wall. When I saw my two Cards Against Humanity buddies tackle the table and the other two chairs, I pulled my jacket on. "I had a great time tonight. Tessa, thanks so much for the excellent eats and both of you for being great sports. I haven't laughed so hard in a long time. Perfect way to blow off a little steam."

Tess straightened, resting the half-folded card table against her thighs. "I'm happy you came. I hope we can do this again."

"Me too." Theo leaned the chairs against mine and took the table from Tess.

Before I realized what was happening, Tessa wrapped me in a bear hug. "Come on, ya big lug. Give me some love."

I hugged her back and glanced at Theo as I was being squashed. She looked like a deer caught in the headlights of one of Minnesota's gigantic snowplows. I felt the same way she did. I wasn't sure I could control myself if I touched her, even after almost three hours had passed. How dumb was that? Maybe this was how adolescent boys felt, jacked up all the time.

Tess released me, walked over to Theo, and shoved her toward me. "Be nice and say goodbye to the company."

Theo stumbled as her foot stubbed the corner of the coffee table. She yelped and almost caught her balance before running full tilt into me. I caught her before we both toppled and, against my better judgment, I pulled her to me.

Her touch was like exhaling. Then the exhale was interrupted as Theo quickly broke our embrace. Good thing, because I could've stood there with her in my arms all night long. Those devastating eyes blazed again, and she mouthed, "You owe me."

If Tessa hadn't been right there with us, I was pretty sure we'd have been rolling on the floor, ripping off each other's clothes. I was so wound up I didn't even care about friend agreements or getting hurt.

Theo opened the door and shooed me out, desire burning in her eyes.

* * *

"Morning." I handed Nash the two cups of coffee I'd picked up from Caribou and climbed into the Explorer. "How was your night?"

Once I was strapped in, he returned a cup.

"Boring." Nash pulled out onto the road. "Yours? Wondered if I was going to have to nab you from The Mashed Spud."

How much did I want to fess up to? Somehow, he always knew when I was not being completely honest. If I didn't come clean, he'd be more irritating than a mosquito, buzzing in my ear until I caved. Guess it was better for a friend to have that trait and not a parent, but still.

"Well?"

"Patience. I'm thinking." I took the lid off the coffee and blew on it to buy myself some time.

"Hey, I know your stalling tactics. Out with it."

I replaced the lid and took a tentative sip. "We got caught kissing in the kitchen by one of Theo's employees."

"You what now?" His eyes went comically wide. "Kissing? You kissed Theo? Like with tongue and shit? How did that happen?"

"I dunno." I leaned against the headrest and put a hand over my face. "It was an accident."

He barked a laugh that sounded more seal than human. "How is making out an accident? Oh, wait. I can see it now. 'Oops, I didn't mean for my lips to run into yours, Theo.' No, no, here's a better one. 'Oh, Theo, I need to inspect your mouth, make sure your tongue is working correctly.'" By this time, Nash was laughing so hard he was weaving between the lines.

I braced a hand on the dash. "Nash. Eyes on the road."

He managed to straighten out before we rammed into oncoming traffic and I'd no longer be able to investigate any tongues at all.

"So did it?"

"Did what?"

"Her tongue function appropriately?"

I smacked him. "You're an asshole."

"I know." He rearranged his face, but only managed a semiserious expression. "All right, lemme get this straight. You kissed 'just a friend' Theo. The woman you weren't going to allow yourself to get tangled up with. What the fuck, Bec?"

"I'm not sure. She grabbed my jacket and kissed me."

"Hold on," he said. "She grabbed your jacket? You didn't even put up a fight?"

"Come on, Nash. It happened so fast I didn't think."

"Oh, sounds like you were thinking about something, all right." He hooted. "You're killing me, Harrison."

"Seriously. One second nothing was happening, the next, whammo." All night long, as I lay in bed staring up at the ceiling, I wondered myself how it had escalated so far so fast. I'd replayed everything, every breath, every touch, every taste, in vivid, looping detail. The memory of that intense, fiery, full-bodied contact flipped the switch on my low-key libido and desire had nearly blindsided me.

Humor faded from his face. "You all right with that?"

"Yes. No. I don't know. Honestly, I've never felt anything quite like…" I grimaced, trying to find the right words. Gave up. "Whatever it was."

He was quiet for a drawn-out moment. "I'm going to play devil's advocate here since I'm the kinda guy who cares about you and your big old soft heart. I know you're afraid of being hurt. But on the flip side, does fear mean you should turn away from what could be the best thing you've ever had the chance to experience? Besides, relationships are good for one's mental health."

"Some. *Some* relationships are good for one's mental health. Jeez, Nash. Did you get up early and study the DSM-5 this morning?"

"No. Buzzfeed."

"Your choices for advice are a bit iffy." I huffed. "Seriously, I thought about what-ifs all night long. The only thing I know for certain is I have never, ever felt such an insanely strong connection and attraction to someone as I have with Theo. I'm terrified. And definitely in a whole lotta lust."

"TMI." Nash put his hand on my knee and squeezed. "I'm here. You need me to talk you into or out of anything or if she hurts you, I'm your man."

I laughed. "We'll see what Sherry thinks about her man being my man too. Speaking of families, it was different, but in a good way. Theo and Tess were hilarious. They laugh. A lot. Poke fun at each other. We played Cards Against Humanity, and no one got into a fight."

Danna and I were both headstrong, and we liked to win in games and in life, which had caused a lot of rancor. Nash had witnessed a few of our less-than-stellar moments. What happened last night, though. The laughter, teasing, the obvious joy in the way they interacted, no angry undercurrent. I liked it. A lot. "They had great dynamics. It was loving, kind. Something I haven't been around in a long time."

"You won't like this, but maybe you should try and see your bro—"

"Let's not even go there. You know my brothers and I are much better at a distance."

We lapsed into silence the rest of the way to work. Zeus strike me down, but I ached for more. For more of Theo. For more laughter. For more fun. I wanted to kiss Theo blind and then investigate the rest of her.

*Well, shit.*

# CHAPTER TWENTY-TWO

Three hours before opening, Theo needed a job to knock her brain off-track. Or, rather, knock it back on track. She wasn't obsessing about the fantastic food Tessa made last night, or the games they'd played with Bec, or the laughter they'd shared. Her brain was doing battle with itself.

Lascivious thoughts flooded through her, then were shunted aside by logic. *You can't let this happen. Too much is at stake. What if she finds out? Then you wouldn't be joking about jail. You'd be in it.*

She hadn't been able to concentrate on her semiregular *New York Times* games session. She hadn't managed to think through filling out the week's booze order. She hadn't managed to go online and update the Spud's Facebook page. She'd catch herself drifting off, thinking of how Bec's warm, inviting mouth had tasted, how she ached to touch, well, everything. How Bec felt pressed fully against her. The bliss of Bec's tongue and lips slipping ever so slowly across her skin right before they'd been caught.

She'd settled on doing some mindless cleaning so she could say she'd done something. The stepladder shifted under her feet as she reached for another bottle of liquor on the literal top shelf behind the bar and took her towel to it. Newly emancipated cobwebs floated through the dusty air.

"What are you doing up there?" Tessa's voice startled her and she grabbed the shelf for balance.

"Jesus Christ, Tessa. You're gonna kill me."

"Your reflexes are too good to allow that to happen. What's going on with you? You hate dusting."

*Tell Tess? Don't tell Tess?* One of the cruxes of the mind battle she'd waged all morning now stood below her in dimly lit Technicolor.

"Theo, stop thinking so hard. Get down here and talk to me."

*Should have been twins*, Theo thought, the way Tess could sometimes read her mind. She didn't have many secrets from her sister. Well, aside from the big one. Tessa was good for batting ideas around, and her advice was usually rock solid. When it came to other people's issues, of course. She was a work in progress on her own but improving every day she was away from that bastard.

With an aggrieved sigh, Theo tossed the rag over her shoulder and descended.

Tessa slid onto a stool. "Step into my office. Bad advice only five cents. Good advice ten."

Theo leaned on the counter. "You've raised your rates."

"It's the tariffs."

"But you're not importing anything."

"Hey, advice comes from all over."

"It's complicated."

"You like to make things complicated."

"No, I don't."

"Sometimes you do."

"Not very often."

"Stop arguing and spit it out."

Theo stared at her. Hazel eyes, so much like her own, were soft and kind.

"All right then, let me put on my mind-reading headscarf." Then Tessa stroked an imaginary mustache. "This has something to do with why you and Bec showed up last night looking dazed and disheveled, like a couple frisky teens caught making out in the barn."

"In the kitchen," she muttered, but Tess wasn't paying attention. The memory lit a fuse. Heat crept up her neck to her cheeks.

Tess pointed at her, expression beyond gleeful. "Oh, I've got your number, lady. You and Bec canoodled before you came upstairs." She rubbed her hands briskly together. "This is going to be good. Where did it happen? In the alley?"

"Canoodled?" Theo pulled an Elvis lip. "I told you. In the kitchen."

"You did? The kitchen? Here? Like right behind that wall?"

"Right behind that wall. Clare walked in on us."

"Oh, my god. You got caught. This keeps getting better."

"If she hadn't…Well, let's say it was good timing." Theo proceeded to lay out the dirty truth. "This is not me. I don't know what I'm doing. I've never felt like this before. It was…beyond breathtaking."

Tess stared evenly at her for what felt like a century. "You're right. This isn't like you. But then, Bec isn't like anyone you've ever spent time with. Because you never spend time with anyone. Christ, Theo, you can't keep hiding from your own heart."

She knew Tessa was right.

"You can't outrun Sofie's memory forever, Theo."

If she only knew. "I haven't thought about Sof for a while."

Tess laughed right in her face. "Bullshit you haven't. You can't tell me, in all the time you've known Bec you haven't given a single thought to the person who was your best friend, who was the love of your life, who lost in a horrible way? Theo, Sofie's why you refuse to get close to anyone."

Tess sure knew how to call someone out. "Yeah. I know. But…"

"But what?"

"I've never felt like I could, I don't know, get close before. With any of the women I've seen. Bec hits different somehow, and that scares the shit out of me."

"But you feel like you could get close to her?"

"I don't know."

Tess leaned back and studied Theo. "You have it bad, don't you?"

"Let's say I'm hot and bothered, which could be bad or could be good. Very, very good."

"Oh, Theo." Tess brightened. "That's it."

"What's it?"

"This. For once in your life, I dare you to go out on a limb and follow your heart. Or your hormones."

Theo narrowed her eyes. "What do I get if I accept?"

"Maybe, smart-ass, you might find a love to keep instead of a one-night stand to dump."

* * *

Theo finished cleaning the top shelf, returned the ladder to its assigned home, and retreated to the office for another go-round at social media. Maybe the cramped office was messing with her mojo. Not much had changed since she had taken the place over from her mom and dad over a dozen years ago.

An ancient wooden rolling desk chair and three filing cabinets original to the bar were crammed behind a desk of the same lineage. Another chair from out front, its padding flattened, was the guest throne.

Instead of working on Facebook and Bluesky posts, Theo found herself chasing Tessa's words as they vortexed around in her head.

She desperately wanted to text Bec, but maybe because she felt so desperate she shouldn't. Her very real, never-ending fear of having her past exposed was being overridden, though, by an insistent batch of hellaciously raging hormones and the overriding need to hear Bec's voice.

Or see her words.

Either or both.

She was flirting with disaster and she knew it, but something she couldn't fathom kept dragging her in for more. Something deeply buried stirred every time she thought of Bec, saw Bec, texted Bec, and honestly, lately, dreamed of Bec. The feeling went beyond bodily chemicals.

Or maybe it was one and the same.

The chair creaked as she shifted, trying to ease the frustration her thoughts had caused. Maybe she needed to seek out a willing partner and take care of business. But...did she want to have another mindless fling with a face she'd only see once?

Did she?

That was a question she hadn't needed to think about in years. After Sofie, she had structured life in a way that wouldn't put her heart, her emotions, her very being at risk. Now, despite herself, the front gate of her fortified castle had been breached. Not by a battering ram, but by a good cop. By a beautiful woman with a beautiful heart. By a human being who was trying to do some right in the world.

Fuck it. She picked up her phone and texted, **Hey you. Wanted to check in and see how you're recovering after last night.**

She hit send before she chickened out.

In all of the next six minutes, she managed to get one sentence written. Then her phone vibrated. Theo scooped it up, only to discover it was some stupid news notification. *Back to work, you overexcited crazy woman.*

She managed to write and publish a full post before the cell rumbled again. Text message or notification? She flipped it over.

Bec.

Her shoulders relaxed, but her heart did not.

**im walking slightly bowlegged thanks to certain sensitivities checking some leads catching up on crap how about you**

If only she dared speak the whole truth and nothing but the truth. It'd go something like: Last night was electrifying. I can't wait to kiss you again, to touch— *OMG, Theo, stop.* She stared at the tiny keyboard, then tapped out, **Doing okay, although I can't say I've been unaffected by what happened. It was an eye-opening night and ridiculously fun.**

Now she was going to stroke out waiting for a reply. Those three dots danced forever as Bec responded.

**made me realize how nice it is to be able to kid around with people I care about have to admit I loved the unexpected appetizer**

Whoa. Her thumbs flew over the keys and hit send as if they had a mind of their own.

**Me too. Like to partake in such an appetizer again.**

Had she honestly written that? And hit send? Yessiree, Bob.

Appetizers. That was it. Appetizers were a light treat before the main course. Maybe if she and Bec kept whatever might be happening between them at appetizer level, she could hang on to some semblance of dignity and safety. Keep her heart safe and her secrets protected.

Then she realized she'd missed two texts.

**the more appetizers the merrier for the moment we're assigned rotating days off mine are sunday and Monday**

**so I've been thinking**

Uh oh.

**hey I can think when I have to I have an idea**

Hmm.

**What kind of idea?**

**can you get this coming sunday and monday off back tuesday midmorning**

Sunday to Tuesday? An overnight excursion? With Bec? A good chance for more appetizers, for sure. The thought alone heated her blood. Even with this little notice she knew she could take the time off—those were slow nights and Clare had been wanting some extra hours. And Tess would be around to put out any fires.

But did she dare? Forging a friendship with Bec was already playing with fire. Then Tess's words rattled through her mind: "You might find a love to keep instead of a one-night stand to dump." She typed **yes, yes, and yes** and stared at the words, frozen by their implications.

**theo you there**

She hit send.

# CHAPTER TWENTY-THREE

Still in shock that last Tuesday I'd gone through with asking Theo to go away with me, I idled the rusted maroon truck in the alley behind The Mashed Spud. The sunny, autumn warm spell we were having boosted my good mood higher and pushed down some of the anxiety about what might and might not happen over the next two days.

No expectations.

No pressure.

Cell service and Wi-Fi didn't exist where we were headed. I had a satellite phone in case of emergency, but otherwise, my hope was we'd both have a chance to chill and get to know each other better. Theo, thankfully, hadn't sounded like she wanted to strangle me when I told her there'd be no mobile service.

After I'd talked with Nash, I thought hard about what he'd said. Was I willing to walk away from what could possibly, maybe be the best thing to happen to me because I was a chickenshit? The answer wound up being a harder no than I'd expected.

Then, when we'd received our days off, the plan fell into place so easily that it felt meant to be. I figured a mini vacay would be nice, and Chu had helped me work out the lodging.

I knew the next couple days would probably either make or break Theo and me, and I was almost sure I was ready to find out which.

Promptly at ten thirty, Theo emerged, sunglasses nestled in her curls, wearing a purple puffy jacket and carrying a stuffed backpack. Her features hovered on the edge of surprise and horror as she caught sight of our ride. The passenger door screeched like a barn owl when she pulled it open and dumped her pack on the floorboard. Over the rumble of the engine, she yelled, "Where did you find this thing?"

"My crap car's in the shop. One of these days I need to find a new one. Shingo did me a solid and found this amazing vehicle for me to borrow. An uncle of her dad's brother's mother or something. When I saw it, I thought we'd blend right in with the good ole boys."

"Definitely not attention-grabbing, and yes, I'm being sarcastic."

"I concede the point."

The decades-old rust bucket had been outfitted with glass-pack mufflers and oversized tires which made accessing the cab an athletic event. Theo navigated the ascent and yanked the door shut, eliciting a reverse squawk. She shouldered the door to make sure it stayed closed and pushed down the old-fashioned lock.

"Do you have more surprises up your sleeve?"

"Of course. Do you trust me?"

"We made it safely through the Haunted Ship, so I suppose so." Theo snapped the seat belt into place and tugged on it. "On the other hand, you did haul me down to the slammer and give me the third degree about Arne's murder." She glanced dubiously around the cabin. "You sure this vehicle is road-safe? Judging from its appearance, I'm not sure we'll make it to your surprise in one piece."

"It was an interview. Not the third degree."

"I'm like a mosquito in the summer."

"Stop making me itch and quit deflecting. Do you trust me or not?"

"Me? Deflect? Never."

"It's a yes or no question."

"Maybe."

"I'll bet you were a willful, stubborn, obstinate kid."

The sound of Theo's laughter was delightful. Since when did a laugh delight me? When did the word "delighted" come into my lexicon?

"I'll bet I wasn't the only trying child. Yes. Of course I trust you."

"Good answer." I stepped on the clutch, shifted the three-on-the-tree into first, and prayed I wouldn't kill the engine as I eased up and pressed on the gas. With a roar reminiscent of a sick stock car, we rolled down the alley.

Once I navigated the city streets and merged onto I-35 heading north, I began to get used to the rhythms and quirks of the truck and to relax. To our right, Lake Superior stretched into infinity. At the moment, the lake was placid, reflecting the bright blue sky. But things could take a bad turn faster than Olympic sprinting champ Flo-Jo, as plenty of wrecks resting on the rocky lake bed could attest.

"Hey, look." I pointed out my window. The leaves, almost past their peak, were beautiful. Saturated reds, oranges, and yellows of all shades blazed on the hillside across the expanse of highway.

Theo leaned toward me to get a better look. "If only we could bottle this view. I think humans too often get swallowed up by the hectic crazy and miss out on moments like this. In the end, I think moments are what make life livable."

We came out of a curve, and both sides of the road were lined with preening trees showing off their neon colors.

"Agreed. Especially these days. Maybe I should appreciate Danna for helping me realize it really is the moments in life that matter, not how much money you earn, how much success you have, how many goddamn Amazon packages you get." I laughed bitterly. "It's the precious moments."

Intentionally or not, Theo brushed her fingertips on my arm as she withdrew, raising immediate goose bumps. Maybe it was her way of saying we'd had a moment. Or maybe it'd been an accident.

"Whoa." Theo grabbed the oh-shit handle as we bounced energetically over a row of potholes, breaking the spell of moments. Or lack thereof. "We're heading to—let me guess—Betty's Pies."

Betty's Pies was an iconic roadside café north of Two Harbors. "Close but no dice. I haven't been there, but I'd sure like to try a slice."

"You're a poet and ya didn't even know it. Depending on whatever wonderous thing you're getting us into, maybe we can stop by later."

"Anything's possible." We lapsed into silence. After a few minutes I realized, at least from my perspective, the silence we shared didn't feel uncomfortable, and I wondered how Theo felt. Eventually, I said, "I'd ask if you like music, but there's no radio in here."

"I see that. And I do. Like music, that is." Her sunglasses were now hiding those spectacular eyes, a good thing since my own should be on the road.

"How about this then?" I thought fast, which was about ten times slower than usual. "Pick door number one, door number two, or door number three."

"Okay, what do we have behind door number two?"

"For your edification, door number two is all about musical tastes. Tell me yours."

"I can do that. I like some of today's pop if it's not too whiny. Jazz, blues, of course '80s and '90s rock, not the pop stuff but actual rock. Hair bands. Classical, not opera. No way, no how. That fresh hell will pop your brain like a zit and it'll leak out your eardrums. Cajun, zydeco, world music. Drumming. I did a drumming circle once. It was cool. I can't carry a tune if you held a gun to my head"—she sent me a sly smile—"or play an instrument, not unless you want the wolves to howl, but I sure appreciate people who understand and share it. Your turn."

"Same on today's music. I'm a huge Taylor Swift fan. I like rock, pop too. Classical and opera?" I made a face. "Yuck. No blues, yes jazz."

I braked for a car turning onto a side road and sped up again. Traveling northbound on a Sunday was perfect. The opposite side of the road was packed with cars, trucks, and SUVs heading south, many pulling boats and trailers, lined up like ants marching back to the colony after a weekend of sipping suds and trolling for walleye.

The sun reflected off Theo's glasses as she shifted to face me as much as the seat belt would allow. "Here's the big question. What kind of music can you absolutely not stand?"

"Country."

"Same. What else?"

I always caught hell for this one. "Musicals."

"How can you not like musicals? Weirdo. And?"

"Like I said, opera could kill me."

For the next twenty minutes, we compared musical notes, artists, albums, songs. By the time we hit Two Harbors, we'd pretty well hashed out the thumbs-up and thumbs-down. At the top of our list was Journey, The Eagles, Shinedown, P!NK, Lady Gaga, Melissa Etheridge, Brandi Carlile, the Indigo Girls, Sofie Hawkins, Dua Lipa, Bad Bunny, and Ricky Martin.

The turnoff I needed was coming up quick. "Okay, Theo. Trust time."

She pulled her sunglasses off. "What's up your sleeve now?"

I smiled benignly. "Close those eyes and don't open them until I say so."

"Seriously?"

"Yeah."

"Ay. All right." She slouched into her seat and put her hands over her eyes. "I can't see anything. Mostly."

"Good." I turned on Fifth and followed the silenced map app I'd pulled up on my phone as I wound my way through small town streets to our destination.

I'd seen the Lighthouse Bed & Breakfast online, but pictures didn't do it justice. The sun burnished the building's red brick. The snow up against the building hadn't melted yet, and the contrast of white and red against the blue sky was stunning. I hoped Theo would think so too.

The lighthouse and attached keeper's quarters had been built in 1892, and the lighthouse itself was square instead of tube-shaped, which I thought was kind of odd. A few outbuildings were scattered on the grounds around it.

I stopped in a parking lot a few hundred feet below the outpost. "Open 'em up."

Theo slid her hands from her face. It took about two seconds for her to comprehend what she was seeing. "No way. How did you? But I thought—" She glanced at me. "I've heard about this place. It's the Lighthouse Bed and Breakfast, right?"

"Give the lassie a prize." I touched my nose and pointed at her. "Oldest lighthouse still in operation in the state." For a heartbeat, the raunchy part of me considered exactly what kind of prize I could give Theo. My face and other places grew warm. *Knock it off*, I lectured my recalcitrant libido. *Think about hockey. About the moon. About Mountain Dew.* Where did that come from? I didn't even like Mountain Dew.

"I've always wanted to come up here and check it out. Never had time. Or never made time is more accurate, I suppose."

*Way to go, Bec.* I gave myself an imaginary pat on the back. "Chu, at the PD, knows people. The place is owned by the local historical society and he's friends with the son of one of the big dogs who specifically run the bed and breakfast. They usually shut down the B&B October first, but the lighthouse remains in service year round. They agreed to open it up for us. The only thing about this place other than no cell service or Internet is the breakfast part of the B&B. Instead of having a host make food, they provide a gift certificate for the café in town. Fine by me, I don't like to get up early on my time off from work anyway."

"I'm with you all the way on sleeping in. You are something else." Theo leaned over the bench seat, plastered a wet one on my lips, and pulled away before I had a chance to realize I'd been smooched.

"Uh, I, thanks." A split second of Theo was enough to undo me. For the fifty-eighth time, I thought about what-if. What if something more than friendship developed between Theo and me?

What if I got hurt?

What if I didn't?

"Come on, Bec. I assume we're not parking this far away."

"Nope. Patience." I followed a winding gravel drive and pulled up to a white, wood-slat garage about fifty feet from our destination.

We grabbed our bags and the sack of snacks I'd brought and followed a narrow walkway to a side entrance of the Keeper's Quarters. I opened the screen door to an enclosed vestibule. Overhead, a dim light came on. Four concrete steps brought us up to a whitewashed entrance door, solid and snug within its frame. No one would be breaking in here without a fight.

A modern keypad had been mounted above the doorknob. I keyed in the code I'd been given, and with a whirr, a deadbolt retracted. The door opened to a foyer with a beautifully refinished red-oak hardwood floor partially covered by an industrial-sized waterproof rug. A framed "Footwear Parking" sign, written in old-style English, hung on one wall. Below it was a rubber shoe tray with raised edges. We parked our shoes appropriately and hung our jackets on what looked like a 19th-century coatrack. The air was a mix of old house and lemon-scented Pledge, with a faint whiff of eucalyptus.

The foyer gave way to a kitchen, with an eclectic mix of old and new appliances and fixtures. It held a replica wood-burning stove, which I assumed was electric, an antique enamel sink with a built-in drainboard, a stainless dishwasher, and an unusual glass and wood clawfoot cabinet with four shelves. It looked like a tall, skinny, Art Deco jukebox with stacks of plates, cups, saucers, and drinking glasses neatly tucked inside. A freestanding island in the center of the room provided extra counter and gathering space.

I set the bag of eats on the island. "How did anyone cook in a space this size back in the day? A microwave would've come in handy for them. Now too, for that matter."

"You're not 'back in the day' anymore, Opie. There's a microwave right behind you for your radiating pleasure. Look."

Sure enough, tucked almost out of sight in a corner, there was an appliance that might or might not be big enough to hold a full-sized dinner plate.

"Come on." Theo disappeared into the next room. From the sound of her footsteps, I assumed she'd found her way upstairs.

I crossed the threshold to what turned out to be the dining room. A six-person walnut table was the star of the show, along with an ornate and highly polished switchback staircase. A floral carpet runner protected the stairway and gave sock-covered feet some traction and stability, which was probably good for avoiding lawsuits.

At the top of the stairs, the bathroom was immediately on the left, with, of course, a requisite clawfoot bathtub and a modern sink and toilet. Plenty of clawfoot business going on around here.

The first bedroom I passed had a white metal sign mounted on the door, raised black letters on it, designating it as the Keeper's Room. I wondered if the plaque was original or if it'd been added as a reason to charge more money for the big room when this place was running as a typical B&B.

"Bec, check this out," Theo called from down the hall before I could peek inside.

"Where are you?"

"Second bedroom."

I found Theo next door, kneeling at the end of a quilt-covered cast-iron bed and facing an old green steamer trunk situated beneath the bedroom's lone window.

She ran her fingers over the trunk's surface. "This looks nearly identical to the one in my parents' basement."

"No kidding." I crouched beside her.

"My great-grandfather came over from Italy through Ellis Island. After a few years he made enough money to send for his wife. They wound up having seven kids."

"Holy tiny tots. The Zaccardos are prolific."

"The elders were, that's for sure. The number of offspring has decreased with each generation, which is good because if there were any more relatives, I'd never be able to keep anyone's name straight."

The furthest bedroom, we discovered, was a close repeat of the middle room. It was the smallest of the three, but, in its defense, it did have two windows.

Then we backtracked to the Keeper's Room. It felt airier somehow, even if it only had one window overlooking dense pine trees and a glimpse of the lake. A teal-and-white quilt covered a king-sized, silver metal, four-post bed. The rest of the room contained two pine nightstands, an intricately inlaid pine dresser with five drawers, and a rocking chair.

A vision of me tackling Theo onto the bed and kissing her senseless floated through my head. I tried to float it out the way it came. My voice was husky when I said, "Which room do you want?" The sooner we got back downstairs the better.

"I don't care. We can decide later."

I'd half expected her to say something suggestive and wasn't sure if I was relieved or disappointed. *Rebecca Harrison*, I scolded myself, *Theo is a friend. Even if she smooched you earlier in the truck. Buddies, Bec. Pals. Amigas. Homies. Maybe one day, BFFs. Yeah,* said my unfriendly, shoulder-riding devil, *tell that to your heart and your down-below bits.*

*Oh, boy.*

I needed to get far away from any room with a bed. Maybe then I could banish my carnal and heart-ish thoughts. "We still have a downstairs to tour."

Theo followed me down to the dining room. On the far side of the table, under glass, was a replica of the original Fresnel lens used to alert ships. I walked around the table to take a closer look. "The lens kind of looks like one of those brass diving helmets, doesn't it?"

Theo came to stand beside me. "It sure does look like one of those freaky old things." She shivered.

"You cold?"

"No. I used to have nightmares about drowning in one of those contraptions."

"In a helmet?" I tried to visualize how that would work.

"No. In a helmet with the suit attached."

"Oh. Well, that's different."

"Spoken like a true Minnesotan." She sighed. "It's what I get for writing an eighth-grade report on the history of scuba diving."

"Ah-ha. To make you feel better, I can confess you're not alone in the interestingly outlandish fear category."

"Do tell."

"I will never, ever buy a car with windows I can't escape through."

She considered me. "Okay, that's different too."

"Also spoken like a true Minnesotan."

"Ya, sure, you betcha. Tell me more."

"Long before I was born, my great-grandfather ran an auto repair business and owned a Model A tow truck. He was on 24/7, weekends, holidays, whatever. When I was a kid, my grandpa would tell stories about his dad towing broken-down cars, pulling people out of ditches, helping at accident scenes, and stuff like that. The one that still freaks me to this day was about hooking and dragging out vehicles, driven by ice fishermen and others, that broke through lake ice. Especially in the middle of the night."

As if she sensed my discomfort, Theo leaned against my arm. For once the electricity between us didn't blow up. But a wave of—I wasn't even sure what to call it—comfort, maybe, washed over me.

"As a result, I've never driven on a frozen lake, ridden on the ice with someone else, or, for that matter, ever purchased a car with inappropriately sized windows. Just in case."

"Well, that's a certainly a unique worry." Then she hastened to add, "But a logical one in the Land of Ten Thousand Lakes. Note to self, don't take Bec ice fishing." She put her hands on my shoulders and guided me toward the parlor.

Yes, it was literally called the parlor.

I asked, "Do you like to ice fish?"

"Hell, no. But I have enjoyed sitting with my cousins in one of those fancy ice houses they have these days, the insulated and heated kind, and drinking a local brew and eating the catch of the day fried up in beer batter."

"You can bring me the catch of the day on shore." The feel of her fingers seared through the material of my hoodie, and I was overwhelmed by the urge to let myself lean back and melt into her. It took everything I had not to turn around, wrap my arms around her, and hold—

*Hang on, Casanova. No daydreams about holding allowed.*

When was the last time I wanted to hold someone? Since my last lover was my ex-wife, it'd been a very long time. *Trouble's brewing, Bec. Be ready to duck.*

Instead of thinking about holding anyone, making out, breaking through the ice, or doing anything else physically gratifying or psychologically terrifying, I concentrated on the contents of the good old parlor.

The space was filled with period pieces or well-designed replicas, including a couch, a high-back armchair, and an overstuffed recliner, all upholstered in navy-blue velvety cloth with lighter blue flowers and green leaves. A tall lamp with a cobalt blue cloth shade and white dangly strings stood between the two chairs. In front of the couch was a varnished, wood-plank, wrought iron coffee table. Two side tables and a black bookcase containing paperback novels, cards, and board games occupied the rest of the room.

Theo dropped her hands from my shoulders, and I was simultaneously relieved and cast adrift. What the fuck was wrong with me? *When all else fails, Bec, go for food.* "You hungry?"

"Thought you'd never ask. What'd you bring?"

"Snacks. The fridge is already stocked with food and drink. Including Orange Crush." Despite insisting this outing was just a little escape, a tiny break, planned off the cuff, I'd coughed up a pretty penny, some ugly nickels, a few new dimes, four pristine statehood quarters, and many crunchy greenbacks to make this spur-of-the-moment thing happen.

"Holy hell. How'd you manage that?" Then she gave me a sly, knowing look. "Did you come up here and stock it?"

I smiled blandly. "Are you always this nosy?"

\* \* \*

The sun dipped below the horizon. We sat at the dining room table eating cold cuts and cheese on Telera rolls, and one of my favorites, Old Dutch Rip-L Chips with Top the Tater.

"Wanna play a game?" Theo asked as I crammed a chip with a sizeable load of dip into my mouth.

I nodded and wandered over to assess the options. Maybe playing something would distract me from myself. "We have Jenga, Risk, Operation, Clue, Trivial Pursuit 90's Edition, Life, or cards." When she didn't answer, I found her staring intently at me, but mute for some reason. Her mouth wasn't even full of food. "Theo?"

Her eyes refocused. "Jenga."

Maybe this whole thing would be easier if we both laid our cards on the table and fessed up to the fact we had some serious chemistry and were out and out attracted to each other. So much attraction.

But then things would get complicated.

*Bec, things are already complicated. You're the one who invited her up here, unsupervised, the two of you, all by yourselves.*

All this mindfuckery was exhausting. Play the damn game, finish your sandwich, and eat some more chips and Top the Tater.

The emotional/sexual/whatever tension between us eased once we set up the Jenga tower and took turns removing wood blocks and stacking them on top. When it toppled, thanks to a misaimed tap on my turn, I set it up again. We laughed and snacked and laughed some more.

I'd downloaded some music onto my phone when I found out there'd be no cell service and was happy I'd guessed more or less right about what Theo might like. Between Dua Lipa and Cher, P!NK and Brandi Carlile, we slipped into an easy back-and-forth.

However, the easy didn't stop me from admiring the grace with which Theo moved when she carefully slid out a Jenga block or how her face softened when she glanced my way. When she spoke, her lips mesmerized me.

Okay.

I did have a few thoughts about what those lips would feel like against mine again, so maybe I wasn't as calm as I thought.

The tower fell on me a second time.

Theo gathered the scattered pieces and pulled them toward her. "You want another go, loser?"

I stood and stretched. "I'm a good loser."

"I've got an idea for a different game."

"What is it?"

"You'll see."

"But I haven't said yes yet."

"I'm clairvoyant."

"Uh huh." If she could read my mind, we'd be sweeping those Jenga pieces onto the floor and having at it right there on top of the table. However, I held my base self in check and helped put the wooden blocks away. "All right-o, Ms. Mind Reader, I need something to drink. You want anything?"

"What kind of snacks do you bring in your magic bag?"

"Sweet or salty?"

"Sweet."

"Dark-chocolate Oreos, brownies with chocolate chips and maraschino cherries—"

"Back up the golf cart. Maraschino cherries? In brownies?"

"Yeah. One of my mom's specialties."

"You made them?"

"I did. All by myself. Pretty sure you'll survive the experience if you want to try one."

"Yes, please."

In the kitchen, I rounded the booty up and thought about our Jenga-ing experience. One way to get a real feel of the way someone ticked was how they acted when they played games. A person could be super intense, a gloating winner, a sore loser, the one in a group who hated games, or maybe they were simply indifferent altogether.

The flip side was the easy-going game-players. Sure, they could be as intense as the negative noodles, but these folks usually didn't get bent into various pretzel shapes about a rule or a play. They tended to cheer-for-one-cheer-for-all, were gracious winners, and usually decent losers.

My mom had been like that, always wanting to make sure everyone had a chance to come out on top. Of course, she only played one game, the original Trivial Pursuit, and she, like the Zaccardo family, created new rules on the fly to help her achieve her desired outcome.

Sure, I liked to win. But I wasn't the take-it-to-extremes sort. So far, it seemed Theo's style of play was similar. Of course, if she morphed into a temper-tantrum playing fool, I could threaten her with arrest.

Unless she liked cuffs.

Then it could be an entirely different story.

Shit. My overstimulated self was off and running yet again.

When I returned with two brownies and two bottles of water, Theo was on the couch in the schmancy parlor, crossed feet propped on the coffee table. A computer was open on her lap. I hoped she remembered we had zip for connectivity.

"Looks like you've made yourself comfortable."

Theo looked up. "I have." She set the computer aside and grabbed a brownie from me. "These look great."

"Lemme know what you think."

I sat beside her, not too close for comfort, not too far away, and watched her take her first bite.

For a second, she stared straight ahead. Then her eyes widened and she chewed faster, nodding and making some very interesting sounds in the back of her throat. If anyone could be turned on by listening to someone eat, this would do it.

It certainly did it for me.

"Ohmigod." She took another bite. "These are so good. How many more of these incredibly dangerous brownies do you have?"

"An entire pan, now minus two. Thumbs-up?"

"So many thumbs. I thought you didn't cook."

"I don't much, but these I can bake. Not hard with a boxed mix, a bottle of cherries, and chocolate chips." I took a bite of my own brownie. "Okay, boss, what ya got?"

Theo wiped her fingers and retrieved the laptop. "I was listening when you told me we wouldn't have service and grabbed a few games from the interwebs before I left home. How about a little Truth or Dare?"

I stared at her. Was she kidding? "Truth or Dare? Don't you think that could be a little dangerous?"

"Are you a chicken?" She gave me a broad smile.

"Chicken?" My mind raced, thinking about the implications.

She tilted her head and brought those breathtaking eyes to mine. In this light, they were a glittering brownish green. Her teasing demeanor vanished, replaced with a palpable look of raw hunger, which disappeared as fast as it came.

Theo broke our gaze. "Seriously, if one of us doesn't want to answer something, we'll skip it. Easy as that. I'm sure we both have things we'd rather not revisit."

Right. Easy as that, my ass. But, on the flip side, this could be a whole lot of fun. "All right. But it's only fair we both see the questions, so you don't cheat and make something up."

"Me? Cheat?" Theo put her hand to her chest. "I'm wounded."

"Don't tell me you haven't learned a thing or two with that crew of siblings you have."

"You might have me on that one."

I scooted a bit closer so I could see the screen. Five buttons across the top were labeled TAME, PG-13, SAUCY, WICKED, and MISCELLANEOUS. Below them were the TRUTH or DARE buttons. "Okay, I'll go first. I'm no chicken."

She shot me a side-eye. "I'll stick to the PG-13 ones. Or would you rather the tame ones?" The little shit smiled sweetly at me.

I stuck my tongue out at her.

The sides of her mouth curled as she fought not to smile. "I could think of a million things to say about that tongue of yours, but since we're friends, I'll refrain."

A delicious, sensory memory of that tongue meeting hers hit hard. This was so not a good idea. Especially when I could feel the heat of her right beside me.

"Truth or Dare, hotshot?"

"Truth."

She clicked the button. Random words scrolled, then aligned into a sentence. *Relate a funny childhood memory.* "See? Not so bad. Lay something funny on me."

"Okay. Let's see. I was maybe three. Or four. Staying at my grandparents. I can't remember where anyone else was. My great-grandfather owned a combined Pontiac dealership and auto repair garage."

"I remember."

"After he died, the business was handed down to my grandpa. He wasn't all that into selling cars, so he turned the showroom into a parts store." The memory made me melancholy, but in a good way, if that was possible. "For some reason, the floor in the showroom was red. Red clay? I don't know. But if you bounced a tennis ball on it, it would turn this dusty red color. So strange, now I look back on it. Anyway, on a tall counter, tall to me at the time, were two big, and I mean, like, foot-thick parts catalogues, in these big metal holders.

Theo nodded.

"Two old wooden rocking chairs sat in the middle of the showroom, and I'd sit in one of them and watch him flip through those pages when someone came in but he didn't have what they wanted in stock. So, one day, I was over at the station—it was right across the yard from my grandparents' house—and he had to go to the bathroom or something. I don't remember exactly. He left me happily rocking. Man, to think about it, no one would leave a kid alone like that these days."

"True." Theo shifted to sit sideways on the couch. "I think I can see where this is going."

"Oh, yeah. Someone came in asking for…" I threw up a hand, tried to squint the memory into focus. "For…some part. I vividly remember pushing a chair over to the counter, climbing up, flipping through the pages and proceeding to try and sell him some deadlights, a cranky shaft, or a calli-pooper. The customer thought it was hilarious and so did my grandpa."

She grinned. "You were a precocious, take-charge thing even then."

"I guess. Your turn. Truth or Dare?"

"Dare." Theo clicked the button. *Talk like a robot for the next round.*

She monotoned, "I am a robot. My name is not R2-D2."

"Then what's your name?"

Theo looked straight ahead, then made a buzzing sound as she looked left, came back to center, and then looked to the right. "My name is Pee Wee."

"Pee Wee?"

She buzzed her head to the left again to look at me. "Do not make fun of my name. It is your turn, human."

"I would never. I'll try a dare, too."

"All right. One Dare for you." She made a whirr as she pivoted her head to center and clicked DARE. "You must reveal the last text message you sent. There will be no cheating."

Her voice cracked me up and my mind raced as I retrieved my phone. Who'd I text last? No one since we'd left Duluth. I opened messages. Nash was on top, with a blue dot indicating an unread message. "Hang on. This could be important police business." I made a show of sneakily looking at it, but, without cell service or Internet, the message wouldn't download. I handed my phone to Theo. "Here's the last thing I messaged. To Nash."

She read, "'On the way to pick Theo up. See you in a couple of days.'" She slipped out of robot speak. "Dang. Nothing juicy."

"But I live such a juicy life."

"Ha."

For the next hour we barked like a dog, gobbled like a turkey, and I did a handstand against the wall. A few secrets were shared, some stories were told. I liked watching the way Theo's eyes grew unfocused as she recalled a past event, how animated she could become when she was passionate about something. When she found something over-the-top funny, she had this deep-from-the-belly laugh which made me howl, and soon we were leaning against each other in a vain attempt to control ourselves.

It'd been so long since I'd let go. Let it all go. I didn't know if it was because we were here, somewhat isolated, in this place, at this particular time. The world was reduced to just Theo and me and an incredibly historic building birthed of strength, ingenuity, and independence. Where hopes and dreams overcame unspeakable challenges and brutal realities.

My own brutal reality had revealed itself over the course of the evening. I couldn't kid myself any longer. I was completely, totally infatuated with this bar-owning ass kicker and I was scared shitless.

* * *

Dinnertime came, and we debated walking into town to find a bite but settled instead on a frozen pizza and more of my now-famous brownies. We ate the entire pizza and half the pan of brownies and cleaned the kitchen together when we were done, chatting amiably as we worked.

I wanted to bring up the Spud kitchen kiss, find out what, if anything, it'd meant to Theo. Maybe this charged air between us could become wholly physical and nothing else. But something inside me had changed. No. Changed was too simple a word for what I felt.

"Transformed" much more accurately described the jumbled mess inside me. I liked everything about Theo. Her kindness, her snarkiness. The way she handled herself under pressure. Her loyalty to her family. But as fast as all of that stormed through my mind, so did the memories and heartache of the betrayal Danna had left in her wake. The idea that we could pull off "something just physical" was as likely as the Vikings winning the Super Bowl.

Theo halfheartedly snapped me with a dishtowel. "Everything's dried and put away. You can drain the sink unless you want to stand there staring at the wall the rest of the night as your hands turn into wrinkled plums."

I flung some suds at her. "You're older. You'll turn into a prune before me."

"Might be true. But I've earned every white hair in this red head, and I have some finely honed skills."

"Might be true," I echoed and splashed her again. Then we went to town, water and suds flying, and I was dodging the business end of Theo's dishtowel. I put my hands up, giggling like a five-year-old. "I surrender, I surrender."

Theo looked in the sink. "Surrender, my ass. You're out of suds." She snapped at me again.

This time I caught the end of the towel and jerked it out of her hands. "Oh, I've got you now, lady."

She streaked out the kitchen and I chased after her, both of us chortling like naughty kids.

I moved one way around the dining room table, she moved the other. "Come on, Theo," I taunted. "Make a move. I owe you a few."

"Nope." Her eyes were locked on mine, looking for an indication of my next angle of attack.

We pressed forward and retreated, rounding the table twice. I deked, came back fast, and snapped. Theo leaped out of the way, but the end of my towel tagged the glass case protecting the Fresnel lens. "Oops."

"You break, you buy." Theo used my distraction to charge in the opposite direction, around the far end of the table, and vanish up the stairs.

"You sneak," I shouted and raced after her, taking the steps two at a time. At the top I stopped. She was nowhere to be seen. "Oh, that's how it's going to be, is it?" I did a fast check of the bathroom, but it was empty.

"Theo, come out, come out, wherever you are."

I scanned the big bedroom. Our bags were still there; she wasn't.

"I'm gonna find you." I held the kitchen towel at opposite corners and twirled it tight, armed, and ready. I sidled up to the door of the middle bedroom, did a quick peek and retreat.

"Where are you, Theo? Don't you want to come out and play?" I moved on to the last room. "I've got you now, my pretty. Bwahahahah. Come out, come out wherever you are."

I felt a tap on my shoulder. As I spun around, Theo grabbed the towel I still held clenched in my fists and yanked. I stumbled forward, right into her arms, her face two inches from mine. She whispered, "Did anyone ever tell you that you're adorable when you're on the hunt?"

"Did anyone ever tell you that you talk too much?" I crushed my mouth to hers.

After a stunningly short amount of time, she pulled back, breathing hard, searching my eyes. "If we don't stop this now, I don't think I'll be able to."

"Train left the station a while ago."

Then we were trying to keep our lips together as we attempted to peel off each other's clothes.

Theo tried to tug my shirt up, and I broke away long enough to pull it over my head and fling it.

Our lips still locked, I went for the button on her jeans. We stumbled, nearly fell, but didn't break apart. I couldn't get enough of the sweet taste of her. It was hot and electric and crazy and I loved every second of it.

We bounced off the walls as items of clothing littered the hall. I pulled her into the Keeper's Room, managing to avoid our bags as she endeavored to divest me of my pants.

Somehow, we landed on the bed, then she was on top of me and my hands were finally on her, sliding down the smooth suppleness of her back, feeling ridges and curves and muscle that flexed and relaxed as we rolled against each other. Moans and soft cries and gasps fueled by ever-increasing desire filled the room.

Goddamn, I was so fucking hot, aching like I hadn't ached in years. I needed more, so much more, and bucked up against Theo's hips, trying to reverse our positions.

"Mmm-mm," she hummed into my mouth. In an instant, she slid off me and then her hand was there. Right fucking there. All thoughts of turning tables vanished. Every single one of my senses was now focused on Theo's exploring fingers. I surged against her, wanting, needing, desperate for her touch.

Theo found exactly the right spot and played me like a concert pianist. One of us began keening. Me? Her? The pleasure was so intense I didn't think I'd survive the firestorm, but as hard as I tried, I couldn't hold on another second. Release slammed me so hard I threw my head back and opened my mouth in a silent scream that became a ragged wail. My body undulated, riding out the waves of passion, the pleasure blinding. Theo stayed with me until I was completely, undeniably, totally wrecked.

Still panting, I opened my eyes. Theo was right there, her forehead against mine. She whispered, "You might not be able to carry a tune, baby, but you sounded like an angel."

# CHAPTER TWENTY-FOUR

Theo awoke to an inferno-like heat enveloping her back and legs. It took Theo a second to place where she was and whose very warm body was snuggled up tight against her back, legs entwined with her own. Sunlight leaked through the sides of the blind on the window. Then it all came back in a rush of tangled limbs, lips, hips, thighs. The intoxicating taste of Bec's mouth, her exquisite fingers, the body Theo couldn't get enough of. The memory alone sent a rush of desire through her. She tried not to tense. She needed a little more time to sort things out before Bec roused and asked her how she was.

*That's the question, isn't it, Theo. How the hell are you?*

Yesterday had been a great day, indescribably amazing sex aside. Her idea to play Truth or Dare on her own terms had worked out perfectly. They'd shared what they'd been comfortable with, the Truths driving conversation, allowing them to learn more about each other, and the Dares bringing plenty of laughter.

*Theo, if you're not careful, you're going to fall head over police badge for this one.* Bec was the whole package. Fun, considerate, understanding. A fun-loving streak three miles wide. She had the ability to flip the script from casual interaction to serious attention.

But she was a cop.

*Maybe she'd understand.*

But she was a cop.

*Maybe her heart was bigger than the law.*

But she was a cop.

"Hey," a sleepy voice behind her rumbled. A warm hand slid over her waist, across the tops of her breasts, and came to a rest below her clavicle. "You okay?"

With a sigh, Theo wrapped her fingers gently around Bec's wrist and kissed the top of her hand. "I am."

She felt Bec's cheek press against her back and then lips on her skin. "Felt like you were restless."

If Bec only knew why. *Knock it off, Theo*, she scolded herself. This was one of those fleeting moments they'd talked about yesterday on the way up here. *Take it for what it is and enjoy it.* She tightened her fingers on Bec's wrist, lifted her arm, and rolled over so they were face-to-face. Bec's eyes were closed, She looked well-loved and exhausted.

"Hey." Theo kissed her nose.

Bec tightened her grip and slid her thigh between Theo's legs, snuggling up tight. "Do we have to get up now?"

"Nope." Theo tucked Bec's head against her chest, smiling when she felt Bec exhale and heard a barely audible, "Good."

\* \* \*

When Theo woke again, she was still on her side, but now her head tucked in the crook of Bec's neck. Fingers softly played with her curls. She hummed in contentment. Her arm was sprawled across Bec's abdomen, and her knee was resting on top of Bec's thighs.

"Good morning again," Bec whispered, more coherently than earlier.

Theo tried to lift her head, but her cheek had adhered itself to Bec's shoulder. "Morning. Or is it afternoon?"

"Dunno. I haven't wanted to move to check the time."

With care, Theo peeled her cheek off Bec, then flopped onto her back. "Holy shit."

Bec reached for Theo's hand, and she threaded their fingers together.

"No shit."

"That was some shit."

"Amazing shit."

They lapsed into silence as they both studied the popcorn on the ceiling.

Theo said, "Does this mean we're going steady now?"

"Maybe. Or maybe it's only a hookup."

Was that what she wanted it to be? A hookup like all the rest? Fun, casual, no strings. No, Theo decided. That's not what she wanted. She wanted to see Bec again. And again.

Then her stomach growled.

Bec rolled on her side and her hand glided onto Theo's belly. "Sounds like someone's hungry." Her hand slid lower. "What are you hungry for?"

Theo's hips twitched and she moaned as wandering fingers found her happy place. "Blueberry pancakes. Eventually."

\* \* \*

"Those were the best damn blueberry pancakes I've ever had." Theo set down her fork and wiped her lips.

"The ones upstairs or the ones down here?"

Visceral memory nearly made Theo groan. "Both."

"That's what I like to hear. Since we're out of bed, what do you wanna do today?" Bec forked the last of her pancakes into her mouth.

"I suppose going back to bed isn't an option, seeing as it's two in the afternoon."

The heated gaze Bec gave her made her rethink their options. "Stop. You are so bad. We're adults. We should be able to control ourselves for"—she checked her watch—"longer than forty-two minutes. How about we go down and walk that breakwater, then maybe head into town and give Castle Danger Brewery a try?"

"Perfect. Bonus points if a ship comes in."

Between the two of them, it didn't take long to take care of breakfast, bundle up, and head down the hill toward the harbor, the sun warming their backs as they walked. The grassy slope between the B&B and the water's edge was turning brown as nature readied itself for another brutal winter on the rugged shores of Superior. The thought made Theo's insides contract, and no, not in *that* way. Life on the North Shore during the winter months wasn't easy. Could be nice to have someone warm to crawl into bed with. *If that someone is Bec.* Then Serious Theo lectured Smitten Theo to stop those kind of thoughts already.

Two picnic tables were positioned near the head of the breakwater, which was essentially a chevron-shaped concrete dock about three hundred feet long. An informational sign near the picnic tables informed the historically curious that the breakwater had been built in 1887, and the mini lighthouse was called the Two Harbors Breakwater Light.

The breakwater had a seven-foot-wide walkway with a cable strung between posts set three or four feet apart forming a sketchy handrail.

"Up close," Bec said, "with the sun shining, this sprawling behemoth doesn't feel all that intimidating. But I bet when the water's roiling and you add some snow and gale-force winds, it'd be a hellish walk for the poor sod who has to maintain things out there."

"A braver soul than I."

Bec held out her gloved hand. "Would you care to accompany me down to the end of this situation?"

"Why yes, I'd love to experience this with you." Theo slid her mittened hand into Bec's.

Jagged, bluish-black boulders were piled on either side of the walkway, spread out wider near the shore and tapering to an end about a quarter of the way into the bay. From that point, it was all concrete versus water. Gentle ripples lapped the outside edge of the break, and the water on the inside was smooth as glass. Smooth or not, Theo wanted nothing to do with the forbiddingly dark, hypothermic depths. Memories she wanted nothing to do with roiled her gut. She tugged Bec closer to the railing.

Bec gazed at the empty docks across the bay. "I wonder if the shipping season's over."

"Pretty darn close, I bet."

They ambled past the point where the boulders ended, and now nothing stood between them and the lake except the walkway itself. "You've heard a bunch of BS about my family, but I've only gotten bits and pieces. You grew up in the Twin Cities, right?"

"Right." Bec smiled wanly. "I was born in Minneapolis, moved to Richfield when I was a baby. Two older brothers. Mom and Dad were killed when a drunk driver going the wrong way down I-94 in St. Paul hit them head-on as they were coming back from a Wild game. The drunk driver died too. God, we were a hockey-obsessed family." She went quiet a moment, eyes unfocused. "Anyway, both my brothers were in the American Hockey League, the league immediately below the NHL. I played hockey at the U of M, with two top-four appearances in the NCAA tournament. Television journalism major, of all things, with a minor in criminal justice, blah blah, long story. I graduated from college after swapping my major and minor around. Detroit was hiring at the time, and that's where I wound up. And here I am."

"Oh my god, Bec. I'm so sorry. I don't even know what to say." The horror Theo felt about Bec's loss was crushing. She cast a concerned glance at her. Her short hair ruffled in the breeze as she gazed contemplatively across the lake. Bec squeezed her hand and let go as they reached the middle of the chevron and continued down the span leading to the breakwater light.

Theo reached for Bec's hand again, not sure if she'd take it or not. She did.

"I know. I know you don't know what to say. Not really anything to say. What happened, happened. Took me awhile not to want to kill the guy. Probably a good thing he was already dead."

"What about your brothers?"

"They didn't take it well. Blamed me for bringing about our parents' deaths."

"What?"

"Because I'm a gay sinner."

"My first instinct is to say fuck them." Theo slid her hand free and threaded her arm through Bec's. "I'm sorry. That's out of line."

"No, it's not. It's the truth. Fuck them. They live in Florida. Perfect place for families who never wanted queer relatives."

They arrived at the breakwater light and slowed to a stop near its base.

"Sounds like it was a shit show for everyone, but I can't imagine how unspeakably awful it had to be for you."

"Thanks to a major amount of therapy and some anger management, actually, a lot of anger management training, I'm well aware that, ultimately, I was lucky to have had them as long as I did."

"You are an incredible human, Rebecca…What's your middle name?"

Bec raised her eyebrows and said nothing.

"That bad?"

Bec's face grew pink, then red.

"Come on, now you gotta fess up."

"Remember *Rocky and Bullwinkle*?"

"The show? Oh, yeah. My family loved those reruns. In fact, Bullwinkle became a running joke. 'Where's Theo and Tessa? Oh, they're Bullwinkling again.' Bullwinkling became the term for lazing around and essentially doing nothing constructive."

"That's funny. My mom was a Bullwinkle freak. Back to middle names. How about the spies from Pottsylvania?"

"Yes—oh, no. No no no. Which one did you get stuck with?"

"Natasha, of course. Boris would've made me trans and my brothers' heads would've exploded."

Something about the way Bec said that caught Theo's funny bone, and her chest heaved as she tried to hold in her mirth. She clapped a hand over her mouth, but she couldn't hold it in. Her laughter skipped across the water like a smooth, flat stone tossed just right.

The hysterics were contagious and uncontrollable. One of them would almost pull it together, catch the other's eye, and they'd both lose it again. Holy crap, Theo's stomach hurt so good.

When she managed to pry her teary eyes open, she saw Bec had nearly laughed herself right over the edge of the walkway. "Oh, shit." She grabbed Bec's arm and twirled her around, pinning her against the battered ladder leading up to the watch room of the Lilliputian lighthouse.

"I—" Bec cut herself off and pressed her lips tightly together to smother more hilarity. "I nearly peed my pants."

And away they went again. It took some time, but once Theo was able to look at Bec with a straight face, she moved her hands up the ladder. She stopped when they were even with the sides of Bec's head. Slowly, she leaned in. "You are a seriously dangerous chucklefuck, Rebecca Natasha."

"Chucklefuck? That's a new one."

"You heard me."

It was as if the mirth they'd shared had supercharged Theo's lust. The next second her lips found Bec's.

Bec's hands cupped Theo's face, holding her in place.

Time screeched to a halt.

Theo's world narrowed to Bec's intoxicating mouth, her warm, seeking tongue. The nipping teeth thoroughly plundered everything Theo was.

It was Bec who broke off, breathless. "House."

They bolted back the way they'd come.

Theo realized as she ran flat out, it was Bec.

*It's always been Bec.*

She'd loved Sofie so much, but it was Bec she'd been waiting for.

She just hadn't known it till now.

# CHAPTER TWENTY-FIVE

Castle Danger was an entire complex of buildings. Several were presumably for production, and one was the public beer hall. Its interior was appropriately woodsy, constructed of reclaimed boards in various stages of weathering.

The vaulted ceiling, covered with shiny gold-colored, three-inch wood slats, felt immense. A mix of regular and tall tables filled the space, with more seating outside—when it was warm enough—on a patio overlooking Lake Superior. Castle Danger shirts and other logoed merch was available for those who wanted to take home a memory or two. The air was filled with the aromas of yeast and hops, with a subtle pine undertone.

The taproom was quiet on a Monday evening, leaving plenty of space at the bar to pull up a stool and survey their options. Twenty-plus taps offered a crazy variety, from Castle Cream Ale to Aurora Haze, White Pine Project to Shredder Session IPAs.

A tall, slender bartender with black hair and a matching goatee wandered over. "Hey, I'm Bart. What'll it be for you two on this fine evening?"

We both settled on the brewery's signature ale, Castle Cream. After he pulled us our pints, Theo asked him about the brewing process, and pretty soon they were throwing around words like mashing, lautering, germination, enzymes, and conditioning. Too much information for my sex-saturated brain to take in. So I happily sipped the smooth, creamy ale and appreciated watching Theo light up as she and Bart jawed about craft brewing's ins and outs.

Light danced across the planes of Theo's features, and I vividly recalled how her lips had felt skimming down my body. The kitchen kiss at The Mashed Spud hadn't been a one-off after all. That question had been answered quite satisfactorily. However, the answer led to more questions, questions I wasn't sure I was ready to face.

Theo brought out the fun in life I thought I'd lost a long time ago. I felt like me around her. I didn't need to play a role or put on a certain kind of facade. She'd seen me in action as a cop, and she'd seen beyond that, deep into me, into a place I swore I'd never expose again. The thing that was scaring me the most was that I didn't care. I didn't care that she was charming her way into my heart. The more I hung around her, the more I wanted. It was totally worth the risk. Goddamn Nash had been right after all, not that I was going to tell him so.

"Hey," Theo said. "Sorry to get all caught up in the beer biz."

"No worries. It was fun hearing how excited you got about germy grain."

She bumped her shoulder into me. "Not germy, germinating."

"Germination smermination. It tastes good."

"Yes, indeed it does." She took a swallow, and some of the foam caught on her upper lip. It took everything I had not to lean over and lick it off. She caught me staring, and I pointed. An evil gleam appeared, and slowly, sensuously, she licked it off herself.

I almost fell off my chair. "Okay. Time for a subject change. Tell me why you're a serial one-night-stander."

Theo side-eyed me with a raised brow. "Okay. I might need another one of these, though." She waved at Bart. In a flash he had another beer for each of us.

Theo's lips tightened, and her hand trembled as she reached for her mug, making me reconsider my question. The seconds ticked by, and I wanted to take my question back.

"When I was a kid, my best friend's name was Sofie. With an 'f,' not a 'ph.' Her mom died when Sofie was seven. Her dad was left to deal with Sofie and her younger sister. Which meant Sofie raised her sister because Daddy-o was too busy being drunk, out fucking around for days, sometimes weeks, to do any of that parenting bullshit. Then the bastard began sexually abusing Sof, I found out later. It started when we were ten." She stared at the wall. "I stayed overnight as often as I could because when I was there, he didn't try anything."

"Jesus, Theo. That's awful." My heart pounded, and the impulse to strike out at that horrific wrong rose up in me like fire creeps up the walls of a building.

"When we were fourteen, Sof and I realized we had feelings for each other beyond friendship. You know, the kind of feelings you should never have, especially in a small town in northern Minnesota."

"I know those feelings well, minus the small town. Go on."

"I guess what was growing between us made me even more protective of her. I hated that man, Bec." She went pale, eyes blazing. "I detested that sonofabitch."

Her fury, so unexpected, hit me like a blast from a firehose, staggering in its intensity. She straightened, sucked a deep breath. Blew it out hard. "Sorry. The very thought of him…" She trailed off, shuddering. "He…took off for good when we were in tenth grade."

"He just left? Never came back? That's so much goddamn bullshit. Was he ever charged?"

Softly, she said, "No. Sofie begged me not to tell anyone, said he'd literally kill her if he found out. So I didn't. We stayed together through high school, into college. During our sophomore year, her…depression, I guess, got the better of her. She killed herself."

That sucked the air out of the room.

"Whoa. Theo. I am so very, very sorry." I put a hand on her forearm. She was so tense her muscles were rock hard under my palm.

"I loved Sofie so much. I tried so hard to help her, but my love wasn't enough. It wasn't enough, Bec." Tears glittered in the corners of her eyes. She looked away and downed half her ale. "After I found her—"

"Oh shit, you found her?"

"Yeah. She'd gone into the woods behind the college to a spot we often went when we needed a time-out. A small clearing, flowers, butterflies, it was peaceful."

Her eyes went glassy. I realized she wasn't here with me anymore. She was back in that divergent space of serenity and horrendous tragedy.

"If this is too hard, you don't have to say another word."

She continued as if she hadn't heard me. "I found her sitting on the ground, leaning against our favorite tree, an empty pint of whisky and an empty pill bottle next to her. Oxy. It wasn't hers, I don't know where she got her hands on it. Neither one of us had a prescription. She'd left a note. How sorry she was, how much she loved me. But she couldn't—" Theo choked up, then said in a rush, "She couldn't take the pain anymore."

I couldn't stand it another second. I pulled her into a hug right there at the bar, fuck what anyone might think. She leaned her head against me, trembling as she struggled not to fall apart. My heart imploded with the depth of her agony and something else I couldn't define. But that something else shook me to the core. After a few long moments, I kissed the top of her head and returned to my seat.

Theo sniffed hard and her jaw clenched and relaxed, clenched and relaxed. "After that, I wouldn't allow myself to get involved with anyone. Not like that."

"Never?"

"Never."

"Holy shit, that takes my breath away. You don't have to tell me, but what happened to Sofie's sister? Was she abused too?"

Theo gave me a wan smile. "It's okay. Yeah, she was. Sofie would always try to divert her dad's attention. Get Sara, her sister, out of the house as often as she could. But she couldn't be there all the time. An aunt of their mom's took them in after someone from the school realized they were living at home alone. Then Sara, she got in with the wrong crowd. Barely graduated from high school. Drugs, alcohol, I'm sure you're familiar with that slippery slope."

"I am."

"The summer she graduated, she took off with one of her various druggie boyfriends. Bounced from Florida to New Jersey, back to Florida. I don't know where else. Once in a while she'd let Sofie know she was okay, usually by postcard of all things. Probably didn't have enough money for a cell phone. Someone managed to get a hold of her after Sof died." Theo took a deep breath. "Sara showed up for the funeral. Jesus, Bec, she was a shell." Theo put her hand over her eyes and then let it drop. "She was painfully thin. Her face, god, it was a mess of scabs and scars. She didn't stop to talk to anyone. Just walked up to the casket, laid a white rose on it. Caught sight of me and gave me a nod. I swear her eyes looked totally blank, almost dead. And then she walked out. I followed her, tried to catch her. But she got onto the back of a Harley with a huge, bearded dude wearing one of those black leather vests with a motorcycle club patch on the back and they roared off. I never saw or heard from her again."

Silence echoed between us for a few long beats. "Finish your beer." My voice registered lower. "I have an overwhelming need to make slow, sweet love to you and I'd rather not do it in a brewery." I ached to ease Theo's pain, which, in turn, might ease my own.

* * *

The next morning around ten we packed up and left the B&B. I was sore and tired in an extraordinary way. Last night had been magical, raw, emotional, life-affirming. I was pretty sure, by this point, I could trust Theo. I thought I could see a way clear to ease up on my "never another relationship" mantra. The thought scared me to death, but on the flip side, not taking a chance on this evolving thing between me and Theo scared me even more.

But then the what-ifs showed up. I drummed my thumb on the steering wheel, half to the beat of the B-52s on Theo's phone and half in anxiety.

I cleared my throat and glanced at Theo. "I was thinking."

"Good or bad?"

I opened my mouth and shut it again. *Spit it out, for chrissake.* "I like you, Theo. A lot."

"I hadn't noticed." The smirk Theo got when she teased me flashed, then faded fast. "I…feel the same."

Relief and extreme terror were two ends of a fast-fraying rope. *Easy does it, Bec. What Nash said. Be brave.* "Okay. I think we might both be a bit freaked out."

"Whatever gave you that idea?"

I allowed my need for her to fully show in my eyes.

"Jesus, Bec. I don't know what you do to me. If you aren't careful, I'm not responsible for what might happen in this crappy truck."

"Goddamn, Theo. All righty then, let's think this through before our hormones take over again. I don't want to invite another round of devastation into my life, and, if I've got this right, you're afraid to open your heart again because you might not survive another life-leeching loss."

"Essentially."

"So how about if we compare deal-breakers? Either that'll help settle these initial concerns, or we find out now we should call it a day." My heart began to pump, and I failed to keep my breathing even.

After a second, Theo nodded long and slow. "Yeah. You go first."

I ran my list of no-gos through my head. Better start off with a not-too-traumatic one. "Dark chocolate."

Theo snickered. "Dark chocolate? If someone didn't like that, you'd dump them?"

"Well, it would depend on other criteria. But maybe. Definitely a possibility."

She twisted toward me, brought a knee up onto the bench seat. "You would turn down the love of a lifetime for chocolate?"

The outrage in her voice made me laugh. "Never know. Your turn."

"Let's see. A hard no would be an active alcoholic."

"Totally, yeah," I said. "Apart from our initial introduction, I'm really not a big drinker. Anymore, anyway. College was a good time, but then I pulled my act together. Until Danna dumped me. But I rallied. Okay. My turn. So...Someone with narcissistic tendencies. That one has the big D written all over it."

"The bitch. Maybe we should take a road trip to Detroit."

"Now you're talking," I said. "Hmm. In the same vein, a clingy, can't-do-anything-alone lover."

"Bingo. That's a no-way-in-hell. I get itchy thinking about it. What else?"

"Neediness," I threw out. "I once had a girlfriend in college who I'd broken up with, a crazy clingy-ass stalker. She'd hide and wait for me to leave class, I suppose, to see if I walked out with anyone. Once she even tried to physically attack Nash when he followed me to my car so I could give him a class handout he'd missed."

"Holy crap. That's needy-insane-obsessive."

"She was a loon. But boy she was good in the sack."

"You sound like a horny guy."

"I speak truth." I threw her a leer. "You're rather insatiable yourself." We blew past Glensheen Mansion-turned museum—the site of an infamous murder—and then slowed as I cut off onto East Superior Street.

"Here's one," Theo said. "No recluses. I'd like someone who wants to get out and do shit, at least some of the time."

"Cheers to that." I grabbed my water bottle from the holder and held it out.

Theo bumped mine with hers. "Here's another must-have. A partner who's genuine. No putting on airs, no mightier than thou, no know-it-alls. Affectionate. Kind. Is willing to talk about their day and not blow me off with a, 'Oh, it was fine,' and then shut down."

"Cops are notorious for not doing that sharing shit. I never told much with Danna because she didn't want to hear it." I glanced at Theo.

Her eyes blazed. "The more I hear about her the more I'd like to wrap my fingers around her neck. She sure didn't get the memo, did she?"

"Nope. She got the delivery driver. Seriously, I'm not sure how we managed to get together in the first place. She was from the greener side of the pasture. She often made me feel like I couldn't measure up to her standards, being a lowly blue-collar cop and all."

Theo looked at me in disbelief. "Where did you meet this piece of work?"

"She'd been hauled into the precinct on a shoplifting charge—"

A shrill "What?" echoed through the cab, and I cringed. "Hey, don't judge. I was young and impressionable, and she was hot."

"Young and impressionable?"

"That was then, this is now. I'm older and wiser." Downtown traffic wasn't too bad, and in minutes I rolled to a stop in front of The Mashed Spud.

"That makes me permanently older and wiser than you."

"You zinged yourself on that one."

"I did. So, what else is a giant stop sign?"

I pressed my lips together as I thought about it. "Honesty. No liars. I learned my lesson with one criminal. Those are two hard lines I'll never cross again."

Theo gathered her water bottle and, ducking her head, slid it into the backpack at her feet. "In all sincerity, thank you for a very hot time."

I broke into a wide grin, wanting nothing more than to pull her to me and kiss her breathless, right here, right now. As if she'd read my mind, she touched her finger to her lips, then pressed it against mine.

"Be careful out there, Detective." She slid out of the truck and slammed the door.

I lifted my hand to wave, but she didn't look back as she pulled open the door and disappeared inside.

# CHAPTER TWENTY-SIX

Theo beat a quick path through the bar to the stairs. If history rang true, Tess would be busy crunching weekend numbers in the office.

She unlocked the door to the apartment and called out, "I'm home."

No one answered, and a miniscule piece of the weight she carried dissipated. She shuffled to her bedroom, every bone inside her dissolving with each step. The backpack slipped through numb fingers and hit the floor with a thud. She closed the door and slid down it, head in her hands. She didn't bother to wipe away the tears sliding down her cheeks.

* * *

"Theo, can I please come in?"

"No. I'm okay." What was okay, anyway?

"You've been in there three days. Maybe you need to go to the doctor."

"It's just food poisoning."

"Then why do you sound like you have a cold?"

*Yeah, Theo, you big, bad lesbian. Why do you sound like Snuffleupagus?* Not a soul who knew her would believe she'd spent the last thirty-four hours bawling like a three-year-old who'd lost her favorite teddy bear.

"Allergies."

"You don't have allergies."

Damn. Tess had a memory like an elephant.

A thunk sounded against the door. Probably Tessa's head.

Theo tried to open her eyes, but they were so gritty it was easier to keep them shut.

"I've had it, Theo."

Uh-oh. She knew that tone of voice. She dragged a pillow over her head.

"I'm coming in."

The door opened, and for a second, silence reigned. Then, "Jesus Christ. You need some light in here. And fresh air."

The blind rattled as it was drawn up, and with a grunt, Tess slid the window open.

"I like the dark." Theo's voice was muffled. "I don't want to get you sick."

The pillow was plucked off her and dropped next to her.

"Too bright." Through slitted eyes, she could see Tess looming over her.

"Have you been crying?"

"I don't cry." Theo flopped her hand around for the pillow and pulled it back into place.

"Shove over." The mattress dipped.

Theo shifted her legs half an inch.

"All right, tell me what's going on. You don't have food poisoning. Did something happen in Two Harbors with Bec? She's texted me about seventy times in the last three days, wondering why you aren't answering her."

After a few long moments, Theo dragged the pillow off and screwed her eyes shut against the now-bright room.

"You two have a fight?"

"No." Theo's voice was lower than usual, gravelly from disuse. "I'd rather not talk about it."

"I'm going to lay your own advice on you. Hiding in your bedroom is no solution. Whatever the fuck is going on, you need to face it." More softly, she added, "I've never known you to run away from anything."

Theo did a long exhale and managed to sit most of the way up, the sheet and blanket pooling around her hips. Tess's brows were furrowed, her expression filled with empathy. Why was it easier to say something like that to a loved one than to hear a loved one say it to you? She made a grumpy noise.

"Going Neanderthal on me now?"

"Maybe."

"Well, then, you sad sack of misery, tell me what happened."

Theo played with the edge of the comforter. "We got along great."

"That's good news. So what has you in this state?" She waved a hand around the room.

"Maybe it was too great."

"Too great?" A glimmer of comprehension flickered across Tessa's face. "I see. You really like Bec." It wasn't a question.

"Maybe."

"You gotta lot of maybes going on here. Is your hesitation because you're holding on to Sofie?"

Theo's head began to pound. Goddammit. If only Tess knew. Shame, fear, frustration, the piercing pain of loss swirled sickly in her gut. She couldn't do it.

A hand rested lightly on her knee. The touch made her think of Bec's perfectly perfect knees, how it'd felt to run her fingers over them, tracing her kneecap until Bec jerked away in a fit of tickle-induced giggles. Her heart constricted even more. "I don't know, Tess." She begrudgingly met her gaze. "I haven't felt anything so perfect. Even with Sofie."

Tessa stilled. "Oh, shit."

"Yeah." Might as well play off the fear angle. No better way to distract. Besides, what she was saying was the truth. Part of it, at least. "I'm petrified."

"Makes sense. You've kept yourself away from love, from someone who might care about you, for so damn long your sense of comfort in a relationship is stunted."

"You a shrink, now?"

"No, silly goose. I'm someone who loves you and wants to see you happy, not clinging to a memory of love that died a long time ago."

"That hurts. But you're right. I know you are. I'm just not ready."

"When do you think you'll be ready to let love in, Theo? When you're ninety?"

If only it was as easy as letting love in. Why did Bec have to be a detective? Have to be involved in law enforcement at all? Morality battled with self-preservation, the clash thumping through her with every beat of her heart. She groaned and fell sideways, pulling the covers over her head yet again.

Tess sighed and squeezed her leg. "When you think you can face reality, we need to work on renewing our liquor license, and I had to reschedule your meeting with Dawn'isha from QueerMedia about next year's marketing plan. I'd rather not have to do it again." In a less stern voice, she said, "I love you, Theo. I'm here, okay?"

"I know."

The bed leveled as Tessa stood. Theo barely heard the closing snick of the door as she added the pillow to the covers over her head.

* * *

The next morning, Theo didn't feel a whole lot better, but she managed to drag herself to the shower and get dressed. She wandered down to the office, which was devoid of Tessa, and called Dawn'isha to apologize and confirm the next meeting date. Then she began to pull together the files she'd need for the liquor renewal.

A tap on the doorframe startled her.

"Hey, sorry." A-Team Alex hovered outside the door, and Theo waved her in. "What's up?"

"Bec's here asking if you're available."

The chair squeaked as she straightened. Options were limited. Go out and talk to her? Theo would rather break her leg. Ignore the request completely? Send her away? It wasn't fair to Alex have her do the dirty work. And it wasn't fair to Bec. But, damn it, she absolutely could not face her right now.

"Would you mind telling her I'm caught up in work, but I'll text her later?"

"Sure." With a wave, Alex disappeared down the hall.

She was obligated now to text Bec, but at least it wouldn't be a face-to-face blow off.

Theo searched her pockets for her cell, then patted down the mess of paperwork on the desk. She found it on the credenza beside the desk, right where she'd left it.

**Hey Bec, sorry I didn't thank you sooner for the mind-blowing time in Two Harbors. I had a rocking good time with you. But I've come to realize I can't do a relationship. I just can't. I'm sorry, so very sorry.**

She read it three times before she worked up the courage to hit send. With a whoosh, the message vanished into the ether.

# CHAPTER TWENTY-SEVEN

The squad room was busy on a Friday midafternoon. Nash, Shingo, Chu, and I tried to look like we were busy too. We'd taken care of a massive backlog of scut work over the last few days and were hoping today to be able to focus on our murder and drug-running case. Fingers crossed, we were due for another update from MPD.

I crumpled up the third version of the note I was trying to write to Theo and lobbed it toward the garbage on the side of Nash's desk. The wadded paper ringed the top of the can and spun to the floor, landing beside my other two attempts.

"I'm sick and fucking tired of waiting."

Nash glanced at me, hands hovering over his keyboard. "Good grief, Bec. Go over to The Mashed Spud and talk to Theo."

I propped my feet on the edge of my desk and petulantly crossed my arms. "Already did. She won't see me."

Shingo spun her chair around. "You have every right to be pissy. You walked in here Tuesday evening with that bright and shiny just-got-laid glow, and whomp, the rug's pulled out from under you. I guess women are as bad as men." She grabbed one of the banana Laffy Taffys Nash had filched for me from the Halloween candy bowl at the reception desk out front, unwrapped it and stuck it in her mouth. I was so distracted over the state of my love life, I didn't even bother to give her shit about swiping my favorite candy.

"Bashing men again, huh, Shingo?" Chu shoved off his desk and rolled over, helping himself to my taffy stash too.

"Hey." I swatted the candy out of his hand. "No one wants the banana ones until I have them. Why is that?"

Shingo shrugged, chewing noisily, her lips clamped tight so she wouldn't drool.

"It's because the good stuff's all gone." Chu nabbed another, and this time I let him have it.

"Hey, Nash," I said as I grabbed the last two pieces of my taffy and stowed them in my drawer. "What's Baby Harper going to be for Halloween? You don't have much time to decide."

"We're torn between a sunflower costume and Sherlock Holmes."

"Uh." Shingo finally swallowed. "You gotta go with Sherlock."

Chu braced his elbows on his knees. "I can see her waving one of those huge magnifying glasses around."

"And"—I put a finger to my cheek—"one of those adorable Sherlock hats. You know, the ones with the flaps."

Nash's eyes lit up. "Good ideas—"

The squad door banged open, interrupting Nash. Sergeant Alvarez marched into the room, followed by Wizzer from drugs and the head SWAT guy. I couldn't remember his name, but he looked like a human Shrek. Laughed like him too but wasn't nearly as cranky.

"All right, gang," Alvarez said. "Briefing in the conference room in five." Then the three of them sequestered themselves in Alvarez's office with the door shut.

Five minutes later we assembled in the con room. Ten minutes after that, Alvarez, Wizzer, and the man who I now knew was Sergeant Adam VanValkenberg, or plain old Van, came in.

Alvarez looked better today. Instead of a grayish pallor, his cheeks were ruddy brown and angsty energy rolled off him. Maybe he was getting laid too. The thought of getting laid led me to a flash of Theo, her head thrown back, the veins and tendons in her neck stretched taut as she rode the wave and crashed hard.

*Oh, sweet mother of all that's unholy.* I needed to rinse that girl right out of my mind.

"I suppose this isn't a meeting for shits and giggles." Nash threaded his hands behind his neck.

"I'd love some shits and giggles right about now," Wiz said. "Minneapolis just notified us Jimmy Boy's heading up here to do a drop at an address in East Hillside tonight about eleven. Side note, the idiot's been bragging to anyone who'll listen, including two snitches from the Cities your CI gave us, Nash, about how he'd come up to Duluth and had followed Ivorsen for two full days, waiting for his opportunity to snuff the guy. The night of the murder, Jimmy followed him into The Mashed Spud. He watched Ivorsen have a racist, homophobic rant and then get himself tossed. During the scuffle between Ivorsen and Theo Zaccardo Jimmy heisted a pizza cutter that she'd tossed on the top of the bar when she came out of the kitchen to deal with Sir Lippy. Had the bright idea to pin the murder on the manager—"

"Owner," I interrupted.

Wiz gave me a nod. "He had the idea to pin the murder on her after he heard her tell Ivorsen he'd be dead meat if he came back. He seems to be very proud of his ingenuity in writing 'dead meat' on the guy's head. Anyway, as soon as Ivorsen was out the door, he followed him to his car, pulled a gun, and forced him to drive to his home. There, he made Ivorsen gather all the cash he had and put it in a bag. Hustled him back out to the car and made him drive to the Spud and park in the alley by the bar's back door. He took him out with the pizza cutter, fingerpainted Ivorsen's forehead and heaved him into the dumpster along with the cutter. With his prints on it in Ivorsen's blood."

"What a complete and utter dumb fuck," Shingo said.

"You got that right, Shing," Wiz said. "And it gets better. Apparently, Jimmy really loves reliving what he did. He's been using pizza terminology to describe what happened to anyone who's willing to listen. I won't share those details here. You're welcome."

"Jesus," I said. "That's disgusting. What time did he kill Arne?"

Wiz lifted a shoulder. "Didn't get it pinned down yet, but somewhere between two a.m. and four, maybe five."

If I'd ever be able to talk to her again, Theo would be happy to hear she was completely and unequivocally in the clear.

"All right, down to biz." VanValkenberg riffled through the pages of a rumpled yellow pad. "We have eyes on the address now. We'll coordinate here at 1900 in the back lot."

Alvarez's smile looked more like a wolf bearing its fangs. "Figured you four might want to be in on the takedown."

"Hell, yeah." Chu leaned forward with his arms splayed out like he was ready to army crawl across the table. "I'm ready."

Agreement rumbled.

"Here's how it'll go down," Van said. "My team goes in first. They clear the place, and then you folks can have at it."

For the next half hour, we talked technical details, mission planning, and tactical response. Once we were dismissed, we regrouped at our desks.

Shingo twirled a pen between her fingers. "I'm stoked. But I'm going back home, need to center and ground."

Nash and Chu decided to kill time shooting hoops in the gym. I stayed behind to try to write an entire note to Theo.

For the life of me, I couldn't figure out what had freaked her enough to completely drop out of sight. Not one of my texts had been answered, and the two times I'd dropped by, she was either out or too busy to see me.

God knew I'd had my own nightmares about pursuing anything more than fuck-buddy status with her. Some serious stewing had kept me up after Two Harbors, but I realized I was already half gone, intoxicated by everything Theo was and everything she wasn't. I was no longer afraid to say that I wanted—no, that word didn't do my feelings justice—that I *hungered* to see where things might lead.

*Okay, Bec, now you need to convey how you feel to Theo.*

I could've messaged her but felt this decision was too momentous to be reduced to shorthand texts and dumb emojis. Who knew if she'd actually read it, anyway? If Theo was having second thoughts, well, actually, having no thoughts at all about pursuing the tentative connection we'd made, I planned on hitting her with six players on the ice and no goalie.

*Heartbreak, cut me some slack.* I decided not to worry about anything beyond getting the damn letter written and delivered before drug-dealing clowns threw things into a raging opioid circus.

After a few more false starts and a number of hand cramps, it was done. A beginning, a middle, and an end. I picked up the sheet of paper and read it through one last time before calling it good enough.

*Hey, Theo,*

*I'm not sure what's going on, but I hope you're okay. It's a sad day when I don't see a text from you, aside from your brief message about our Two Harbors adventure and your no relationship declaration. I've been thinking long and musing hard about everything we shared during our lighthouse excursion. Then I thought about it some more. I know I might be talking to a walled-off fortress here, but I hope you'll at least consider my words.*

*Theo, you make me laugh. You make me scream. You make me think. You give me the chance to experience the world in ways I never have before. You fill me in places I didn't know were empty. One look from you and I melt like the Wicked Witch, without the wicked or witch parts. A simple touch from you is somehow reassuring, and I wasn't aware I wanted or needed to be reassured.*

*I know relationships don't come with guarantees. But I'm hoping you'll consider exploring our connection, see where it might lead. This time, maybe for the first time, my heart is open and I'm trying to come at this without any preconceived notions.*

*What might blossom will blossom.*

*What might grow brilliant, like those glorious, electric, autumn leaves we saw, might flame out and fall, like leaves inevitably will. But wouldn't it be worth it to live the truth of something so intensely beautiful, even if only for a limited time? Or, flip side, what if it isn't limited at all?*

*After my ex ripped me apart more completely than a medieval torture device might've, I never, ever wanted to be in another position to expose the deepest parts of myself to anyone. Yet somehow, I've found I'm willing to do that with you. You make me feel safe, needed but not needy. Strong, but weak.*

*Please, think about it. Think about the possibilities.*

*B*

*PS who knew a cop could come up with such mushy shit?*

Before I could talk myself out of it, I slid the letter into an envelope, taped it shut, and wrote Theo's name on the front in block letters. As I stuffed it in my pocket, I realized I hadn't mailed an actual letter for a long time. Didn't even know if I had stamps. Oh, well.

My watch read two minutes after four. Plenty of time to fire up the beater and make a special delivery.

\* \* \*

I pulled into an open spot half a block from the bar and hoofed it toward the front door before I could chicken out. *You saunter right on in there like you own the place, Bec. Throw your shoulders back, hold your head high, and stroll inside as if you're not feeling like a scared shitless kid.*

As ever, when I entered The Spud, I paused to let my eyes adjust. The weekend crowd was already ratcheting up the rowdy.

My query for Theo got me nowhere. Then I saw Tessa descending the stairway from the apartment.

*Don't think, do.*

I caught up with her as she headed down the hall, either to the office or the bathroom. "Hey, Tess."

"Yeah—Bec." She glanced around, but we were alone. "What's up?" Her face was unreadable.

"I know this is awkward. I don't know what Theo's told you, but I'd like you to—no, I need you to, please—give her this." I withdrew the crumpled letter and thrust it into her hands. "I can't stay. Tonight's the night we make our move."

Tess caught my meaning and squeezed my arm. "I'll give this to her, but I can't guarantee she'll read it. But, Bec, please know, she cares so much."

At her words, my heart swelled. "Nothing in life's guaranteed. I know that. But as stupid, naïve, and"—I grasped for another appropriate word—"cliched as it sounds, I swear on all I am that I've never felt like this before." Impulsively, I hugged her and hightailed my ass out of there.

# CHAPTER TWENTY-EIGHT

After reading Bec's letter—and it was an honest to god letter—Theo went to bed. She didn't think she'd ever fall asleep. Her resolve to run had been strong, but as she read what Bec had carefully written, that resolve crumbled, word by word. What if Bec would understand why she'd done what she'd done? Then again, what if she didn't? Shades of gray danced behind her closed eyelids. Secrets filled with complicated layers of danger.

She eventually fell into a dream where nothing was as it seemed. She opened her refrigerator and walked into another dimension. Everything was familiar, yet not. Colors swirled before her as if she could reach out and grab them. Then she saw Bec across the cavernlike space. She tried to call to her, to yell, to scream, but Bec didn't react. Could she not hear her? Or did she not want to?

An irritating sound wouldn't stop, dragging her away from Bec. She didn't want to leave. She tried to ignore it, but the further from magical space she was pulled the louder the sound became.

She awoke with a jerk, gasping for air.

*Phone.*

The phone was ringing. It was Bec's ringtone. She fumbled on the bedside table. Why would she be calling now? In the middle of the—holy shit. Tessa had told her the bust was tonight. She bolted upright and answered.

"Bec?" Her voice was sleep-hoarse. The background was noisy with sirens, voices shouting. Louder, she said, "Bec?"

"Theo? Hey, hang on."

That voice was not Bec's.

Her thudding heartbeat tripled-timed.

"Theo, this is Detective Shingobe. Shingo. I work with Bec."

"Shingo, yeah."

The cacophony grew louder, then faded, as if she was moving away from it.

"Can you hear me better now?"

"Yes."

"Gotta be quick. Bec's been shot."

The very air around Theo mutated from a gas to a solid. She couldn't inhale, couldn't exhale.

"Theo? You there? Listen. She's headed to Saint Luke—" Shingo cut herself off as an indistinct voice came across the line. Then, "Check that. They're airlifting her to HCMC. Hennepin County Medical Center, in Minneapolis. Theo, you got it? HCM—" The call disconnected.

Theo's hands shook as she tried to call back, but Shingo didn't pick up. Then some kind of unreal, preternatural calm enveloped her.

*Get up.*

*Get dressed.*

*Wake Tess.*

*Map the hospital.*

*Grab the phone and car keys.*

*Go.*

*Now.*

\* \* \*

The trip down to Hennepin County Medical Center in Minneapolis was interminable, though she somehow made it in two hours, cutting thirty minutes from the usual driving time. Tessa had decided she should stay behind and keep close to the bar since it was the weekend, so Theo was on her own.

She'd tried a multitude of ways to drown her thoughts out, from music to rolling down the window, which had only frozen her hands, to listening to the news, which pissed her off, and now she sat in relative silence, drumming her fingers on the steering wheel. No matter how hard she tried to block them, what-if scenarios screamed at light speed through her imagination. By the time she pulled into the HCMC parking ramp, she'd killed Bec so many ways she was sure she really was dead by now.

On the way down, Shingo had texted her Nash's phone number because he'd flown with Bec and was already there. Theo had saved the information to her contacts and texted him now.

**Hey, it's Theo. I'm in the parking ramp at the hospital. Where do I need to go?**

Three minutes which felt like fifty-nine hours later, he responded with the floor he was on and where the surgery waiting room was.

**How is she?**

**The surgeons haven't come out yet, but with the extent of her injuries, it'll probably be a while.**

His words hit her like a bomb. The extent of her injuries. Theo put a hand on her chest to make sure her heart didn't pound its way right through her ribs. Part of her brain managed to maintain some semblance of rationality, because she understood Nash had to be having a heart attack of his own.

**I'll wait for the specifics till I see you.**

The hospital was a maze, but after asking two people for directions, she found the right elevator and rode up to the med-surg floor. She passed a bustling nurse's station to a door with a Trauma Waiting Room sign above it.

After some slow, calming breaths, she entered.

A dozen people, divided in three main groups, were scattered throughout the space, along with a few loners. The walls were beige, the carpet was beige, the chairs were beige. A bank of rectangular windows looked like blank, black eyes.

Theo caught Nash's wave. He stood at her approach, hugged her long and hard, then sunk back into his chair as if his bones had been removed. She sat beside him, wondering if she was going to have to catch him if he passed out. Poor guy looked like hell. His eyes were sunken, and he had streaks of something black on his face. He wore an ash-gray, long-sleeved T-shirt and jeans, stained dark at the knees and thighs. She didn't want to think about what kind of stains they might be. Or where they came from.

She opened her mouth, and Nash held up a hand. "Thanks for coming. I know you have a shitload of questions, but I need to tell you this first." His fingertips rasped across the stubble on his cheeks as he stared blankly over Theo's shoulder. "I don't want to get between you and Bec, with whatever you two have going on." Then he met Theo's eyes with a ferocity that made her want to retreat. "I've known Bec most of my life, and I'd do anything for her. Which is why I had Shingo call you. Over the years I've seen Bec with a few women, including Danna. She had a bad picker on that one." He scowled. "Then there's you. I have never seen her so intense, so singularly focused on anyone. I mean, she actually wrote you a letter today. Or yesterday. I don't know anymore."

"You know about that?" Theo's insides squirmed. *Come on, Nash. Get to the point already.*

"The floor at the station was littered with rejected drafts. I told her to go talk to you, but in her usual stubborn way, she refused."

"Okay." This afternoon if Bec had tried to talk to her, Theo figured she would've blown her off. Now, everything was an entirely different story.

"I guess what I'm trying to say is I've seen so much change in her, for the better, since you came into her life. I know it was a strained beginning, but you two really hit it off. You're good for her, and I'm pretty sure she's head over heels. You need to know that."

Theo nodded, not sure if he was trying to say these things before he told her Bec was on her deathbed. Or not. "I appreciate that, Nash, thank you. All points are taken to heart. Now, please, tell me what the hell happened."

He leaned back, shoulders drooping, looking utterly and completely spent. "I can't go into a lot of the specifics, but first off, I can tell you that as of three-and-a-half hours ago, the guy who killed Arne Ivorsen is out of commission."

"Good."

"The SWAT team cleared the building. We picked up four dope peddlers, but not the guy we were looking for. As we went through the house for evidence, he ambushed Bec."

"How?"

"He hid behind a false wall SWAT missed in one of the upstairs closets." He scrubbed his cheeks with his palms. "God, they're beside themselves. But the wall was really well concealed. We know there's risks of something like this happening as we come in behind them. Usually, it's all good. This time…Bec happened to be searching the wrong room in the wrong moment. He came out shooting blind. The bullet missed her ballistic vest by a fucking quarter inch. Her lung collapsed, but the air ambulance medics got it reinflated. As soon as we landed, they took her into surgery." He looked at his watch. "They've been in there for about an hour and forty-five minutes. One of the nurses told me this could take an hour or it could take many. Depends on the damage."

"What happened to the son of a bitch?"

"She managed to get a shot off before she collapsed, hit him in the neck. As far as I know, he's still kicking. They got him out of there before I could kill him myself."

"Holy hell." This was so much better and so much worse than she'd expected. She slumped in her not-well-cushioned seat. They lapsed into silence, each lost in their thoughts.

Bec was alive. Theo had known, intellectually, that police work was dangerous, but, in all of her worries about Sofie and whether or not to confide her damning secret to Bec, she'd never considered the fact Bec could be hurt or killed on the job.

How utterly, completely, catastrophically stupid was she? *Unfuckingbelievable.*

She was an idiot. That much had been confirmed. This was a dumb-ass time to be asking herself the question, but…could she truly see herself in a relationship with a cop? And…how did the answer change if the question was about being in a relationship with Bec?

Truth be told, she couldn't imagine not having Bec in her life, in her bed, in her heart. It was amazing how fast clarity came when enough insanity hit an industrial-sized fan.

That was it then, she decided. To have a shot at a relationship with the woman she was in love with, she was not willing to confess her sins. She was compelled to. She'd explain everything, place her fate in Bec's hands. The time had come to risk it all, including her freedom.

*  *  *

At some point she dozed. The scent of coffee woke her, and she blinked her eyes open. Hazy morning sunlight streamed through the windows, and a woman in scrubs and a white coat was walking toward them.

"Nash." She elbowed him and they both rose. Standing was somehow better than sitting to take in whatever news was coming their way.

The woman asked, "You're with Rebecca Harrison?"

*Bec*, Theo screamed in her head. *She goes by Bec!* However, she kept her mouth shut.

"We are," Nash said. "I'm Detective Ryan Nash, and this is Theo Zaccardo. She's Bec's partner." Theo hadn't realized she didn't know Nash's first name. She'd thank Ryan later for giving her the in.

The doc shook Nash's hand, then Theo's. The contrast of tawny skin against Theo's olive undertones was strangely fascinating. Holy shit, she needed some coffee.

"I'm Dr. Patel, the cardiac trauma surgeon who worked on Rebecca. She'll be sent to ICU soon."

The doc's intense eyes were deep brown, almost black, and the quiet confidence they exuded gave Theo a sense of relief. Dr.

Patel had a competent, commanding presence, and she knew Bec was in the right hands.

"A little privacy would be nice. Please, come with me and I'll fill you in." Her slight accent had a distinct sense of musicality, and her tone was steady and sure.

They followed her to a room barely large enough to hold a table and four chairs.

Once they were seated, she said, "First of all, you should know Rebecca is in critical but stable condition. She'll remain in an induced coma for the next twelve- to twenty-four hours. How she responds will dictate the direction we will go. The bullet ricocheted off two ribs, cracking one, deflated her left lung, and nicked her pulmonary artery. It ended up lodged very close to her aorta. She is one very fortunate woman."

Doctor Patel paused, allowing them a few seconds to digest the very complex and terrifying information she'd imparted. "I was able to repair her lung, the pulmonary artery, and successfully remove the bullet. From here it is up to her. She is strong. Her heart is strong, her body is strong." The doc met Theo's eyes again. "Ms. Zaccardo, I'm probably not telling you anything you don't already know, but your partner is a fighter. We'll be doing everything we can to help her get through this."

\* \* \*

As they waited for Bec to be moved to the ICU, Theo called Tessa and brought her up to date, hearing in return that all was well at the Spud and she should stay with Bec as long as it took. If she needed anything, she was to text Tessa and she'd find a way to get it to her. She loved her sister's strength fiercely. But sometimes, like now, Theo loved her empathy and understanding even more.

Bec lived up to Doctor Patel's assessment of her fighting ability and after only eighteen hours in ICU, was extubated and moved into a private room on the med-surg floor. The nurses moved a sleeper couch into the room for Theo, who had done nothing to disabuse them of the notion she was Bec's partner. She'd have gone crazy if they'd barred her from being by her side.

Nash had taken off once he heard Bec would be moved out of ICU, promising to come back as soon as he checked in with his wife and baby and caught some sleep. Duluth's chief of police had visited while Bec was still in ICU, as had Sgt. Alvarez, Shingo, and Chu.

Finally, Theo was blessedly alone with Bec or as alone as one could be with incredibly kind nurses coming in on the regular to make sure they were both doing okay. She pulled a chair next to the bed and held Bec's hand, watching the gentle rise and fall of her chest. So many wires and tubes sprouted from her she looked like a bizarre Frankenstein experiment.

Bec had stirred twice, squeezed Theo's fingers once, and fallen asleep again. As Theo sat gently stroking the soft skin on top of Bec's hand, she wondered why neither of Bec's brothers had shown up. She couldn't imagine they wouldn't have come had they known, even if they were assholes. Something to ask Nash.

A million thoughts swirled like a tornado in her head. When to tell Bec, how to say it. Imagining what her reaction would be, both good and bad. Earlier, she'd once again considered not sharing her story, but then Bec's words haunted her: "Honesty. No liars. I learned my lesson with one criminal. Those are two hard lines I'll never cross again." She had to. She had to tell Bec everything. Afterward she would either be on the road to redemption or on the road to hell.

She dozed off with her head on the edge of Bec's bed.

Familiar pressure on her fingers woke her sometime later. Then she felt it again. She tried to slip her hand away but Bec held on with a surprisingly strong grip. Her eyes were slits, but they were open.

"Hey, okay. There you are," Theo whispered. She stood, moving closer, not letting go. She kissed Bec's knuckles and leaned in.

A raspy, "Ew talkin to me now?" made Theo suppress a hysteric giggle.

"I am."

Bec's eyes drooped. "'ood. Don lego." She squeezed Theo's fingers again.

"I won't. Sleep, baby."

She did.

The next time Theo woke up, weak light filtered through open blinds. The hand holding Bec's was numb, and her neck might never be the same. Her bladder was screaming. She carefully slid her hand away, waiting to see if Bec awoke. She didn't stir.

As quietly as she could, she snuck out of the room, stretching her neck one way and then the other. After getting directions to the nearest restroom, she found a vending area, got some water, Coke, and some blueberry Pop-Tarts. Ironic, wasn't it, how hospitals stocked their vending machines with shit food which caused health issues that brought some people into the hospital in the first place?

She walked up and down the hallway near Bec's room for a few minutes while she ate her Pop-Tarts, then headed back into the room. To her surprise, Nash was beside Bec's bed, bent close, whispering something to her, but she appeared to still be asleep.

He straightened when he saw Theo and smiled. He was showered, in clean clothes, and smelled good when he hugged her, no longer appearing on the verge of keeling over.

They stepped out of the room and Theo pulled the door shut behind them. Nash leaned a shoulder against the wall. "What's the latest?"

"Not a whole lot. She kind of woke up at one point and made me promise not to let go of her hand, then knocked off again. The nurses say she's doing fine. You get any sleep?"

He flashed a grin. "Some. I'm kind of used to it with the baby, so I'm okay. I've coordinated visits from most of the department so no more than two cops will come by each hour during visiting time. Between me and you we can be the red light/green light, depending on how she's doing. If I didn't organize things, we'd be overrun. Everyone wants to stop by, even if it is a five-hour round trip."

"I'd call that serious support." Theo yawned.

"You have to be zonked. But, I do have some news that might wake you up. You want to hear it?"

She shut her mouth so fast her teeth clacked. "Hell, yeah."

"You're really going to like this."

Theo raised her brows at his smirk. "Okay, big guy, let me have it."

"Jimmy Boy's doing fine. In fact, he's so fine he's still squealing on everything he's done wrong since he was nine."

"I assume you are going to narrow that down for me."

The smirk slid into a delighted grin that lit Nash's face. "Oh, yeah. Get this. Jimmy was in the bar tailing Arne when Arne lipped off and you threw him out."

The lightbulb started to glow. "If he was in the bar he had to have heard me tell Arne if he came back he'd be dead meat."

He pointed at Theo. "Bingo. He'd been looking for the right time to do Arne in, and he fell into the perfect storm of random occurrences that became a spur of the moment decision. Do you remember what you were doing before the altercation with Arne?"

"I was in back washing dishes."

"Then what did you do?"

"Came out front, and you know the rest."

"Ah, yes. Indeed, I do. And now you will too. Did you have anything in your hands when you came out of the kitchen?"

"In my hands?"

"Yeah."

She rubbed her forehead, trying to remember. One minute she was scrubbing something, and then she was out front. "I have no idea."

"You set something on the top of the bar."

"A rag?" Where the hell was crazy boy going with this? "Jesus, Nash, come on."

"A customer was sitting on the last stool at the end of the bar by, you know, the place servers pick drinks up from. Whatever it's called."

"Technically, the service area." She peered over his shoulder for a couple seconds. "I vaguely recall passing by a guy as I charged out of the back when I heard the commotion."

"Yeah." Nash's head bobbed enthusiastically. "You did. Now think. What did you set down at the service area?"

She opened her mouth, closed it, shrugged. "I still have no idea."

Goddamn if his eyes weren't twinkling. "How about a pizza cutter?"

She stared at him as the pieces fell together. "For fuck's sake." She'd been washing that damn cutter. Now, in her mind's eye, she could see herself flinging it onto the rubber mat as she ran hell bent toward the ruckus. "The guy at the end of the bar was after Arne. And he saw me leave the cutter there."

"Give the girl a dollar."

"Oh, come on. It's gotta be ten bucks by now, with inflation. So, the murder was some kind of spur-of-the-moment decision on Jimmy Boy's part?"

"Yes!" Nash said with enough volume and enthusiasm the nurses at the desk glanced up at them as one.

Theo waved at them. "Sorry, he gets excited sometimes." She refocused on Nash's face. "Carry on."

"As soon as 'dead meat' came out of your mouth he saw an easy opportunity to pin the murder on you. He grabbed the cutter and beat a hasty exit as you were shooing everyone out. Then he caught up with Arne at his car and made him drive home. Forced him to cough up all the drug money he had and drive back to the bar, where Jimmy killed him. He was pretty proud he'd come up with the 'dead meat' touch on Arne's forehead, figuring that would seal the deal and we'd only look at you."

"Boy, talk about random series of actions coming together."

"I know. He's also ratted out half his associates. Minneapolis now has a chance to take down that particular drug ring, not that three more won't pop up in the meantime, but one battle at a time. I don't think prison's going to be a very safe place for him. He also stole a bunch of money from Arne that belonged to the gang he was running dope for, and they are not happy about that."

"Holy shit." Theo slapped her hand over her mouth and widened her eyes. "Jesus, Nash, if I hadn't left the cutter there, none of this would've ever happened. Bec wouldn't have been shot."

The amusement on his face faded. "No. No, Theo. Canceling one act doesn't mean others wouldn't happen anyway. Besides, if you hadn't found the body, you wouldn't have met Bec."

After a moment she cracked a weak grin. "No. I wouldn't have met her if you hadn't decided to choose the Spud to celebrate her promotion."

He stared at her. "Actually, if you hadn't invented the BB, you wouldn't have met her."

"Ya got me there. Let's call it happy coincidences, then."

He checked his watch. "If she's still sleeping, there's a bit over three hours before visiting time ramps up. That couch in there didn't look used. You wanna lay down for a while and I'll keep watch?"

"You drive a hard bargain, Nash." She paused, debating on voicing her question, then said, "Why haven't Bec's brothers shown up?"

Nash pressed his lips together hard enough that a white rim appeared around them. "Bec doesn't want them notified unless she's in imminent danger of dying."

"Seriously?"

"Yup."

"Is it that bad between them? She told me they're in Florida, and they don't see eye to eye regarding her sexual orientation."

"All true. They weren't so bad as kids, but later…I don't know what happened. They're essentially, well, assholes. I haven't seen or spoken to either one of them in years."

Theo blew out a heavy breath. "Well, between me and Tess and you, Sherry, and Harper, and the rest of her cop family, she's not alone anymore."

"Nope, she sure isn't."

They hugged again and went back in Bec's room. The burden of fear Theo carried had taken a back seat in the immediacy of Nash's news, but now that fear clawed its way back and felt even heavier and more hopeless than it had before.

Bec was still out, occasionally emitting quiet pooing sounds, which Theo thought were endearing as hell. Nash took the chair, and she settled on the couch, conked out almost before her head hit the pillow.

* * *

The rest of the day flew by, between cops visiting, nurses doing vitals, and an appearance from Dr. Patel, who did some poking and prodding, then assured everyone Bec was on the right track.

After that, the patient had awoken a few times, but otherwise had slept like the dead, as Nash had said unironically at one point.

The longer Theo hung out with him, the more she liked him. He was fiercely loyal to Bec and included Theo in that loyalty when he talked to cops who came to check in. Theo appreciated it. Turned out he had a wicked sense of humor too; she could understand why he and Bec were so tight. It went a long way to dispelling the constant, low-grade unease she was carrying.

By eight that evening, Nash headed home and Theo was thoroughly wrung out. Her head itched, and she needed a change of clothes, but she'd be damned if she was going anywhere until she talked to Bec while the woman was actually coherent. She glanced around the room as she swallowed three ibuprofen. Thanks to Bec's police family, the place was so loaded with balloons, bears, and flowers it could serve as a gift shop.

She picked out a fluffy purple dragon and tucked it next to Bec's shoulder, settled in the chair at the edge of the bed, and again clasped her hand. She drifted, half-asleep, half-awake, half-asleep throughout the night until the sound of the morning nurse doing her thing made her stir. She dozed some more. Sometime later, gentle fingers running through her hair fully woke her. She opened her eyes. Bec was gazing at her with a look that stole her breath.

"Hello," she said softly.

Bec croaked, "Otter," and smacked her lips.

Theo grabbed the water glass and straw off the tray and held them while Bec sucked up most of the water and then licked her lips. "Thanks."

"Anytime."

Bec's eyes were clear, she was aware.

Theo smiled. "It's good to see you."

"Better to see you." Her voice was still gravelly. "I feel like I was run over by a bad guy who then ripped my throat out."

"The throat's because you were intubated. The rest of you is because Doc Patel fixed you up after Jimmy Boy pulled the trigger and you got in the way. And I do admire your ability to maintain your sense of levity."

Bec held her hand up, and Theo took it again. Bec croaked, "I couldn't—can't—believe you're here."

"Believe it." *At least for the next few minutes.* "Are you sleepy?"

She seemed to think about it, then locked eyes with Theo. "Not bad. You're here."

Theo wrapped both hands around Bec's. Good thing they were in a hospital in case the confession she was about to lay on Bec gave her a four-alarm heart attack. Or a stroke. Or both.

Oh god. Theo could hardly breathe. Did she really want to do this? Was she ready to reveal the soul-sucking secret she'd been harboring for most of her life?

No. Not at all. But if there was any chance, even the smallest sliver of hope that something with Bec could work out, she did not have a choice but to confess. She was head over heels for the pale, beautiful woman lying in front of her.

Then the argument in her head reversed itself. She should wait till Bec was stronger and better able to absorb the shock her forthcoming confession would bring. The poor woman just came out of major surgery, after all. After she'd been shot in the line of duty. She had seen lucidity in Bec's eyes when she awoke just now. But was it right to hit her, right this moment, with this bombshell?

Then again, if she didn't, she might not ever again find the courage to tell Bec any of the sordid story. She'd never know the reason Theo walked away. How was that fair to either one of them? Was she willing to live the rest of her life with the biggest, most important what-if in her life unanswered? And do the same to Bec?

The unabashed affection Bec was radiating at her, to her, for her, helped her make the decision.

"Bec, I need to tell you why I broke off our relationship. I know this is really shit timing."

A frown flickered and her gaze sharpened. "What? Yes. Tell me."

"I swore to myself I'd never, ever say anything about this. To anyone. Tessa doesn't even know. But you mean too much to me. I have to." Theo closed her eyes and clenched her teeth. "Remember that comment you made when you dropped me off at the Spud the day we came back from Two Harbors?"

"No." Now Bec's eyebrows rose in tandem. "What'd I say?"

"You said you drew the line at viewing liars and criminals as girlfriend material."

"Okay, yeah." Now her tone was wary. "You gonna tell me you're not really the owner of the bar, your sister's not related to you, and you've been embezzling money?"

That made Theo smile. A little. "Not exactly." She forced herself to maintain eye contact. "I need to tell you a little more about Sofie and me."

"I already know you were together."

"Yes. But I left some details out."

"You're looking at me like you might throw up. Which would only be fair. But I can't get out of the way."

"I won't. Promise. But this is really hard."

Bec squeezed her hand in encouragement and repeated, "Tell me."

"Okay." Theo cleared her throat. "We'd been together a couple years. I was spending the night, like I told you I did, trying to do whatever I could to keep Sofie's dad away from her. Sof had sent her little sister to a sleepover for the weekend to keep her away from that sleaze ass. Her dad was drunk out of his mind. He came upstairs, started pounding on Sofie's door, screaming at her to let him in."

"Oh, Theo."

She didn't stop to acknowledge what Bec said. If she did, she was afraid she wouldn't be able to start again, so she rushed on. "Sofie's room was right across from the stairs. That son of a bitch yelled that he wanted some fresh meat, fresh meat by the name of Theo, and that nothing Sofie could do would stop him. He was going to make her watch. That was the first time he'd ever specifically called me out, to my knowledge, anyway. Sofie fucking lost it. She ripped the door open and charged at him." Theo closed her eyes, replaying her worst nightmare. "Because of Sofie's momentum, they tumbled down the stairs. When they hit the bottom, Sofie was banged up but okay. Her dad's head, oh god. It was at an awful angle. It was obvious his neck was broken."

Bec's hand tightened and she croaked, "I'm so sorry both of you had to go through that."

Theo locked eyes with her. Here was the part that might end up with her in prison.

"Sofie was terrified she was going to get charged with murder and be locked up the rest of her life. She was so worried about who'd take care of her sister. Like I mentioned before, their aunt came through on that one, but at sixteen, neither of us knew what would happen." Theo pursed her lips. "And, honestly? I didn't want to lose Sof. She'd already been through so much. It wasn't fair. And I loved her. So much."

Bec's eyes reflected only empathy and curiosity, not disgust. Yet. She softly asked, "Then?"

Theo stared at the dark ceiling, then turned her attention back to the object of her desperation.

She could do this.

She had to. Rip off the Band-Aid and lay the wound right out there in the open.

"We managed somehow to get him loaded into the bed of his rusted out old truck. Sofie's mom had had her driving that thing since she was old enough to see over the windshield and reach the gas. I think it was because she wanted Sofie to have a way to run if she had to."

Bec gave her a startled look, and she smiled faintly. "We start 'em young up there in the north woods. My dad had me sitting on his lap steering when I was five, and I soloed when I was twelve. Anyway, we followed a trail through their property to a fire road. Sofie drove to an off-the-map quarry pit and we dumped him in it. Jesus. I can still hear his body splashing into the water."

There it was. "I'm not only a liar, at least by nondisclosure, but I aided and abetted in the disposal of a murder victim. I don't know if you want to arrest me or not, but I won't run."

She watched, holding her breath, as Bec eyed the metal stand holding various IV bags and multiple tubes going every which way like wild vines of ivy, and raised a brow.

"I'm not much up to chasing after you right now, so breathe." Beat up and battered, Bec could still convey unspoken sarcasm like a champ. She gave Theo's hand an encouraging squeeze. "Was the body ever found?"

"Not to my knowledge. I did go out there once. After Sofie died. Nothing to see, no floating remains or anything. I stood on the edge of that fucking pit and cursed his ass for essentially killing his own daughter."

Theo had to sit before her legs gave out. She hadn't realized Bec was still holding tight to her hand until she pulled away. The silence beat a steady rhythm in her head.

"Theo. Come back." She slapped her hands on the mattress in frustration. "Goddamn, I hate being trapped by all this shit."

Reluctantly, she slid the chair to the edge of the bed.

Bec's gaze wasn't harsh or angry or disappointed. It was filled with compassion. "I've got three things to say, and then I think I need to take a nap.

"Number one, that fall down the stairs was an accident. Sofie was not a murderer. Number two, yeah, you guys should not have messed with the body. But considering the totality of the circumstances, I don't blame you for what you did. And I don't think the police would either." She squeezed her eyes shut. "I don't remember the statute number, but I do know interfering with a body or the scene of a death is only considered a gross misdemeanor."

Theo opened her mouth, but a sharp glance from Bec had her snapping it shut.

"I'm pretty sure the statute of limitations for something like that is three years, which expired a long-ass time ago. The two of you were minors. Put it all together, and I doubt much if anything would have happened to either of you had this come out back then. In any case, as of this moment, I haven't heard this story. Officially. Unofficially, we can talk about this anytime you want or need to.

"Number three, and most importantly, I'm head over heels for you, Theo. I'm in love. With you. I don't want you going anywhere. I know we have a lot of things to work through, but if you're willing to see where this might go, so am I. That's a load of traumatic crap you've been carrying all these years. Alone. I can see now why you instituted your one-date-only rule. But know this."

Bec crooked her finger for Theo to come closer. When she did, Bec reached up and grabbed the collar of Theo's hoodie and pulled her down so they were face-to-face. "You are not alone in this anymore. Despite myself and my sometimes overly rigid thinking, I want to be with you."

Theo didn't know whether to laugh or cry and wound up doing both. She felt Bec's callused palm skim her face, her ear, and stop at the back of her head. She pulled Theo toward her until their foreheads touched. "I love you, Theo. I didn't survive only to lose you."

Thankfully, her confession hadn't gone the way she'd feared. "You're not the only one. I'm thoroughly besotted, infatuated, smitten, enchanted, entranced, one hundred percent under your spell."

"Sheesh. You sound like a thesaurus."

"I might have referred to one in my more hopeful moments."

"I'd kiss you, but I don't think you'd like it very much."

Theo broke into a grin.

Bec looked so inordinately delighted to see her grin she couldn't help but do the same.

"You're right, I wouldn't. But I will kiss you here." She laid a gentle one on the tip of Bec's nose.

"Aw, what the hell? You two need to get a room. Happy Halloween, by the way."

They broke apart to find Nash at the end of the bed, a hand clamped over his eyes.

"You can let go of the peepers, partner," Bec rasped.

He opened said peepers to see Bec flipping him off. "Oh, look, and from an invalid at that. You know, I don't think anyone's ever going to beat your initiation into the Hornet's Nest. Seriously." He put a hand on Bec's foot. "I've never been so happy you're okay." He coughed to cover the fact he'd choked up.

"Even more happy than the time you thought I broke my neck falling out of the treehouse?"

"Well, seeing as I was the one who pushed you out and I had nothing to do with shooting you, not quite. Hey, you want to see Harper as Sherlock Holmes?" He pulled his phone from his back pocket.

"Of course," Theo said.

Bec smiled. "You actually found a teensy Sherlock outfit?"

"Well, no. Sherry improvised. Here." He held the phone so they could both see the picture. Little Harper sat in a highchair, wearing a tiny aviator hat complete with earmuffs. Sherry was kneeling beside her making a funny face. An oversized magnifying glass clutched in Harper's chubby fist was coming straight toward the side of her head. It didn't appear as if Sherry saw it coming.

"Yep." Nash nodded when they looked up at him in alarm. "Harper clobbered her and gave Mommy a shiner."

"Ow." Theo put her hand to her own face, imagining how badly that had to have hurt.

Bec and Nash fell into an easy back-and-forth about the various injuries they'd sustained on the job and off. Theo gazed affectionately from one detective to the other. In exposing her biggest fear, she'd gained not only a love of hopefully a lifetime, but a rock-solid friend in Nash. Pretty good two-fer, if anyone asked.

Actually, a three-fer, since today was her birthday, not that she intended to mention it, considering the circumstances. But this, the people in this room—especially Bec, of course—and the outcome of her confession was the best present she could ever have hoped for.

Eventually, Bec's eyelids slid halfway shut.

"Okay," Theo said. "Let's reconvene this party after someone here one has a nap." She leaned over and gently planted a smooch on Bec's soft lips. "The more you rest, the faster you'll heal, and the faster you heal, the quicker they'll spring you. Then we'll take you home."

"I like the sound of that." Bec allowed her eyes to close all the way, but a smile still pulled on the corners of her mouth. "Who can get any rest with the two of you hovering over me like a couple of mama bears? Get outta here for a while." Her voice trailed into a whisper. "But don't forget to come back."

Nash and Theo exchanged happy glances, as for once, their girl obeyed.

She and Bec were embarking on an imperfect, messy, complicated, and no doubt occasionally frustrating path. They'd need to face down plenty of uncertainties, insecurities, and all the changes, good and bad, that new love brought. But they'd take the time to do it right. To make sure honesty, kindness, and communication were the overarching themes in their lives.

The one thing Theo knew for certain, despite herself and her singular ways, was that she didn't want to go through the rest of her life with anyone other than Bec at her side.

# EPILOGUE

## *One Year Later*

Since Halloween was Theo's favorite day and, as I'd discovered last year, her birthday all rolled into one, I wanted this year's holiday to be an unforgettable lollapalooza. Three hundred sixty-whatever days ago she'd spent her tandem holiday with me in my hospital room, where I'd been attached to so many tubes I'd looked perfectly monstrous.

To brighten things up, at some point in the day, Theo had brought in two strings of orange lights with skeletons dangling from them and draped them on the various machines surrounding me like wagons circling a campfire. The nurses got a kick out of Theo's Halloween enthusiasm, and when they found out it was also her birthday, they'd snuck in treats. After that came weeks of hellish physical therapy, but I was back to work by February and was almost good as new.

I'd learned so many things over the last year, including the fact Halloween at The Mashed Spud was usually a paid holiday for Theo's staff of nine, even if it was her birthday. She and Tess would dress up, work the bar alongside each other until ten p.m., serving up the one-day-only Phantasmic BB. Then they closed up early so Theo could watch her beloved horror movies the rest of the night while Tess put earplugs in and read.

Not my idea of a fun time, but it was the way Theo wanted it, and what she wanted for herself I wanted for her too.

This year Theo and I had tag-teamed the holiday at the Spud. This allowed Tessa to spend the afternoon taking their pint-sized nieces and nephews Trunk-or-Treating in one of the Miller Hill Mall parking lots. In balmy twenty-five-degree weather. Tessa had costumed herself as a roly-poly doctor because she could fit a lab coat over her parka.

I'd dug out my old Lindsey Whalen Lynx jersey, a pair of basketball shorts, and a blue terrycloth sweatband, which was the perfect getup to charge around in the bar all day.

Each and every year since Theo had taken over the bar, she'd turned herself into the Wicked Spud of the North. Her costume consisted of her usual work uniform of black T-shirt and jeans, and the addition of a lumpy, strangely shaped potato hat that someone had made her. I found it especially hilarious because the damn thing was too big and Theo was constantly pushing it off her face with her forearm. Regardless, she loved it.

At ten p.m. on the dot Theo ushered the last stragglers out and locked the door. By ten thirty, I finished cleaning the kitchen while Theo took care of things out front. She'd killed the main lights and was now back in the office tallying numbers for the nightly deposit.

While she was preoccupied with finances, I was sweating like a polar bear in Florida despite my air-conditioned wear. Time to check in on her one last time, then put my hopefully well-laid plans into action. I tossed the wipe-down rag I'd been using in the laundry bag and headed for the office.

I stuck my head through the doorway, unable to keep my heart from thumping harder than it already was. God, I loved her. "Howdy, birthday girl."

Theo looked up and broke into a wide smile. "Hey, baby. You all done?"

"Almost."

"I should be finished in ten or fifteen, then we can go home and search for bogeymen under the bed after we watch *Halloween* and *Psycho*." Her eyebrow arched suggestively and my insides shuddered in response. Jesus, when was I going to be able to control the flames she ignited in me with nothing more than a heated gaze? This absolutely wasn't the time to think about bogeymen, birthday suits, or rose petals. All that good stuff would most certainly come later.

"You're gonna be the death of me." I came around the desk, lifted up her potato hat, kissed the top of her red curls, replaced it, wished her happy birthday for the eightieth time and fled.

Back in the kitchen I turned up the radio and unlocked the alley door. Nash, his wife, Sherry, and little Harper as Sherlock, without magnifying glass this year, were first to slink in, followed by Shingo, Chu, and Alvarez, then Tessa, Mom and Dad Zaccardo, three more of Theo's siblings, two of Theo's nieces and two of their friends. Half the guests were in costume and half weren't. This was going to be the surprise party of a lifetime if we could pull it off.

In the front of house, the purple, fuchsia, and orange lights strung behind the bar as part of the Spud's Halloween makeover cast a glow which didn't quite reach the booths. Silently, I gestured for part of the group to head for them.

Nash's wife, Sherry, remained just inside the kitchen doorway bouncing a sleepy Harper on her hip. Nash, Theo's dad, Lorenzo Sr., and her brother, Enzo—Lorenzo Jr. to their mother—had broken off and scooted behind the bar. Lorenzo quietly tried to keep Enzo from presampling the whiskey selection, which made me clap a hand over my mouth to stifle a deranged giggle. I leaned against the end of the counter, half shielding them if Theo decided to pop out from the office sooner than expected. My hand strayed to the pocket of my shorts and I patted the lump within, assuring myself the surprise was right where it belonged.

"Jesus, Bec," Nash whispered from behind me. "I hope you haven't been doing that all night. I can hear the tapping from here. She's gonna say yes."

"You don't know that," I muttered and adjusted the fake spider web hanging from the ceiling. To make up for last year, Tess had gone overboard with lights, plastic skeletons, orange, purple, and green pumpkins with bizarre faces, and enough fake cobwebs and plastic spiders to house every real spider in Minnesota.

"I do know that." He poked me in the back. "Theo looks at you like you fart sunshine and glitter."

"Fart sunshine and glitter? When did you become so, so—"

"Wordy?"

"Yeah, that." Through the hall, I caught the slightest glimpse of my girlfriend. She was right in the office where she belonged, hopefully oblivious to the goings-on taking place only a few yards away.

"Tessa loaned me a book."

I stifled a snort. "Oh no. Don't tell me you're reading romances now?"

"No, not romances. Romantasy. More fantasy than romance. Sometimes."

"I do love you. Is the term metrosexual still in style?"

"Look in the dictionary. You'll see my picture."

Of that I had no doubt. Eileen Zaccardo caught my eye and gave me a thumbs-up. Theo's mom had been in on this plan from the day I concocted it. I swear the woman was more excited than I was.

A bright light flashed, and I realized Tess and Theo's sisters, Gina and Naya, were taking selfies with Chu, who was dressed as a vampire and, from the look of it, taking his role very seriously. Tess and Eileen both turned around gave them the mom stink eye, which worked amazingly well.

Movement in the office caught my attention. "She's coming!" I whisper-hissed.

Aside from the music coming from the kitchen, the room fell silent except for Shingo occasionally gnashing her fake fangs. Chu wasn't the only one who was vamping tonight.

It was easy to see Alvarez grinning at me, his blood-red lips wildly contrasting from the zombie-white grease paint on his face.

Theo backed out of the office into the hall, pulling a two-wheeler stacked with cases of beer from Castle Danger. As soon as she came out of the hall into the main room, Sherry hit the lights and we all shouted, "SURPRISE!"

It was fucking perfect. She jumped about three feet in the air, her potato hat tumbling to the floor. She almost lost her load but righted the stack before it hit the floor and spun around. "What the hell—Mom? Dad? What are you all doing here?"

"Happy birthday, honey!" Eileen charged forward and wrapped her in a hug that lifted her clear off her feet.

The next few minutes were the best kind of chaos. Theo was tossed between people for hugs as if she was the steelie in a pinball machine. Enzo launched into a story about his new girlfriend while Gina and Naya debated who had the sexier pirate costume, trying to pull Chu in, but he was smart and refused to take sides in the sibling rivalry.

Nash cranked up some creepy Halloween music, and then Sherry handed a very unhappy-to-be-woken Harper off to him. He tried to explain to the kid why everyone was being so loud, but when she spotted the spiders embedded in all the webs around the joint she forgot she'd been upset.

I hung back, watching Theo's face light up. This was exactly what I wanted, all the people who mattered most to her, all together, all happy.

The perfect moment.

Except my hands were shaking.

Shingo appeared at my elbow. "You good?" she asked through her fangs.

"Yeah, just…you know."

She stared silently at me in the way she did when she was interrogating suspects. I had to admit it was terrifying to be on the receiving end. "Okay, yes. I'm fucking freaking."

"She's head over bootstraps, Harrison."

I knew she was right. I'd known Theo loved me for months. She told me so every morning when we were drinking coffee in our kitchen in the cozy little house we rented in West Duluth six months ago. She showed me every time she laughed at my terrible jokes or let me pick the movie on Netflix. Once her dirty laundry had been aired out, she'd become a different person. Willing to commit, more open, more easy going, never subtle about her feelings.

But knowing someone loves you and knowing they wanted to marry you were two different things. We'd never really talked about marriage. We'd talked about everything else, like what we'd name a dog. There was an ongoing debate between the names Potato and Detective Fluffernut—maybe the answer to that was getting two dogs. And whether she might want to expand the bar or maybe someday open a second location. Or something else entirely.

But marriage? That was the huge unspoken floating between us.

Until tonight.

Papa Lorenzo's boisterous voice caught my attention. He was telling some story about Theo as a kid that involved a garden hose, the neighbor's cat, and an attempt at a bath that turned into a bloody massacre. The cat managed to escape unharmed. Everyone laughed, including Theo, who said she was only trying to squirt the smell of skunk off the poor feline. She caught my eye and grinned. My heart did that fluttery thing again.

This was it. This was the moment.

I reached into my pocket, closed my fingers around the ring box, and took what I hoped wouldn't be my last deep breath. Then I marched over to where Theo stood in the center of everyone, still arguing with her dad about the garden hose incident, and I dropped to one knee.

The room went dead silent.

Theo looked down at me, her expression flickering through fifteen different emotions in three seconds. Then she laughed.

"Oh, come on, Bec. Very funny. You're not seriously—" She stopped midsentence when I pulled out the black velvet box. "Oh, shit."

"Language, Theodora," Eileen said automatically, but she looked fit to burst with excitement.

"Theo"—my voice came out steadier than I expected—"a little over a year ago, I walked into this bar to, well, in the long run, investigate a murder. I had no idea who I was about to meet."

"Oh my god," Theo whispered. "You're serious. You're actually serious right now."

I smiled up at her. "You're dead on. You make me laugh every single day. I get through even the worst days at work because I get to come home to you."

Tears began streaming down her face and I had to clear my throat before continuing.

"I love how you put whipped cream on everything, even corn on the cob, which is disgusting yet, because it's you, cute. I love how you sing off-key in the shower and how you always steal my hoodies. I love that you're brave enough to run your own business and stubborn and kind enough to make it work. I love that you see the potential in everyone. In me. In us."

Someone behind me sniffled. I wondered if it was Nash.

"And," I continued, "I love how you make friends with every dog in the neighborhood and how you always know exactly what to say when I've had a bad day. I love that you're fun and smart and generous and absolutely terrible at mini golf, but you keep trying anyway."

"I'm getting better at mini golf," Theo protested weakly.

"You are." I couldn't stop the smile. "And I love that too. Theo, I want you to steal my hoodies for the rest of my life. I want to build something amazing with you, right here in this bar, in this city, with these people who love us both."

I opened the ring box.

Theo gasped.

The simple white-gold band tucked in the box had an embedded diamond so it wouldn't get caught on anything. The facets reflected multiple colors from the Halloween lights.

"Theodora Zaccardo, will you marry me?"

For a second, the only sound was the radio in the background and Shingo's fangs.

Then Theo dropped to her knees in front of me, grabbed my face, and kissed me so hard we tipped over onto the floor.

"Yes," she said against my lips. "Yes, yes, obviously yes."

The room exploded. Everyone cheered and laughed. Nash was indeed crying, even harder than Eileen. Gina and Naya hauled Chu and Shingo to one of the booths to start planning the bachelorette party. Or would it be parties? Enzo asked to officiate because he could get a license or a permit or whatever they called it online, and Sgt. Alvarez took pictures of us with his phone while declaring he knew this was coming months ago.

Still on the floor with Theo in my arms, I tried to jam the ring on her finger while she kissed my face and called me a crazy goofball between smooches. "I can't believe you did this in front of everyone," she said, finally allowing me sit up enough to slide the ring onto her finger. It fit perfectly, thanks to Tessa.

She held up her hand to admire the bling, and the small stone caught the light again. "Oh my god, Bec, it's…just…exactly right."

"So it's a yes?" I asked, even though she'd already said yes about fifteen times.

"The biggest yes in the history of yeses." She plastered me with another juicy one.

Lorenzo tapped a pen on a Solo cup and began to sing "Happy Birthday." Everyone joined in. As we serenaded Theo, Eileen came out of the kitchen carrying a homemade red velvet cake with crackling birthday candles.

Theo blew the flames out and cheers erupted again.

Someone turned the music back up, and within minutes the party was simultaneously a birthday celebration and an impromptu engagement party. Enzo found the good whiskey and the stash of plastic cups. Eileen, after cutting the cake and serving it on Minion paper plates, called relatives who couldn't make it to tell them Theo was now engaged, even if it was a quarter to eleven on Halloween night. A half-tipsy Chu tried out a toast that involved way too many vampire references. Later, when the party finally wound down, Tessa headed for bed, and the last of our blended family left for home.

We tossed the cups in recycling, cleared plates and napkins, put liquor bottles away, and discussed whether the skeleton in the corner was playing the guitar or the banjo.

"So." Theo perched on a stool while I finished wiping down the top of the bar. "Marriage, huh?"

"Having second thoughts?"

"No way. I just keep thinking about how this all started. A year ago you walked in here to celebrate a promotion, had one or three too many BBs, and showed up the next day to investigate a murder. I was sure you were going to throw the book at me after the 'dead meat' thing came out."

"To be fair, the whole thing was kind of dodgy until I interviewed Tess."

"You were doing your job. And you brought me something to drink while you guys were raking me over the coals."

"Because I was good cop of the day and trying to bribe you for more info. Considering it was the stale stuff from the break room, I'm not sure it was the best approach."

"It wasn't."

I walked around the bar to her, resting my hands on her thighs. She wrapped her arms around my neck and pulled me against her. I leaned back so I could look her in the eye. "No regrets?"

"Hell no. I've been ready to marry you for months."

"Why didn't you say anything?"

"Because I wanted you to ask when you were ready, Bec, not because I pressured you into it." She paused. "Also, because I was terrified you'd panic and run."

"I'm not going anywhere. You're my home."

Theo kissed me soft and sweet, tasting like birthday cake and whiskey.

"So what now?" she asked when we broke apart.

"I dunno. Plan a wedding, I guess. Fair warning, Nash wants to be your mister of honor."

"Mister of honor?"

"That does sound really funny, doesn't it? Mister of honor. Anyway, yeah, he thinks we should turn the whole straight marriage thing on its head. He also thinks he got us back together after he talked to you at the hospital, so he's decided he gets the right to help us get hitched."

Theo gave me a gentle smile. "He's crazy. I like his crazy. And he did help me see things more clearly, that's for sure."

How could she make me dissolve like ice cream in ninety-degree weather with one look? "God, I love you. So you're up for an inside-out marriage?"

"Yeah, sure. But then Tessa gets to be your woman of honor."

"You like turning this marriage thing inside out, don't you?"

"Hell, yeah. My sister wouldn't take kindly to being a matron of honor, and she'd refuse to be an 'old' maid. So woman of honor it is."

"Do you think your dad would walk us both down the aisle?"

Theo peered at me, her eyes soft. "I know he would."

A year ago I was convinced I was too damaged for love, too cynical, too angry, too afraid. After Danna, I was sure me and relationships and me and love had parted ways for good.

Turned out I just needed to walk into the right bar and meet the right crazy, big-hearted, amazing woman with the most mesmerizing eyes ever, who would love me as I was—with room for improvement, of course.

"Happy birthday, future Mrs. Harrison," I said.

"Happy Halloween, future Mrs. Zaccardo."

I pulled her against me, pressing my lips against the silky skin on her cheek. A thought hit me, and I pulled away. "We should probably keep our own names so that they match our birth certificates in case the joker who's president decides to stop people from voting if the two don't match."

"Well, shit. Good point. I can't believe how fast this country is devolving. I'm sure same-sex marriage will be coming up on the chopping block at some point real soon."

I rested my forehead against hers. "I've heard the rumblings. But there are still plenty of places we could go and get legally hitched."

Theo warbled "O Canada!" Off-key as usual.

"The fifty-first state. Not." I sighed. "Life's going to be rough for a while for so many people. But together I know we can deal with anything that comes our way."

She pulled me in tighter and rested her head on my shoulder. "Damn right we will. Love conquers all, baby. Love conquers all."

Bella Books

*Happy Endings Live Here*

P.O. Box 10543
Tallahassee, FL 32302
Phone: (800) 729-4992
**www.BellaBooks.com**

## *More Titles from Bella Books*

**Jones – Gerri Hill**
*978-1-64247-598-2 | 260 pages | Mystery*
One weekend getaway, six friends, and a deadly secret that will wash away everything they thought they knew.

**Merry Weihnachten – E. J. Noyes**
*978-1-64247-610-1 | 292 pages | Romance*
Christmas traditions aren't the only things getting mixed up when these two hearts collide beneath the mistletoe.

**Sweet Home Alabarden Park – TJ O'Shea**
*978-1-64247-570-8 | 362 pages | Romance*
She came to restore a royal estate—she never expected to rebuild her heart.

**Dr. Margaret Morgan – Christy Hadfield**
*978-1-64247-628-6 | 286 pages | Romance*
Facing the professor on campus everyone hates is terrifying—but falling for her might be even worse.

**Overtime – Tracey Richardson**
*978-1-64247-630-9 | 278 pages | Romance*
A charming romance about second chances, found family, and scoring the goal that matters most.

**The Big Guilt – Renée J. Lukas**
*978-1-64247-657-6 | 206 pages | Romance*
What if the one who got away became the one you can't have?